THE POPULARITY PACT

CAMP CLIQUE

❧ BOOK ONE ❧

EILEEN MOSKOWITZ-PALMA

RP | KIDS

PHILADELPHIA

FOR DOUGLAS AND MOLLY, MY BEST FRIENDS

Running Press Kids
Hachette Book Group
1290 Avenue of the Americas, New York, NY 10104
www.runningpress.com/rpkids
@RP_Kids

Printed in the United States of America

First Paperback Edition: March 2021

Published by Running Press Kids, an imprint of Perseus Books, LLC, a subsidiary of Hachette Book Group, Inc. The Running Press Kids name and logo is a trademark of the Hachette Book Group.

The Hachette Speakers Bureau provides a wide range of authors for speaking events. To find out more, go to www.hachettespeakersbureau.com or call (866) 376-6591.

The publisher is not responsible for websites (or their content) that are not owned by the publisher.

Print book cover and interior design by Marissa Raybuck.

Library of Congress Control Number: 2020940919

ISBNs: 978-0-7624-6743-3 (paperback), 978-0-7624-6745-7 (hardcover), 978-0-7624-6746-4 (ebook)

LSC-C

Printing 1, 2021

⇥⋯ CHAPTER ONE ⋯⇤

MAISY

"COME ON! IT'S A STOP SIGN, NOT A RED LIGHT!" DAD POUNDED the dashboard and muttered under his breath, "We can't miss this bus."

We have to miss the bus. We have to miss the bus. Please, God, let us miss this bus.

Dad turned into the parking lot and my palms started sweating when I saw the ancient yellow school bus with Camp Amelia painted in dark green letters on the side.

Dad whooped. "We made it!"

"They were too cheap to send a coach bus, which means the camp is definitely a dump. Are you okay sending me to a third-rate camp?" I asked.

"It beats having you sit around watching Netflix all summer," Dad said, as he turned the ignition off.

I slid further into my seat while Dad grabbed my stuff from the back of the Jeep and brought it to the bus. He had bought me a monogrammed sleeping bag and duffle set from Pottery Barn Teen in steel gray, my favorite color. Like that would make up for shipping me off to wilderness boot camp.

When Dad got back to the car, I didn't budge. The second I got out of the seat, my summer would be over.

Dad opened my door. "Come on, Maisy. You don't want the bus leaving without you."

I narrowed my eyes and folded my arms. "Would that really be so bad?"

Dad opened my car door wider. "You can't stay home alone all summer while your sister's away at gymnastics camp."

I tried to keep my voice calm because Dad can't deal when I get too emotional on him. "As if I would sit home all summer? I'd be at the pool with the M & Ms."

The M & Ms are my friend group. We all have names that start with *M*—Mia, Madison, Meghan, Madeline, and of course me. I joined the group later than the other girls, so it's a good thing my parents named me Maisy.

"You know I'm at work twelve hours a day." Dad looked sorry-ish. "Even longer on surgery days."

All of Dad's patients think he's a genius, but when it comes to parenting stuff, he doesn't know how to think outside the box—which is something my English teacher says about me, so I must get it from him.

"I'll hang out at Mia's house and you can pick me up when you get off work. Mia's mom won't care. She's never home anyway," I said.

Dad shook his head and his hair flopped over his eyes. He was in desperate need of a haircut, not to mention a shave. He'd stopped caring what he looked like when Mom left. "I don't want you running around with that crew at Mia's house all summer. I don't like the guys her brother hangs out with."

"If you're gonna get rid of me for the summer, can you at least send me to rock band camp?"

"You know this. All the music and drama camps book up a year in advance. When I bumped into Bea's mother at Stop and Shop and she told me about Camp Amelia, it sounded—"

"Bea Thompson and I haven't been friends since fifth grade!"

Dad spoke in that tone he used when he didn't want to sound judgy but totally did. "Which I still don't get. You guys were like two peas in a pod and then suddenly you weren't friends."

Sometimes the only way to respond is with an eye roll.

"Come on, Maise." Dad opened my door wider. "You're going to have a great summer."

My legs felt like rubber as I climbed out of the car. It didn't help that Dad's Jeep is super high off the ground, and I'm literally the shortest almost-seventh grader in existence.

"You're ruining my life," I said as soon as my feet touched the pavement.

Dad pulled me in for a hug, but I stood completely still because hugging him would make him think I was okay with this. "I love you, Mini. Even when you think you don't love me back."

As if he wasn't being annoying enough calling me by my baby nickname, Dad grabbed my arms and wrapped them around him like he used to when I was a little kid. Then he gave me a hard squeeze, even though I kept my arms limp like wet spaghetti. "I know things have been really hard. But when you get back from camp, Mom will be home and everything will be back to normal."

Things hadn't been normal in our house in a really long time. The days when Mom was PTA president, team mom for my sister Addy's gymnastics club, and my Brownie troop leader felt like they had never happened.

Dad let go and gave me a gentle push toward the bus. "You better run before they leave without you."

I shuffled my feet toward the bus as slow as humanly possible, hoping the driver would pull away before I got there.

Dad called after me, "Don't forget to write Mom. I put the address in the front pocket of your bag."

As *if* I would write to the person who was responsible for ruining my entire summer.

A college girl wearing a gray Camp Amelia T-shirt and ripped jean shorts with a grubby flannel tied around her waist, scuffed blue Converse, and a big silver whistle on a chain around her neck waited on the bus steps. She had shoulder-length brown hair with homemade bangs that were higher over her right eyebrow than her left, so it looked like she was winking at me.

"The bus is full, but you can sit with me in the counselor section," she said, and smiled so wide I could see a chipped molar.

Sitting with the counselors seemed like a pretty newb-like thing to do, but it had to be better than sitting with Bea, so I followed the girl up the stairs into a bus full of the strangers I would be stuck spending my whole summer with.

The girl kept talking as if my summer wasn't officially over. "My name is Bailey. I'm from upstate New York."

"I'm Maisy."

Bailey pointed to a seat filled with snacks and magazines. "Hold on, I just have to move my stuff."

I heard Bea's voice before I saw her, which is weird because she's so quiet at school. Half the time I don't even notice her. But she was acting like queen of the bus the way she was hugging people and OMGing about how much she missed them.

I lifted my hand in a half-wave, but Bea didn't turn my way.

Seriously? We were literally the *only* two people getting picked up in Mapleton.

I pulled out my phone, and Bailey reached out and took it from my hand. "No phones allowed."

"Wait!" I reached my hand out. "My friends will think I'm ghosting them if I don't tell them."

"Try writing letters," Bailey said, as if we were living in the eighties. Then she dropped my phone in a straw basket on top of a bunch of other phones and smiled at me like she hadn't just taken away my lifeline to civilization. "You can have it back on the last day."

Dad hadn't mentioned this no-phone rule, 'cause there's no way I'd have gotten on that bus if I'd known. It was bad enough I was gonna lose all of my Snapchat streaks, but on top of that, I couldn't go all summer without talking to the M & Ms. I couldn't risk it.

Everyone thinks we're best friends. But it's complicated. Madison's my best friend in the group, but she's family friends with Meghan. Madison idolizes Meghan, but Meghan tells anyone who will listen that she only hangs out with Madison because their moms are besties. So, Madison acts like my best friend when Meghan is ignoring her or being mean to her, and as soon as Meghan decides she likes her again, Madison kind of ditches me. Being away from my phone all summer would mean I wouldn't be able to remind Madison how much she needs me.

Bailey opened a bag of Doritos and the Cool Ranch seasoning mixed with the hot plastic smell of the bus seats started making me queasy. She pushed the bag toward me, but I shook my head, trying not to breathe through my nose. This was going to be a long bus ride.

"Camp newbie?" Bailey asked through a mouthful of Doritos.

I nodded.

Bailey washed down the Doritos with red Gatorade that made her teeth pink. "The bunk tournament is the best. There are four competitions: swimming, kayaking, rope climbing, and trail running. All the bunks live for the competition."

Turns out Dad didn't just leave out the no-phone rule. "Can I just be scorekeeper or something?" I asked.

Bailey laughed and wet Dorito crumbs landed on my arm. "You are so funny. You'll make friends fast."

"Seriously, I'm not such a great swimmer and . . ." I started.

"Hey, Bailey. You got the bunk assignments?" asked a tall counselor with crunchy blond curls.

Bailey turned to me. "One of my camp jobs is to organize the bunks. Sorry, this is privileged info."

I was relieved when Bailey squeezed into the seat across the aisle because I didn't want to hear any more about this tournament thing. Not to mention, it wasn't like I cared what bunk I was in, as long as I wasn't with Bea and her annoying friends, who were now singing a camp song that was giving me a headache. They weren't the only irritating girls on the bus. The girl behind me stuck her bare feet through the space between my seat and the window. She was in serious need of a pedicure and a shower. Some girls in the back of the bus thought it was hilarious to toss around a beach ball to see if they could keep it in the air during the entire bus ride. I ducked every time that ball came near my head. This was going to be the longest summer of my life.

I had been up all night stressing about camp and the Mom situation and suddenly felt like I could sleep for days. I rested my head against the bus window and gave in to the rocking motion of the wheels.

I must have fallen asleep because next thing I knew, we were at a rest stop. The counselors all headed off to grab Burger King, but I decided to go to Quickmart for candy.

It was really weird not to have anyone to talk to. Groups of girls ran past me shrieking and laughing, but it was like they didn't see me, like I didn't exist. I didn't have my phone to hide behind, so I kept my eyes on the ground as I walked.

I went into the Quickmart and grabbed a big bag of Sour Patch Kids Extreme and headed toward the line. Bea was already standing at the register with the exact same thing. I wasn't surprised since she's the one who introduced me to the goodness of Sour Patch Kids.

Bea kept her head down with her hair covering her face. Like I wouldn't recognize her red curly hair and pale freckly arms?

I hate awkward silences, so I had to say something. "Remember the time we ate so many Sour Patch Kids we couldn't taste anything for two days?"

Bea laughed so hard she looked like she was going to pee in her pants, which she may or may not have a history of doing on sleepovers. "My mom made me go to the doctor even though your dad said I would be fine."

Standing there laughing with Bea actually felt good. Kind of like old times—when I had one best friend and didn't have the constant pressure to hold my spot in the popular group. When Mom was still Mom, and I still felt like I could be a kid.

Suddenly, a thick Staten Island accent attached to a tiny girl with shiny black hair interrupted our moment. "You don't talk to Bea at school and now you're nice to her 'cause you got no friends at camp?"

Bea opened her mouth and then closed it quickly. She opened it back up again and shut it. She looked like my sister Addy's goldfish.

I stood up taller, even though I didn't really have to since this little jerk was even shorter than me. "I don't need your permission to talk to Bea. I've known her since preschool."

"Isa!" A tall blond girl who looked like an Abercrombie model ran over to us. "You don't have to be so mean," she whispered.

The girl who was apparently named Isa jabbed her pointer finger at me. "This girl was best friends with Bea their whole lives, then ditches her for the popular girls. And I'm the mean one?"

I felt shame creep up my neck and spread out over the tips of my ears. I wished I could explain to Bea what had really happened. Why I had to cut her out of my life. But it was too late.

Isa said, "It's a big camp. You stick with your bunk. We'll stick with ours."

BEA

Dear Mom,

I'm writing my annual "still on the bus but missing you already" letter. I know you were only trying to be polite to Dr. Winters when you bumped into him and that he isn't to blame for Maisy's Mean Girl ways. But did you really have to give Camp Amelia the hard sell? I go to camp to get out of the Mapleton bubble. Now I'm stuck here for six weeks with my ex-best friend, who is a daily reminder that I am about to start middle school with no friends. I wish we lived in a big town where there are multiple elementary schools feeding into a big middle school. Not this backward village, where middle school doesn't even start till seventh grade. It's impossible to start over with the same kids I've known my whole life, the same kids who already know what a loser I am.

Maisy started jockeying for a spot in the social hierarchy before the bus even pulled out of the parking lot. She actually sat with the counselors, as if that would give her a leg up with the other campers. She clearly doesn't understand camp politics. I've decided to handle her the same way she deals with me at school—by pretending she doesn't exist. Keep your fingers crossed that she ends up in a bunk on the other side of the lake from me.

I miss you and Mr. Pebbles already. Don't forget to give him canned tuna on Tuesdays and Thursdays for a special treat. He only likes the organic kind packed in olive oil from Trader Joe's, so don't get him StarKist—even if it's on sale.

Love always,

Your #1/only daughter Bea

P.S. Here are some care package ideas for the summer:
 -*Eleanor & Park* by Rainbow Rowell
 -*The Perks of Being a Wallflower* by Stephen Chbosky
 -*Everything, Everything* by Nicola Yoon
 -*The Best American Short Stories Collection* (either the 1986 edition edited by Raymond Carver, or the 2014 edited by Jennifer Egan)
 -A new writer's notebook (wide rule)
 -Gel pens (metallic)
 -Sour Patch Kids Extreme
 -Sour Patch Watermelon Slices

P.P.S. Thank you for literally and figuratively being the best mom and friend ever. I would have no hope of surviving the wilderness of middle school without you. I love you and miss you already.

I couldn't help feeling like it was my fault when Isa told Maisy off. Isa had been sticking up for me, but when I saw the look on Maisy's face, I felt guilty, as though *I* should be sticking up for *her*. I had to remind myself during the rest of the bus ride that Maisy wasn't my friend. She hadn't been for an eternity.

Maisy and I had been best friends since the threes class at Mapleton Day Preschool. We did everything together and people called us MaisyandBea, as if it were one big word. But, when I got back from camp the summer before sixth grade, Maisy dropped me for no reason. I had grown accustomed to Maisy writing me at camp every other day with stories about annoying things her sister Addy did, or a top ten list of reasons why she was infatuated with some boy, or best friend quizzes cut out from *American Girl Doll Magazine* with all of her answers filled out and spaces for me to fill in mine.

But Maisy didn't write once last summer, and when I got home in August, she wasn't waiting for me on my doorstep. When I texted her about going back-to-school shopping with Mom and me, she didn't reply. Mom told me not to worry, Maisy was probably in the middle of a guitar lesson or something and that we needed to go shopping anyway because I had outgrown everything. It felt like a punch in the stomach when I walked past Abercrombie and saw Maisy in there with the M & Ms. They were all trying on hats and taking a group selfie. I pulled Mom into Sephora so Maisy wouldn't see me cry.

I don't know if there were always groups and I didn't notice them because I had Maisy, or if they formed that last year of elementary school. But it suddenly felt like everyone was part of a group while I ceased to exist. Before I knew it, I was officially invisible.

———⋅———

Two hours later, when we were finally at camp, I couldn't help sympathizing with Maisy because we had a lot of good years before she joined the evil queen beehive otherwise known as the M & Ms. Although she may have swiftly put me on the wrong side of popular at school, I didn't know if I had it in me to exact revenge by doing the same thing to her at camp.

"What's the matter?" asked Poppy. She's the "pretty girl" of our group with her stick-straight blond hair, blue eyes, and super long legs. On top of being pretty, Poppy is wealthy, the kind of wealthy where her house has a name—Ferwick Manor. You might think that perfect life would make her act entitled, but Poppy is obsessed with social justice. She isn't one of those people who just posts artsy pictures of herself holding up witty posters at a women's march once a year either. This school year she spoke in front of the school board on behalf of a transgender student who wanted to use the bathroom of his transitioning gender. Mom always says that a kid who is brave enough to do those things is going to be unstoppable when she is an adult.

I tilted my head toward "the square," where Maisy stood alone. All the campers were huddled around the big grassy area waiting to get their bunk assignments, but no one talked to her or even looked at her. Word had gotten around about Isa telling Maisy off, so the other campers were steering clear of Maisy to avoid Isa's wrath.

"I know I shouldn't feel bad for Maisy, but I can't help it," I said.

"She had it coming to her," said Isa. Her Staten Island accent makes her sound tough, but she's the most loyal person I know, which is why she hates Maisy. That's the kind of friend Isa is: You hate someone, she hates them, too.

I watched as Maisy pulled her honey-brown hair up into a high ponytail, shook it loose, then pulled it back up again. Maisy fixates on her hair when she's upset.

"I can't fathom why her parents would send her here," I said. "Maisy thinks trying out a new nail salon is adventurous. And she's the least athletic person I know."

"Sucks for the bunk who gets stuck with her," said Hannah, who's definitely the coolest one among us.

Hannah's a trendsetter. One year she wore jelly sandals to camp. By the end of the summer, everyone had a pair. She had recently discovered a love of thrift shops, so she was obsessed with vintage eighties-style rompers, which are kind of like the rompers people wear today, but they come in bold primary colors and feature either rainbows across the chest or athletic stripes running down the sides.

She wore what she called statement sneakers, which were generic Keds in bold prints—the crazier the better. Her first-day-of-camp outfit was a turquoise, terry cloth strapless romper that had a rainbow on the front paired with zebra-striped sneakers. The ends of her chin-length brown hair were dip-dyed blue, and I was taking bets with Isa and Poppy on how many campers were going to beg their moms for blue Kool-Aid mix in their care packages.

"Her bunk won't have a shot at winning the tournament with Maisy dragging them down," I whispered.

Isa bumped fists with Hannah. "That increases our chances of winning the Cup!" We won the bunk tournament every year. If we won again our last year as junior campers, we would be awarded the Amelia Cup, which had only been earned by one other bunk in the past fifty years. It was Poppy's Nana Mary who won the Cup, and she really turned up the pressure on Poppy before she left for camp to bring home the win.

"Better give up now. You don't want to waste your whole summer training for nothing," an annoyingly familiar voice said.

Isa and I whipped around to see the Dandelion Bunk twins, Ali and Alexa, lurking behind us. I wasn't sure which one was talking because they are identical. After years of going to camp with them, we still couldn't tell them apart. Not that we needed to. Their personalities were cloned, along with their appearance. They both had thick New Jersey accents, bobbed curly blond hair, pimply skin, and were solid muscle from the mixed martial arts training they do. Picture any female professional MMA fighter at eleven, give her a twin and an attitude, and that's what these girls were like. We just call them the A twins to keep things simple.

Isa crossed her arms. "You guys lose. Every. Single. Year. To us. Why should this summer be any different?"

Ali and Alexa gave each other knowing looks.

"This is going to be our year. You'll see," said one of the twins.

"You do realize you guys aren't eligible for the Cup, right?" I slowed my speech down so these hunkering bullies could understand me. "We're the *only* bunk who's won the tournament every summer. So, we're the *only* bunk who's eligible for the Cup."

The A twins smiled at us, revealing matching sets of fluorescent-green rubber-banded braces. The one on the left said, "Yeah, but if *we* win the tournament, you guys *can't* win the Cup."

The one on the right cut in, "Keeping you from winning the Cup is basically what it's all about for us."

Isa laughed a little too loudly. "Good luck with that."

The A twins tossed their hair at the same time and one of them said, "Don't think we'll be needing luck this summer."

Bailey blew her whistle. Then she stood on top of a milk crate in the middle of the square, holding her clipboard, which meant one thing—bunk assignments. There was a lot of shushing and one more whistle blow from Bailey before everyone finally quieted down.

"I know you guys are all excited about another summer at Camp Amelia." Bailey pumped both of her hands in the air and everyone cheered with her, except Maisy who was busy french braiding her enviously straight hair. Putting her hair in a ponytail meant she was a little nervous. A french braid meant she was one step away from a total breakdown.

Bailey continued, "Campers, listen up for your bunk assignments."

There were never any surprises for Poppy, Hannah, Isa, and me because we always end up together in the Sunflower Bunk with our counselor, Ainsley, just like the awful A twins are always in the Dandelion Bunk with Bailey. But it was cool to watch the girls step forward as their names were called, especially girls I see every summer. Some were much taller, some had new haircuts, some suddenly had boobs, and some looked exactly the same as last summer.

Our counselor, Ainsley, stepped forward. She has a laissez-faire counselor style because she's more interested in sneaking out to the boys' camp to hang out with the guy counselors at night than she is in bossing us around.

"I'm Ainsley, the Sunflower Bunk counselor," she said, flipping her waist-length blond hair over her back. Ainsley's really a brunette, but she went blond a few summers back, around the same time she went boy crazy. She also has a sporadic British accent because she lived in England until she was five. She wore a faded University of Miami cross-country team T-shirt. She went there on a full cross-country and track-and-field scholarship and worked summers at Camp Amelia to earn spending money for the school year. She woke up every morning before everyone else and ran for miles through the woods to stay in shape, which was impressive considering the late hours she kept sneaking into the boys' camp across the lake.

The four of us didn't wait for our names to be called. We ran over to Ainsley with our game faces on to let the other campers, especially the underhanded Dandelion Bunk girls, know the Amelia Cup was ours.

Ainsley read her bunk assignment off of a small sheet of paper even though we had already flanked her like a small army. "Isa, Hannah, Poppy, Bea."

As I stood up there with the girls, I felt what I had been waiting nine months for—that feeling that I belonged. No more worrying about who to sit with, what to wear, and what to say. I was finally in the one place where I knew where to be and what to do. I had my people.

"*And* Maisy," Ainsley said.

Did I just say I was happy? I take that back. Suddenly, I felt like I was trapped in a nightmare, and no matter how hard I tried, I couldn't wake myself up. Everything was moving in slow motion and all the voices sounded like they were underwater. But I wasn't dreaming. My ex-best friend, the absolute last person I'd want with me at camp, was going to be my bunkmate for the next six weeks.

What was the point of camp if the worst part of school came here with me?

I caught the A twins radiating "I told you so" from every pore. They were standing with their bunkmates: Kaya, who had gotten long black clip-in hair extensions and discovered lip-plumping gloss, and Tinka, who sported her blond hair half up and half down so you could see her hidden rainbow streaks, her new cartilage piercing high up on her left ear, and the multiple silver hoops that lined both her ears. With her gazelle-like legs and track star gait, Tinka was a force to be reckoned with when she was running, which was why she was our fiercest competition on the foot race part of the Cup competition. All four girls wore smirks that said "checkmate."

"This has to be a mistake." Isa grabbed the bunk assignment right out of Ainsley's hands.

Even Poppy was outraged, in her sweet Poppy way. "Not to be rude, Ainsley, but this is our year to win the Amelia Cup. We're going to be the first bunk since my Nana Mary's to win."

Ainsley snatched the paper back from Isa and held it up for us all to see. "It says right here. Maisy Winters is in the Sunflower Bunk."

Hannah stared at me, willing me to fix this, as if it were somehow my fault Maisy was here, as if I could magically send her back to Mapleton.

Poppy wrinkled her brow. "I don't understand. I thought the bunks were capped at four campers."

Ainsley looked at all of us. "There was an uneven number of campers this year. Since Maisy and Bea are from the same town, it made sense for her to get added as a fifth to our bunk."

Isa pressed on. "There's no way we're winning with her dragging us down. She's new *and* Bea told us she sucks at everything."

Ainsley shoved the paper in the back pocket of her jean shorts. "I don't know why you guys care so much about the bunk tournament. It's just one small part of camp."

Maisy stood off to the side, her fingers whipping her hair into a fishtail braid. Sort of with us, sort of not. I knew that pose. I was the master of pulling it off when I knew no one really wanted me around.

I felt sorry for Maisy for a nanosecond. Then I thought about the first day of sixth grade. After that day at the mall, Maisy ignored all my Snapchats and texts. Her Instagram feed was filled with pictures of her at the country club pool, Mia's house, or the mall with the M & Ms. From the day I left until the day I got back, she had spent every second with those girls. Mom said not to worry, that as soon as Maisy saw me at school, things would go back to normal. But on the first day of school, Maisy was hanging out at the flagpole taking selfies with the M & Ms. I walked close enough for Maisy to see me, but she didn't say hi or even look in my direction. You would think the day at the mall would've made me realize Maisy wasn't my friend anymore, but it took seeing her at school to truly grasp Maisy was part of the M & Ms, and I wasn't.

"We need to fix this," I said to Ainsley. "We're not going to win with Maisy in our bunk. Bailey can just switch her somewhere else." I didn't care that Maisy could hear me. It's not like she cared all of those times she walked past me at school without even looking at me.

Ainsley rolled her eyes. "I already talked to Bailey about it because I didn't want to deal with you guys and the tournament drama. I had to sit through a lecture about togetherness and the Amelia way. I am not doing that again."

Poppy's eyes welled up. "Nana Mary's expecting me to bring the Cup to the nursing home so she can show it off to everyone."

Ainsley hoisted her duffle bag on her shoulders and headed toward our bunk. "Why are you counting yourselves out already? You girls are the best athletes at camp. If anyone can help Maisy rise to the occasion, you can. Maybe having someone in the bunk who isn't so obsessed with the tournament will be good for you. It will force you to focus on all the other fun parts of camp."

CHAPTER TWO

MAISY

THERE'S SOMETHING NO ONE KNOWS ABOUT ME. OKAY, THERE ARE a few somethings no one knows about me. But the one that's most important right now is that I don't know how to swim. Bea spent every summer at camp, which means even she didn't know that I have never been in water deeper than my knees. Bea and her squad are gonna hate me even more when they figure that out. It was all I thought about on the long, hot walk to our cabin. I had lots of time to think because it wasn't like anyone was talking to me. It was seriously the most awkward walk of my life.

As we walked through the woods, we passed other groups of girls who were on their way to their cabins. They were all squealing and talking nonstop. I could hear girls talking about new crushes, and old gossip, and making promises about all the cool things they wanted to do ASAP. Not my bunkmates. All they could talk about was the tournament. Not only was I at the wrong camp, I was in the wrong bunk with the wrong girls.

"Does everyone from the bunk have to compete? Can Maisy be exempt 'cause she's a first-year camper?" With her funky vintage store style, you could tell Hannah was the cool girl at camp. At least ten other girls had asked her where she bought her romper, and she wasn't even embarrassed to tell them it was from Goodwill. If she didn't hate me already, she was going to as soon as I failed the swim test. And everyone knows it's social suicide to have the cool girl hate you.

"I already asked Bailey and got a lecture about the," Ainsley did air quotes, "real philosophy behind the bunk tournament."

"Bailey wouldn't be saying that if she were stuck with the newb." Isa had a duffle bag that was bigger than she was strapped to her back and she was dribbling a soccer ball while she walked. I was bunking with a bunch of super freaks.

"Obviously, Bailey stuck us with Maisy on purpose. That's what the A twins were implying," said Bea.

I had forgotten about Bea's habit of using big vocabulary words all the time to show off how smart she is from reading all those books.

I felt like I was going to faint at any moment. I get hypoglycemic for real, even though Addy says I'm just a hypochondriac. She's only a year younger than me, but she thinks she knows everything.

Isa slowed down to my pitiful pace and said, "You're the only other girl in our bunk besides me who isn't the color of a Band-Aid. So what are you?"

People always ask Addy and me this because we both have our dad's deep olive skin, full lips, and large almond-shaped hazel eyes and our mom's thick honey-streaked hair, button nose, and delicate frame. "So my mom's Irish, Scottish, English, and Hungarian, and according to family legend, part Native American. My dad's half Italian and half Filipino," I said, ticking each nationality off on my fingers.

"Okay, let's hope all those international genes help us win the tournament," Isa said, with a smirk. Then she dribbled her soccer ball away from me.

We finally stopped walking when we got to a row of mini log cabins. They were kind of cute, and I would have loved staying in one in any other situation but this one. They had tiny sloped roofs with scalloped shingles like the playhouse Addy and I had when we were little. Each cabin had a cozy porch with bright painted rocking chairs, perfect for hanging out in.

By the time we got there, I thought my back was going to break from my heavy bag. If I had known I would be carrying it a million miles through the woods to get to my bunk, I definitely wouldn't have packed so much.

I watched as the other packs of girls came running out of the woods to their cabins, claiming beds and yelling in excitement. Poppy and Bea got to our cabin first and started jumping up and down and shrieking on the porch. Then Hannah and Isa ran over. Isa did not look like the jump-up-and-down-and-yell kind of girl, but turns out she was.

Ainsley walked right past them. "Leave your stuff on your bunks and get changed for swimming." Ainsley threw her whole body into the door to get it open. "Oh, and Bea, you're bunking with Maisy."

Bea had that phlegmy sound she always gets when she's about to cry. "But I always bunk with Poppy."

"Seriously, Bea?" Ainsley pitched her stuff down onto a single bed by the door that was clearly meant for the counselor. "You're the only one who knows Maisy, so you're bunking with her. The maintenance guy put an extra cot in here. Poppy, you can take that."

Bea put her bag on the bottom bunk without saying a word. Even though she obviously hates me, she still took the bottom bunk because she knows my legit fear of sleeping under someone else. Whenever we stayed at my grandma's house in the Berkshires, Bea always took the bottom bunk because she knew I was terrified that the top bunk would come crashing down on me in the middle of the night. I know it would make perfect sense for me to be scared of heights, but I'm more scared of the top bunk crushing me to death in my sleep. It had been a hard year, separating myself from the one person who knew me better than anyone else. But it's not like I had a choice.

I dragged my duffle to the set of drawers next to our bunk. I unzipped the bag and dug through my shorts and T-shirts to get to my bathing suit. I only wanted to bring bikinis, but Dad made me buy a serious one-piece that looked more like one of Addy's gymnastics leotards. I crossed my fingers that the shiny purple and silver Speedo would make me doggy paddle fast enough to pass the swim test.

No one talked to me as we all shoved our stuff in drawers and changed. At first, I was relieved to see the other girls wearing one-piece bathing suits because I was used to wearing the right thing, but then I realized it didn't matter. It was like I wasn't even in the cabin. I had never been in a situation where everyone else is part of a group and I wasn't.

I hunted through my bag for my goggles and instead found two pink envelopes with Mom's handwriting on them, the two letters she sent me before I left for camp. I had thrown them in the garbage unopened and you could see a red smear of pasta sauce on the corner of one of the envelopes and some sticky Mrs. Butterworth's Lite on the other.

Addy is such a traitor. We both swore we wouldn't read Mom's letters or write her back, but the second those letters came, Addy tore hers open. Then she wrote Mom a letter with lots of hearts and Xs and Os as if none of the bad stuff had happened. As if we hadn't spent two years lying to *everyone* for her. Teachers, Addy's coaches, other moms. We even lied to Dad. But worst of all was lying to Bea.

I told Dad I didn't want to read her letters, but he never listens to me, which is how I ended up at this camp in the first place. Just seeing the envelopes with Mom's perfect cursive made me grit my teeth. You know how people say they can see red when they're really angry? Well, I was seeing red, spitting red, tasting red kind of mad. It was Mom's fault I was here in this bunk, where no one liked me. It was Mom's fault I would be away from my friends all summer. It was Mom's fault I was about to fail this swim test.

I held the envelopes out, ready to make a tear right down the middle of Mom's neat handwriting when Ainsley interrupted the girls from their nonstop talking about the tournament.

"Time to go to the lake," she said.

BEA

Dear Mom,

This is probably the first time in Camp Amelia history that someone wrote home twice before lights out on the first day. But this dismal

27

news can't wait. It's bad enough that my nemesis is going to camp with me. She's also in my bunk!!

Poppy and I bunk together every summer. She sleeps in the bottom bunk and I take the top, and we spend half the night passing notes and candy to each other. Now I'm stuck with Maisy, while Poppy's on the other side of the room with her cot pushed up against Isa and Hannah's bunk. I feel so far away from the girls, I may as well be in a different cabin.

I knew as soon as Ainsley assigned Maisy to my bunk that it was inevitable I would have to give up the top bunk because bottom bunks make Maisy anxious. So do the little dots that show up when someone is replying to your text, Sunday nights, peeing in a public restroom because she gets "stage fright," arriving to a movie during the coming attractions, and furry animals, including harmless Mr. Pebbles. Then there are all the things that give her the creeps: people who dress up like Santa—she calls them Santa impersonators—the cafeteria lady who has four missing teeth, sushi, and jazz music. I learned back when I was friends with Maisy that sometimes it's easier to enable her anxiety than it is to deal with her theatrics. So I took the bottom bunk, which I'm sure will be the first of many compromises I will have to make this summer.

Mom, I don't know how I'm going to make it six weeks with Maisy and her neuroses seeping into my camp life. It was one thing dealing with her when we were friends, but I can't summon empathy for her after she effectively draped me in an invisibility cloak and turned me into the Mapleton School nobody.

I miss you so much. You ALWAYS know what to say to make me feel better. Give Mr. Pebbles a big hug for me. He always cheers me up in these situations too.

Love,

Your #1/only daughter

Bea

P.S. Make sure you go out with the Single Mom Squad as much as possible while I'm gone so you don't get too lonely!

P.P.S. This would also be the perfect time to go on a few blind dates . . .

I thought Maisy was going to faint when a toad jumped across the path on the way to the lake. She held her scream in, but it was written all over her face. She was never going to survive six weeks at Camp Amelia. The sooner she realized that, the better for me.

When we arrived at the lake, Ainsley hung her towel over one of the wooden chairs and pulled off her shorts and T-shirt. She always wore a two-piece bathing suit, usually of the string variety, just in case the boy counselors from the camp across the lake happened to be swimming at the same time as we were. They would have to be watching us with binoculars to see her, but Ainsley wasn't taking any chances.

"You guys do your laps while I give Maisy her swim test," she said.

Maisy turned ashen and swallowed hard. It doesn't take much to set off her anxiety.

Ainsley tightened her bikini straps and laughed. "Nothing to get freaked out about. Everyone passes the swim test. Look at all those little kids over there. Anyone swimming past that blue rope has passed the test."

Ainsley pointed to the hordes of younger campers swimming beyond the blue rope that marked the end of the shallow water. Their shrieks echoed across the lake as they splashed each other and got caught up in the excitement of the first swim of the season.

Maisy didn't look very reassured. She put her towel down on a tree stump, pulled off her shorts and T-shirt, and walked as slowly as humanly possible toward the edge of the water. I had witnessed her using the same tactic in PE class. The girl will do anything to avoid breaking a sweat.

Isa, Poppy, and Hannah were waiting for me at the edge of the dock.

Isa pulled on her goggles and jumped off the dock into the deep water and shot back up like a cannon. "Whoo! I always forget how cold this water is!"

Poppy, Hannah, and I counted down from three and jumped off the dock together. The water was better than air-conditioning on a hot day like this. It felt like my entire body drank a tall glass of Mom's homemade peppermint iced tea.

I was about to lead us in our laps when Isa got in front of me. She was hard to miss in her red Speedo one-piece and her mirror goggles. "New girl should be at the buoy by now."

Hannah cupped her hand over her forehead to block out the sun's glare reflecting off the lake's surface. "She's still only knee-deep. What's she waiting for?"

Poppy huffed as she treaded water. "Please tell me she's not a slow swimmer. The swim race is the Dandelion Bunk's best event."

In all the years I had been friends with Maisy, I had never actually seen her swim. We did spend every Saturday in June on the Slip 'N Slide in her enormous backyard. We drank Capri Suns, ate Sour Patch Kids until we lost the feeling in our tongues, and talked about everything. I had always wanted a sister, and Maisy was the closest I had to one. Losing her and not knowing why was still a slow burn of hurt a year later.

Ainsley's voice was coated with her English accent in a showcase of her annoyance. "You have to go all the way in!"

Isa shook her head. "What's wrong with her?"

"Give the girl a chance. Maybe she's just trying to get used to the cold water," Hannah said. She was upping her retro game, with a fluorescent pink and green one-piece bathing suit with a purple zipper down the front. I'm pretty certain there is a picture of Mom in one of her old photo albums wearing that exact same bathing suit in the early nineties, back when she looked like she went through a bottle of hair spray a day to keep her bangs teased at least six inches above her head.

"Hannah's right. We need to hold back judgment and give her a chance to settle in," said Poppy.

Ainsley sounded 100 percent British now. "You have to get in the water to take the test."

Maisy finally made it to where the water was deep enough to swim. She held her head above the water so her face didn't get wet. Then she cupped both of her hands and pushed them through the water.

"Oh, no." Hannah clapped her hand over her mouth. "She isn't..."

Poppy hovered over my shoulder so close I could feel her breathing in my ear.

"I think you have to actually move for it to be considered doggy paddling," I said.

Ainsley grabbed the red rescue tube, one of those background objects in your environment that you never really think about. I had never seen it used at camp before.

All of the shrieks, yelling, and splashing around stopped suddenly as the younger campers steeled their wide eyes on what was probably the first Camp Amelia lake rescue of the decade.

"That's enough, Maisy," Ainsley said, holding the float out toward her. "Climb aboard."

But Maisy was even high maintenance when she was being rescued. She put both hands out to grab the float and ended up pushing it away from her. Ainsley sighed and grabbed it. She held on tight while Maisy tried to climb aboard, but Maisy has no upper body strength, so she flopped around the tube without actually hoisting herself aboard.

Ainsley held out her hands and said in a nonjudgmental but firm way, "Stop! Just stop."

Maisy looked dejected sitting in the muddy shallow part of the lake in her brand-new swim-team-quality bathing suit.

"Just stand there," said Ainsley.

Maisy stood up and Ainsley lifted the float above Maisy's head and dropped it down so that Maisy was inside the circle. Then she said, "Now sit down."

Maisy sighed. "I can walk back to shore. The water isn't even deep."

"Camp procedure. You fail the swim test, you get a ride back to shore," Ainsley said.

She made a great show of pulling Maisy to the lake's edge. She was probably thinking about the guy counselors across the lake who might see her in lifeguard action.

"The girl doesn't even know how to be rescued the right way," said Isa, as she waded back to shore with the three of us on her heels.

When we all got back to the sandy shore, Maisy jumped off the tube. "I was just warming up. Let me try again. Please?"

Ainsley shook her head and the tips of her hair sprinkled water on us. Her voice was kind. "You should've told me you don't know how to swim. You could've gotten hurt."

"Do you know what this means?" shrieked Poppy.

"What?" Maisy looked around at all of us. "What does it mean?"

I could hear the bite in my own voice. "You're disqualified from the swim race *and* the kayak race."

In that second, I saw something no one else did. A flicker of relief passed over Maisy's face, and I hated her even more than I did before.

CHAPTER THREE

MAISY

GETTING OUT OF KAYAKING WAS THE BEST THING THAT'S HAPPENED to me since I got here. Do you know how often those things tip over?

Ainsley waved the other girls back to the water. "You guys didn't fail the swim test. Nothing's stopping you from doing laps."

I think Ainsley had enough of the girls and their drama, too. They started to complain, but when Isa ran to the dock, they all followed like a bunch of sheep. It was kind of weird to see Bea in a group. I've always thought of her as someone who doesn't need to be part of things. When we were friends, she always wanted to hang out just the two of us. Then when I became part of the M & Ms, she seemed perfectly happy eating lunch alone in the library with a book in her hand.

I was so cold my teeth were chattering and my wet towel wasn't helping the situation, but I was really happy to be out of the water.

Ainsley sat in a wooden chair with chippy blue paint that didn't look very comfortable. She kept her eyes on the other girls in the water, which was pointless because it was obvious that none of them needed to be rescued. "Don't think this means you're getting out of swimming. Starting tomorrow you're gonna use this time slot for lessons with the little kids."

"I thought the little kids are the ones swimming in the deep end over there," I said, pointing to the group of girls who were goofing around with their wacky noodles and inflatable floats.

"I mean the really little kids. The only kids who come here not knowing how to swim are usually first graders," said Ainsley.

"As if failing the swim test wasn't already a blow to my ego?" I said, crumpling to the ground in my wet towel. I pulled it around me as tight as I could. "Why couldn't my dad send me to an adventure camp with a heated pool?"

"This should warm you up." Ainsley pulled a triangle-shaped hunk of aluminum foil from her bag, revealing the biggest slice of pizza I had ever seen. "My step-dad owns a pizzeria. He's always par-anoid I'm gonna starve while I'm here, so he sends me on the bus with a few fresh slices."

She ripped the slice right down the middle and handed half to me. The crust was soft and the cheese was thick, with just a smear of sauce. This pizzeria step-dad knew the right cheese-to-sauce ratio.

I took a bite, expecting cold pizza, but it tasted like it had just come out of the oven. "How is this still warm?"

Ainsley spoke with her mouth full. "Magic pizza shop aluminum foil. My step-dad won't tell anyone where he gets the stuff." She swallowed and cleared her throat. "How'd you end up here?"

I took a really small bite of pizza so I could make it last as long as possible. "My dad waited 'til the last minute to register for camp."

"Oh. I get it." Ainsley tore off a piece of the crust and popped it in her mouth. "Your parents are getting divorced."

As if my life was that easy.

"No. They just thought camp would be good for me. You know, to get me out of my comfort zone," I said.

"You're gonna have to get yourself in a totally different comfort country if you want to make friends here," Ainsley said.

I was so cold that the bones in my fingers hurt, but the pizza was good enough to almost make me forget. "Can't I just switch bunks?"

"There's a strict no-bunk-switching rule. Bailey put you in here on purpose, so her bunk can win the tournament. She can't stand that we win every year and, no offense—but with you in our bunk, she actually has a chance," Ainsley said.

She took a big chug from her water bottle, then tilted it toward me. I was super thirsty. But I shook my head and flashed a no-thank-you smile since backwash freaks me out.

I swallowed the last piece of cheesy goodness. "I have to find a way to convince my dad to let me come home."

Ainsley wiped her greasy hands on her towel. "It'll never happen. The camp director is a pro at talking parents into making their kids stay. I mean, if they let every homesick kid go home, they would be out a boatload of money every summer."

I couldn't handle a whole summer of Bea's side-eye. Doesn't she know that back home she's the lucky one? At the end of the school day, she has her mom to go home to, a mom she can talk to. A mom who's her best friend. The *Gilmore Girls* have nothing on Bea and her mom.

I wiped my hands on my wet legs, which didn't help get the pizza oil off but sort of moisturized my legs. "So, I'm stuck."

"Yeah. You better figure out a way to make it work." Ainsley blew her whistle and waved the girls back to shore.

I don't know what kind of magical powers these girls had, but none of them looked cold as they ran to the path that led to our bunk.

Ainsley hung back at the lake to talk to another counselor who was just starting her bunk's swim time. I was busy concentrating on not stepping on anything gross like a spider, a worm, or, worse, a snake when Bea slowed down to walk with me.

Her wet hair hung down her back in perfect corkscrew curls. Too bad it would turn into a hot mess as soon as she brushed the life out of it.

"You should call your mom," she said. "She'll be speeding up I-95 as soon as she hears what this place is really like."

Bea was basing this theory on the Mom she used to know, the one who had it all together, with her weekly gel manis, Lululemons, and hair blown out at the salon every other day. The Mom who would stay up past midnight responding to emails about playdates and fund-raisers. That Mom had been replaced with someone who wore the same stained sweatpants and didn't wash her hair for days, whose voicemail and email boxes overflowed. That Mom wouldn't be rescuing me anytime soon. That Mom is the reason I'm here.

"My mom's not coming for me," I said.

Bea talked in a voice that was probably supposed to sound encouraging but that just sounded fake and desperate. "She definitely will. There's no way she would make you stay somewhere so remote and physically challenging. She obviously didn't understand what Camp Amelia was like when she registered you."

I tried to ignore my wet feet sliding around in my flip-flops and my Speedo straps digging into my shoulders. So far, everything about camp was uncomfortable.

"It's not gonna happen, Bea. I'm stuck here for the summer," I said. Saying it out loud was awful because it made it really sink in.

It was totally obvious the other girls were eavesdropping because they were the quietest they'd been since we all got to camp.

Bea kept talking in that fake voice. "You can move to a cabin with other girls who are . . . less sporty. You know, girls who aren't as competitive."

Ainsley called out from behind us with a mouth full of pizza. I knew there had to be another piece in that big bag of hers. "Nice try, Bea. You know there's no bunk switching."

I glared at Bea. "Trust me, I would rather be anywhere but here."

Bea's face turned so red it matched her bathing suit. "Trust you? That's funny."

Ainsley stepped in between us. "Maisy, come with me. You need to check in with the nurse for your new camper physical."

Dad would have been shocked at how fast I headed toward that nurse's cabin. As much as needles, tight arm pressure cuffs, and crinkly paper gowns freaked me out, a medical exam had to be better than hanging out with my bunkmates.

BEA

As I watched Maisy and Ainsley walk away, I pretended they were walking deep into the cover of the forest where there was a porthole waiting to take them to a distant realm. But because it was real life and not one of my fantasy novels, they simply made a right at the white birch trees near the center of camp where the nurse's cabin, main office, and therapy cabin were located. Maisy was sure to have a panic attack when they arrived because the mere sight of a Band-Aid is enough to quicken her pulse.

"The best thing Maisy could've done was drop you," said Hannah, breaking me from my thoughts. "She was actually doing you a favor."

I thought about the time Maisy waited in line with me at Barnes and Noble for five hours so I could meet Lana Bello, the author of my favorite YA book series. Maisy doesn't even like postapocalyptic dystopian fiction like the Well Ringer books, but she spent an entire Sunday in line with me so I could get the latest hardcover signed with a personal message from my idol.

"She's actually not that bad," I said. "This place just brings out the worst in her."

I couldn't help wondering if maybe it was bringing the worst out in me, too, because I could feel myself morphing into the kind of gossiping, exclusionary Mean Girl I hated back home.

Poppy put a finger to her mouth to signal us to stop talking. Hannah picked up the cue and lifted her chin in the direction of the scattering of Christmas-tree-worthy white pines. We had trained our ears after years at camp to know the difference between the sound of an animal rustling the leaves and a person walking through the underbrush.

Sure enough, the Dandelion Bunk girls cut through the clearing and stopped in the middle of the path so they obstructed our way.

Hannah groaned. "As if things didn't already suck."

The A twins were wearing long-sleeved swim shirts that accentuated their muscular arms, reminding me what strong adversaries they would be during the bunk tournament. Tinka was wearing a bikini that didn't look like it was going to hold up for laps around the lake. Kaya's glam drama was surely admired by her thousands of Instagram beauty account followers, but it was totally overkill for adventure camp.

Tinka glowered at Hannah. "Nice bathing suit. Are you so poor that you needed to borrow one of your mom's old ones?"

"At least I didn't borrow a bikini from a kindergartner," Hannah shot back.

Tinka was concentrating so hard on a comeback that you could practically see the wheels turning in her head, but one of the A twins beat her to the punch.

"Sorry about the Cup, girls," said the A twin on the left.

"Yeah, you have no chance with that newb in your bunk," said the A twin on the right.

Isa stepped up to them even though she was probably only a quarter of their combined weight. "Sorry about your hair. Heard you guys had to cut it because of the . . ." Isa lowered her voice to a whisper "lice."

"Speaking of rumors." Kaya put her hand on her outstretched hip for emphasis and fluttered her eyelashes in fake surprise.

"Heard the new girl's such a bad swimmer that she had to be saved with the rescue float."

"I always thought that thing was just for decoration. The water is, like, knee-high," said an A twin.

All four of the Dandelion Bunk girls burst into laughter as I cursed the lightning-fast Camp Amelia gossip mill. When I was younger, I had convinced myself there was a bluebird who flew from bunk to bunk sharing camp news. Clearly, I had been watching too many Disney movies with Maisy at the time. Now I'm old enough to know the lake acoustics allowed sound to travel to the far ends of the camp perimeter, making it virtually impossible to keep secrets. Not to mention the mini campers had finished up in just enough time ahead of us to spread the word of our demise on their way back to their cabins.

"I've never heard of anyone failing the swim test. Have you?" Tinka said.

Kaya widened her cartoonish eyes again. "Not since we've been coming here."

The A twins said in unison, "The tournament's ours this year."

Poppy tugged on my arm, pulling me away from our arch enemies. For once, none of us had a witty comeback because they were right. We had no shot at the Cup with Maisy in our bunk. A feeling of doom filled me, exactly the same as I had felt walking into school every day for the past year.

Suddenly, sharp pain radiated through my shin as it came into contact with Kaya's tree trunk of a leg. I flew forward and reached out my hands with just enough time to break my fall, landing face first in a pile of dry pine needles.

Hannah reached down and pulled me up. "Are you okay?"

I wiped my hands on my wet bathing suit and tried to ignore the throbbing in my leg. "I'm fine. Really, I'm fine."

Kaya screwed her face into a synthetic empathetic face. "You should watch where you're going. You don't want to get hurt before the tournament."

I lunged at her. But Isa pulled me back. "She's not worth it. Come on. Let's get out of here."

I followed Isa because I had no choice. The Dandelion girls were twice our size and they fought dirty. Usually, the only way to hurt them was by winning the tournament, which was highly unlikely this year.

I spent the whole walk back to the bunk picking bloody pine needles from the palms of my hands. Usually, as soon as I stepped inside our cabin, I felt like I was home. But as soon as I opened the door, I saw Maisy's pink, fluffy robe hanging over the top bunk and wanted to scream at the top of my lungs.

Isa slammed the cabin door shut. "It's bad enough we're gonna lose the Amelia Cup. But we're practically handing the tournament over to the Dandelion girls."

Poppy rubbed her towel over her wet hair. "Can't you guys see why Maisy's parents sent her here? Camp Amelia sells itself as a girls' empowerment camp. I don't think I've ever met a girl who needs to be empowered as badly as Maisy."

Hannah stripped off her bathing suit and pulled on a pair of vintage gym shorts with a Camp Amelia T-shirt. "I'm all about empowering girls, but Maisy's not going to make it here the whole summer. The girl can't even doggy paddle."

"If we're lucky, she'll fail the nurse's physical and get sent home," said Isa, as she got dressed.

I collapsed on my bunk in my wet bathing suit. I could feel the cold dampness spreading out on my comforter, but I didn't care. "I spend the whole school year being invisible while Maisy and the stupid M & Ms rule the school. Now I'm stuck with her for the entire summer!"

I hate the vulnerability of crying, the loss of control, the weakness it shows. But I could feel it bubbling up inside me and rising to the surface in chokes and sputters until the tears were flowing down my cheeks. All of the sadness, loneliness, and betrayal I had felt for the past year spilled out of me as I wondered how I would survive a summer with the person who had shattered me.

"I know things seem about as sucky as possible now," started Poppy. "But—"

"You don't get it," I cut in. "The way the Dandelion girls treat us. The way they make us feel bad about ourselves. That's horrible enough. But going to school every day and having people look right through me is exponentially worse," I said.

Poppy climbed in the bunk and laid down next to me with her long legs hanging off the edge. She pressed her face into mine. "You're not invisible here. You have us."

I stared up at the gray sheets wrapped around the bottom of Maisy's mattress. "I feel like she's everywhere and I can't get away from her."

Hannah climbed over Poppy and curled up on my other side. "We're the ones who are everywhere."

"She's ruined my summer." I wiped my nose with the back of my hand. "She's ruined my place."

Not a snuggler, Isa knelt on the floor next to the bed. "Maisy won't be here for long if she has no friends. She'll be writing home *begging* for someone to come get her."

"You heard Ainsley. We're stuck with her," I said.

Hannah sighed. "Maybe if we all stop stressing about the Cup, it won't be so bad having Maisy here. Obviously, we won't be friends with her. But if we don't obsess about winning, we can at least live a drama-free summer with her."

I sat up. "Don't you guys get it? The Cup is about the four of us being winners for once in our lives. Back home, I *literally* have no friends. Isa plays soccer even though she's sick to death of it because her parents want her to get a college scholarship. Hannah's mom

46

thinks her dyslexia can be cured with a gluten-free, sugar-free diet. Poppy's mom is putting an immense amount of pressure on her to become a supermodel." I exhaled, then asked, "Are we going to let Maisy take away the one thing we have control of in our lives?"

Hannah groaned. "When you put it like that . . ."

Isa jumped in, "We can't let Maisy keep us from winning."

All of a sudden, a realization came over me. I jumped off the bed and grabbed my stack of donut stationary and a Sharpie. I tried to make my pen move as fast as my brain was.

"What?" Isa stood up. "You're freaking us out."

I held up my hand as I scratched one more thing down. I was processing too rapidly to talk.

"Seriously, Bea. What's going on?" asked Hannah.

I dotted my last few *I*s and crossed my last *T*s and then held up my paper, which was filled with squares and connecting lines with the names of every single tournament-eligible camper and bunk at Camp Amelia. "We may not be able to get rid of Maisy, but we might still have a chance at the Cup."

Poppy let out a huge breath. "Wow! It's not over."

"Okay, I haven't taken Algebra II or whatever you two nerds took to understand that chart. Can you just explain it?" Hannah asked.

Isa cracked up. "It's not math. It's brackets, like in soccer tournaments."

Isa snatched the paper from me and tried to show it to Hannah.

"It's hard to tell with Bea's crazy-town handwriting, but you see . . ."

Hannah, who hates anything with words or numbers, waved the paper away. "Forget the chart. Just tell me what's going on."

The words tumbled from my mouth. "It doesn't matter that Maisy is DQed for the swim and the kayak races. She's our fifth person, and all the other bunks have only four campers, so we can use her as an alternate, which means we only need her to compete in two challenges. As long as she completes the ropes course and is decent on the run, we still have a shot."

Poppy clapped her hands together. "Maybe we won't be losers after all."

⤙ ·· CHAPTER FOUR ··⤚

MAISY

IT TURNS OUT MY NEW-CAMPER CHECKUP WAS REALLY ME GETTING introduced to a psychologist "just in case I want to talk," which is code for "your dad told us what's going on." I have a policy about not talking to therapists because they make me more anxious. The school counselor tried to talk to me right before Mom left, but sitting in her freezing-cold, air-conditioned office while she asked me personal questions made my heart feel like it was beating out of my chest.

But Dr. Beth is different from any counselor I've ever met. Her frizzy gray hair hung all the way down to her waist and she was wearing a tie-dyed Camp Amelia shirt with faded overalls. She was barefoot and had a sun tattooed on the top of one of her tan feet and a moon on the other. She wasn't wearing any makeup, and she had deep wrinkles next to her mouth, which made it seem like she must smile a lot. Her skinny arms were covered with rows of silver bangles and she had thick silver and turquoise rings on practically every finger.

The therapy cabin smelled a little like cat pee, but it had a homey vibe with lots of comfy floor cushions. Even though Dr. Beth looked like someone who shops at Whole Foods, she offered me some french fries from her McDonald's extra value meal. I'm always up for fries, but accepting food would mean I would have to talk. I had spent so long hiding Mom's secret, it felt weird talking about it. Why would it be different with a camp therapist?

I shook my head. "No, thanks."

I looked out the window and saw Ainsley doing burpees on the grass outside while she waited to walk me back to our bunk. It made me even more mad that Dad sent me to such a sporty camp.

"Are you okay?" asked Dr. Beth.

I turned back to her. "I'm not upset about my mom if that's what you were about to ask. I'm just pissed that I'm stuck at a camp where everyone is obsessed with some stupid tournament. Not to mention, my phone got taken away, so I've lost my only connection to the real world."

Dr. Beth took a long sip of her super-sized grape soda, making a loud slurping sound. "Can't help you with the tournament business, but one of the perks of meeting with me is the great Wi-Fi service in the therapy cabin."

I rolled my eyes. "What good is Wi-Fi without a phone?"

Dr. Beth grabbed a laptop off her desk and handed it to me.

"The other perk of meeting with me is that I allow emails as part of the therapy experience," she said. "So, if you don't feel like talking to me, you can email your family or your friends back home."

I had a feeling there was more to this, like she had some kind of trick up her sleeve, but I reached for the laptop anyway. That's how desperate I was for a window outside of this awful camp. I sat down on the floppy floor pillow and opened up the laptop. Next thing I knew, a black cat jumped out of nowhere and curled up on the floor right by my feet, which explained the cat pee smell.

Dr. Beth laughed. "That's Stumpy. He's missing a tail and an eye, but other than that he's in tip-top shape."

I didn't know what was more gross, the missing tail or eye, so I tried not to get a close look.

Dr. Beth kept talking. "You're not allergic to cats, are you?"

Cats make me nervous because you never know if they want to lick you or claw your eyes out. They're kind of like passive-aggressive people that way. But that's not the same thing as actually being allergic, so I shook my head.

"Good, because stray cats have a way of finding me," Dr. Beth said, as she plopped down on a floor cushion near me, but not close enough to look over my shoulder, so I started my email to Dad.

From: dramagirl@gmail.com
To: docwinters@yahoo.com
Subject: Worst camp ever!!

Did you know they would confiscate my phone on the bus?

Did you know I would have to take a swim test?

Did you know that if I failed the test, I would have to take swim lessons with the baby campers?

Did you know that I would have to compete in some kind of athletic tournament?

Did you know that my roommates are champions of this crazy tournament and that they would hate me the second they realized how unathletic I am??????

Signed,
The most miserable daughter in the whole world

After I fired off Dad's email, I looked up at Dr. Beth. She wasn't paying attention. She was too busy polishing off her Big Mac. So, I minimized my email and went on Instagram.

I went on Madison's account because she's the one who posts on the daily. Of course she had already posted a pool pic from Mia's house. The girls were all wearing their new bikinis from our last mall trip. The caption was *A little to the left* with a laughy face emoji, a cupcake emoji, and a clown emoji. Madison always captions her pics with an inside joke from the day. It killed me that I didn't get the joke. This was going to be an entire summer of me on the outside of all of the jokes.

52

Of course Dr. Beth's laptop didn't have emojis on the keyboard, which made it impossible to comment the right way, which would have been: bikini, flame, kissy face, and heart eyes. My only option was to send a DM.

To: @mammamia, @madisonave, @maddywiththegoodhair, @meggylonglegs
From: @maisywintersiscoming

I hate camp. The girls suck and there are bugs EVERYWHERE. They took my phone!!! I feel like I'm in jail. Check your DMs cuz it's my only way to talk. Miss you guys sm. ILY!! XOXO

I didn't mention that Bea was in my bunk, or even that I was at Bea's camp. I didn't like reminding them that I used to hang out with Bea because that only pointed out how new I was to the M & Ms and what a loser I used to be.

I switched back to my email to send Dad another list about why camp sucks. Dad, who never checks his phone during the workday, had already emailed me back.

From: docwinters@yahoo.com
To: dramagirl@gmail.com
Subject: Re: Worst camp ever!!

Hi Mini,

Miss you already. The house is too quiet with all three of my girls gone.

You are so much stronger than you realize, and I know this camp is going to show you that. Give it a chance and you might surprise yourself.

Got to go—in the middle of appointments. Love you to the moon and back.

Love,
Dad

Hadn't I already proved to Dad how strong I am? I was the one who had to deal with the Mom situation when he was working all the time. Now he's acting like competing in some stupid camp tournament was going to be the thing that made me tough. I switched back to Instagram where the M & Ms were commenting back and forth on Madison's post with strings of emojis that I didn't get. There were the obvious ones, like the sun, a pool umbrella, a bikini, and sunglasses. But I didn't get the broccoli, Japanese flag, or hammer. I had been gone for one day, and it already felt like my friends were speaking in a different language.

Meanwhile, no one had responded to my DM, which meant I was missing the M & Ms a lot more than they were missing me.

I snapped the laptop shut and handed it back to Dr. Beth.

"Thanks," I mumbled. "I'm finished."

Dr. Beth took the laptop and put it on her desk next to a stack of manila folders that looked like it was going to topple over any minute. Then she sat back down on the floor cushion and let Stumpy climb in her lap. "You can use my computer anytime. I'm also here anytime you want to talk."

Dr. Beth stared at me, like she was waiting for me to tell her my whole life story. Therapists can be tricky like that. One minute they're looking at you, and next thing you know, you've told them all your business.

I didn't want her to think I was agreeing to talk about the Mom situation, but I really wanted to come back and use her laptop again. So, I asked her the question that had been on my mind since I saw Bea on the camp bus. The one question I couldn't ask anyone who really knew me.

The words felt scary coming out of my mouth, like I was exposing the worst part of myself. "Did you ever do something really bad? But for a good reason?"

Dr. Beth rubbed Stumpy behind his ears while he purred like a car motor. "I've done good things for bad reasons and bad things for good reasons."

"What if you couldn't tell anyone why you did it and you just looked like a mean jerk?" I asked.

"Hmmm. That's a tough one," Dr. Beth said.

I wondered where this lady got her therapy license. Wasn't she supposed to know what to do in situations like this?

"Seriously? What if everyone hated you because of this one terrible thing you did?" I asked.

"You can't change what's already been done," Dr. Beth said. "But if what you did hurt someone else, you could tell them why you did it."

"Not happening." I stood up. "I gotta go."

I waited for Dr. Beth to try to stop me, but she just shrugged and said, "See you next time, kid."

I headed back to the bunk with Ainsley, even though I knew no one wanted me there. Being around people who hate me is better than talking about my problems.

When I realized how long the walk was from the therapy cabin to the bunk and then from the bunk to the ropes course, I almost regretted not hanging out longer with Dr. Beth.

I stayed in front of the girls as we headed down yet another dirt trail toward the ropes course. I was beginning to see that this whole camp was made up of dirt trails leading me to things I would never do in real life. I followed the old wooden signs that were nailed into the trees and hoped the ropes course wasn't as scary as it sounded.

"It's all about the brackets," said Isa.

I wondered what they were talking about.

"So, Isa, Poppy, Bea, and I will do the kayak and swim. We just need to figure out which three girls will compete in the ropes and run with Maisy," said Hannah. "As long as we can get Maisy through her two parts, we can still win this thing."

I realized this was probably not a good time to tell them I was afraid of heights.

I walked a little faster to get away from them. I followed the path deeper into the woods. Suddenly, the air got cooler under the clumps of gigantic trees and goosebumps popped up all over my arms and legs.

Bea ran over to me and gripped my arm. "We don't go that way."

"Of course you don't." I stopped in my tracks and rolled my eyes. Bea just had to make me look stupid when all I was doing was following the super old wooden sign that said ROPES COURSE. She is such a control freak. If you don't do something her way, she's the queen of making you look like a moron.

"No. Seriously, Maisy. We don't go that way," said Isa, her eyes wide.

The girls stood frozen on the path and stared at me like I was standing on top of a zombie pit.

Ainsley shook her head. "You guys are so ridiculous. It's just an urban legend."

I scooted to the other girls as fast as I could. "What's an urban legend?"

Ainsley sighed. "A really long time ago—" she started.

"Back when my Nana Mary went to camp," cut in Poppy.

"There was this girl," added Isa.

Ainsley rolled her eyes. "Why don't you guys just tell the story."

Isa jumped back in. "There was a camper named Amelia."

"Like Camp Amelia?" I asked.

Bea nodded. "They changed the name of the camp after she died to honor her."

"My dad said it was named after Amelia Earhart," I said. "Because she's a good role model for adventurous girls. Ugh. I should've known he was lying."

"Nana Mary said a PR person made that up in the nineties, because they didn't want anyone to know the camp was named after a dead girl," said Bea.

"A dead girl who still haunts the camp to this very day," whispered Poppy.

"Did she die on the ropes course?" I asked, hoping the answer was yes, because then Dad would have to pick me up.

Ainsley rolled her eyes. "You guys are so dramatic. She died from a bee sting. She was allergic and they didn't have EpiPens back then."

Poppy put her hand over her heart and looked off in the direction I had been headed. "And her spirit roams the woods back here, because that's where she got stung and died."

Surprisingly, I am not afraid of ghosts. I'm scared of things that are right in front of me. Elevators I might get stuck in, riding a horse that might throw me off, a top bunk falling on me in my sleep . . . you get the idea. But I'm not scared of things I can't see, things that aren't real. Dad says it's because I spend so much energy being afraid of real-life things, I don't have any left to waste on being worried about imaginary stuff. This might be one of the only things he is actually right about.

"Come on, guys. Stop wasting time," Ainsley said, as she walked away from the haunted woods. Honestly, I would much rather hang out with Amelia the ghost than climb ropes with a crew of girls who hate me.

As soon as we got to the ropes course, Ainsley said, "Everyone get your helmets and harnesses on. Then do safety checks on each other. Bea, you get Maisy set up."

My usual rule is that if something requires a helmet, I'm not doing it, and yes, I even mean bike riding. Now here I was being forced to do an activity that requires a helmet *and* a safety harness.

"This should fit." Bea handed me a bright red helmet. "It's the smallest size."

I took the helmet from her without saying thanks. She was just being nice to me because she wanted me to help them win the stupid Cup.

Bea pulled the straps under my chin and clipped them together.

"Ow!" I rubbed my chin where she had pinched the skin.

She smiled at me in that new fake way of hers. "Sorry. You want it tight, so it doesn't slip off."

My mind started spinning. If this ropes course was sooooo safe, it wouldn't really matter if my helmet was loose—would it?

Ainsley walked over to us and tugged at my helmet. "Nice tight fit."

Seriously, why was everyone so worried about my helmet?

"Since you girls are all certified to belay, you can handle the easy part of the course with Maisy. I'll wait over at the tough part," Ainsley said.

She grabbed a helmet off the ground and jogged into the woods. It sucked watching Ainsley leave because she was probably the only person at camp who didn't hate me.

And what did she mean *tough part*?

Poppy chattered as she pulled on her helmet. "We all took a rope climbing training course last summer so we can spot the younger kids. You're in good hands with us."

Hannah grabbed a helmet. "We're kind of like lifeguards, but for the ropes course."

The fact that this sport required lifeguard-type people was not making me feel any better.

Bea clipped on her helmet. "It starts out easy. You climb the tree and then zipline to that other tree down the field. Once you're on the other side . . ."

She lost me at *zipline*. I have no idea what she said after that because the idea of letting go and flying through the air made it hard to breathe.

"Maisy?" Bea held out a piece of rope. "Here, step into the harness."

The "harness" was really just some looped-together rope. What if Bea hadn't put the harness together right? What if I fell through one of the leg holes? They didn't look like they were meant for little people like me.

Bea could still read my mind. "Isa's just as small as you and she's never fallen through the harness."

"I'll go up with you. Isa will belay for me and Bea will spot you," Hannah said.

"Great, so my life is literally in Bea's hands." I tried to use a jokey tone, but no one laughed, which freaked me out. Did they not laugh because they hated me or because they really thought my life was at stake?

Hannah stood at the base of a tree that had all of these little plastic foot holders nailed into it like a set of stairs. "All you have to do is climb up to the platform. I'll go first so you can see how easy it is."

Sporty people think everything's easy. Hannah tucked her foot into a foothold, then reached up for a plastic thing to hold on to. She flew up the tree like a squirrel. My brain knew exactly what my body had to do, but my mind was having a big freak-out.

I reached for the first plastic hold, but my hands were so sweaty they slipped right off.

"Wipe your hands off on your shorts, then dip them in the chalk bin." Bea nodded to the purple chalk bin next to us.

Of course she didn't think to tell me that *before* I almost slipped and died.

I stuck my hands in the bin, and a cloud of chalk drifted in my face. I started coughing, but then Bea gave me a look that said, "Don't be so dramatic." I took a deep breath and tucked my foot on to the first footrest. I reached my hand high above me and grabbed onto the next plastic thingy. My body was being stretched as far as it could. *Don't look down, don't look down,* I repeated to myself.

Hannah called down, "Great job, Maisy. You can do it!"

I wasn't fooled by Hannah's fake cheers. These girls hated me. All they cared about was the stupid Cup.

I reached up again and dragged my foot to the next rung. The whole time I felt like if I slipped or let go, I would go flying down to the ground. But I kept going because I had no choice. If I didn't at least try, there was no hope for me fitting in here. I wish I was like Bea, who went through every school day with her face buried in a book. She was totally okay ignoring everyone and doing her own thing. I'm not like that. I realized after hanging out with the M & Ms that life is so much better with a squad. Because when I'm alone, I think about things that make me sad.

"You're doing great!" Poppy screamed from below. "Grab the rung to your left and put your foot on the green one to your right."

My arms were burning from holding myself up, but I could see the wooden platform getting closer and closer. The quicker I got there, the sooner this whole nightmare would be over.

"Reach up and Hannah will help you!" Isa yelled from below.

As soon as I got to the platform, Hannah pulled me up. I was fine for the first second or two when I was on my hands and knees. But as soon as I stood up, it was over. The platform was smaller than it looked from the ground. If Hannah came any closer, she would probably knock me off and then Bea would mess up belaying me, and I would fall out of this harness that was supposedly not too big for me.

I wrapped my arms around the tree. The bark rubbed against my face as I pressed my body into it and held tight.

The girls cheered from the bottom—even Bea. But I didn't want to look down because that would mean letting go of the tree.

"You did it!" Hannah yelled. "Next comes the easy part. You just hold on to this bar and zipline to that big tree across the field."

Hannah squeezed in even closer to me. There's seriously no such thing as personal space at camp.

I gripped the tree even tighter.

"You have to let go sometime." Hannah held on to a metal bar with both hands. "I'll go first, then I'll shoot the zipline bar back to you."

"Don't leave me!" I grabbed the tree tighter even though one of my hands was sticky with sap and the other one was getting a splinter.

Hannah laughed, as if she wasn't asking me to possibly jump to my own death. "Watch me do it, then you'll see how easy it is."

I held on tight to the tree but peeked around my arms.

Hannah wrapped her hands around the bar and jumped off the platform with her knees tucked into her body. She flew across the field, and when she reached the other end, she looked like she was going to crash into the tree but then bounced back.

My hands were even sweatier than before, and, of course, there was no chalk bucket up here. What if I slid off the bar? What if I fell out of my harness? What if Bea dropped me? I would probably drop me if I was her.

"All you have to do is jump!" Isa yelled from below.

As if it were really that easy.

"Come on, Maisy!" yelled Hannah from the other platform, pushing the zipline bar back over to me. "I'm waiting on the other side."

I pressed my face against the tree and tried to slow down my breathing. What was scarier, ziplining or climbing back down again?

"You can do it, Maisy! You did the hard part already!" Bea shouted from the ground.

I didn't want to look like a loser in front of Bea, so I loosened my grip on the tree. I inched to the edge of the platform until my toes were sticking over the edge. I wrapped my hands around the zipline bar and gripped as hard as I could. Suddenly, I felt like I was being suffocated, by the helmet, by the rope harness, by my jean shorts.

"I can't do it!" I dropped the zipline bar and turned away from the edge of the platform and grabbed the tree. I pressed my face against the bark so that the deep grooves mashed into my cheeks.

"Come on, Maisy!" Poppy was trying to sound peppy but only sounded stressed.

Even Bea tried to cheer. "You've got this, Maisy. Hannah's waiting on the other side for you."

I knew none of them cared about me. They were only worried about the stupid tournament. Like that was the only thing in the world that mattered.

I hugged that tree as if my life depended on it. "I can't do it!"

Isa called up, "We need you, Maisy! You have to be able to get through the ropes course or we'll all be disqualified from the tournament."

I hate letting people see me cry, but I couldn't help myself. I couldn't even wipe my nose because I was too scared to let go of the tree. I tried to push my words out in between wails. "I . . . can't . . . do . . . it! Get me down from here!"

"It's so easy and super safe," called Hannah from across the field. "You just have to get across so you can see it's not as bad as you think it is."

"I already know it's as bad as I think it is!" I clutched the tree harder. "Please! Bea! You have to get me!"

"Maybe if she stays up there a minute or two, she'll try the zipline. She just needs to get across to see it's not that bad," Isa said.

"Maybe Isa's right," said Poppy.

"Please!" I shrieked.

Even though Bea hated me, she was the one who knew me best. The only one who understood how scared I was. The only one who could get me down.

"Bea! You have to help me!" I screamed. "Don't leave me up here! Bea!!!"

BEA

Maisy's screams were reverberating off the trees. "Bea! . . . Bea! . . . Don't leave me up here!"

The absolute last thing I wanted to do was rescue Maisy. She did nothing this year to liberate me from my friendless existence at school. Now she wanted *me* to save *her*?

Isa's eyes widened. "Is this girl for real? She's screaming like there's a creepy clown killer in the woods."

Maisy's voice sounded more desperate with each yell. "Bea! Get me down from here!"

Poppy blocked the sun from her eyes and looked toward the woods where Ainsley was waiting to spot the harder part of the course. "Ainsley must hear this. Right?"

Hannah climbed down from the tree across the field and ran over to us. "Is she for real?"

Maisy was sounding more desperate with each yell. "Bea! . . . Help me!"

I thought about the day I found out Mom and Dad were getting divorced. I had overheard them talking about their plan to tell me later that day. Maisy's mom was taking us on a Daisy Girl Scout ice skating trip to Rockefeller Center, and my parents didn't want to spoil it for me. They wanted me to have one more pre-divorce innocent day and I didn't have the heart to ruin it for them. So, I hopped in Maisy's mom's minivan like everything was normal. I sang along to the radio with Maisy and the other Daisies so no one would detect anything was wrong. But when we got to the city, my stomach was groaning and rumbling and I desperately needed a bathroom. Some people throw up when they get upset; unfortunately, I have issues with my other end.

Maisy stayed with me in the bathroom while the other girls skated with her mom. Maisy, whose favorite thing was skating, hence the scheduled trip chaperoned by her mother, never even had the opportunity to lace up her skates that day. I told her about my parents' imminent divorce and Dad's plan to move to Nyack. I told her all the things I was worried about, like what if I never saw Dad again? What if he forgot all about me when he moved away? What if he got a new family? Maisy didn't have all the answers that day, but she stayed with me until I got all my questions out.

At the end of the ice skating trip, when the other girls asked where we were, she told everyone she didn't feel well and I had been keeping her company. Maisy knew how embarrassed I was, and she wanted to protect me, even if it meant the whole Daisy troop thought she was the one trapped on the toilet for the entire trip. She always looked out for me back then, even to her own detriment.

"Bea! Help me! Pleeeeeeease!" Maisy yelled for what felt like the hundredth time.

"I'm coming!" I finally yelled back.

"Hurry!"

When I got to the platform, Maisy was crying so hard I thought she was going to vomit. Her hair was plastered to her tear-covered cheeks and she was holding on to the tree as if her life depended on it. I wanted so badly to leave her there and walk away from her like she had done to me every single school day for the past nine months. But I thought about the old Maisy, the one who had sat on the dirty restroom floor for hours that day at Rockefeller Center. That's the girl I was helping.

"I'm here now, Maisy. Let's go back down," I said.

Maisy clutched the tree so hard, her knuckles were bright white. "I can't do it."

I reached out my hand. "I've been climbing this tree since first grade. I'll get you down safely."

"I can't." Maisy grabbed the tree tighter and her voice rose several octaves. "I can't do it, Bea."

I knew there was no way Maisy was moving unless she was confident I had her. I wrapped my arms around her in a tight bear hug. I had forgotten how small she was.

"I'll go down first, then you can come right after. I'll be with you the whole way," I said without letting go of her.

Maisy stopped crying and pulled her face away from the tree. She had crimson bark-shaped ridges imprinted into her cheeks. "Are you sure I'll be okay?"

I sighed. "I got you. Stay with me and you'll be fine."

Maisy's whole body was shaking as I gently unwrapped her freakishly strong fingers from the tree. "You're okay. I have you."

I kept both hands on her arms and walked us to the edge of the platform. "Do you want me to go first? Or do you want to go first?"

"I'm not ziplining!" Maisy shrieked. "There's no way!"

"I know." I sighed again. "But we do need to climb back down the tree. It's the only other way back down."

Maisy took a deep breath and exhaled dramatically. "You first. But don't go too fast."

Obviously, Maisy wanted me to go first so that if she fell she could land on me.

I lowered myself under the platform and positioned my foot on one of the rungs. "It's okay, Maisy. I'm right here."

Her legs trembled as she squatted down to the platform. "I can't do it. I'm going to fall!"

"Come on, Maisy. You got this." No one else was cheering Maisy on with me. They were all done with her hysteria. But I knew it wasn't an act and there's no way to reason with her when she was swept up in a panic attack.

Once she got off the platform, she moved down the tree so fast I had to step up my pace.

Isa threw her helmet, and it bounced before landing at the foot of the tree. "There goes the tournament! It's done. Over."

Poppy sighed. "What am I gonna tell Nana Mary?"

"The Dandelion girls are going to steal the tournament right out from under us!" Isa said. "And they'll be laughing in our faces when they do it."

Maisy sat up and, unclipping her helmet, pulled it off her head so fast, she ripped out a tangled knot of hair. She looked so happy to be back on the ground, she didn't notice.

"You didn't even try." Hannah stepped out of her rope harness. "You gave up as soon as you got on that platform."

The thin blue vein under Isa's left eye thumped and twitched. "All you had to do was zipline! It's the easiest thing in the world. You literally do nothing and the zipline gets you across."

"All those summers winning the tournaments, for nothing," said Poppy.

Maisy ignored everyone and stepped out of her harness. She didn't apologize for not trying harder. She didn't offer to try again. She was still the same Maisy she had been for the past year. Out for herself.

"You're scared of everything! You don't want to be braver or stronger or more independent. You don't belong here." The words burst out of me like hot flames. "Why don't you just go home? Back to the M & Ms! You can sit around the pool and compare tans."

Ainsley ran over from the other side of the field and took one look at Maisy's tear-streaked face before laying into us. "I always thought you were the nice girls here. But you aren't nice, you've just been lucky. You ended up in a bunk where you were all good at everything. You never had to help anyone or wait for someone to catch up. Being lucky means you don't know how to be a team. It doesn't mean you're nice girls. It just means that you can be nice when things are easy."

If Bailey had given us that speech, I wouldn't have been surprised. But Ainsley's never once given us a speech. Speeches take effort and she's always cared more about sneaking off at night than anything else. I think it would've felt better if it had been Bailey doing the lecturing.

Before we could say anything, Maisy took off running into the woods and Ainsley ran after her.

Poppy groaned. "I feel awful. Here I am, the Girls Empowerment Club president at school, and I just made some poor girl at camp feel worthless."

"Maisy is not some poor girl," said Isa. "She spent the past school year making Bea feel like crap. Why is it our job to make her feel good about herself?"

Hannah looked at the ground. "All I know is that I feel kind of like a jerk now."

"This whole situation sucks," I said. "No matter how difficult Maisy is, we're going to look like the bad guys. Here we are feeling guilty about her when we should be having an amazing first day of camp. Maisy has officially ruined our summer."

CHAPTER FIVE

MAISY

AFTER MY NEAR-DEATH EXPERIENCE ON THE ROPES COURSE, I convinced Ainsley to drop me off at Dr. Beth's cabin again. Ainsley had already figured out what an anxious mess I am; I didn't need to explain two trips to the therapy cabin in one day to her.

This time Dr. Beth held a fat orange and black striped cat in her arms. "Say hi to Garfield," she said, as soon as she opened her cabin door. "I'm supposed to be fostering him, but he's so cute I might just end up keeping him."

"Hi, Garfield," I said. It was easy to be nice to a cat when someone else was holding him.

Dr. Beth nodded toward her desk. "Laptop's all yours."

"Thanks," I said, reaching for it. I started typing right away so Dr. Beth wouldn't get the wrong idea and think I was there to talk.

From: dramagirl@gmail.com
To: addyflips@gmail.com
Subject: Hiiiiiiiii!

Hi Addy,

Camp sucks!!! They took away my phone on the bus. I'm not getting it back until the end of the summer. :(

It's only the first day and all the girls in my bunk hate me already!! They stuck me in Bea's cabin with all the girls she's been going to camp with since the summer before second grade. They're all best friends and they hate me because I stopped hanging out with Bea this year.

They also hate me cuz we're going to lose the end-of-summer bunk tournament because of my non-sportiness and anxiety. I don't know why Dad sent me here. This place is meant for brave people who aren't scared of ziplining or swimming in a lake filled with fish you can see. How is it possible that we come from the same parents? Nothing scares you. Not even those crazy level 9 vault moves.

Hope your camp is going better than mine.

XOXO,
Maisy

As soon as I hit send, I looked at Dr. Beth to make sure she wasn't paying attention. She was busy lining up small bowls and filling them with dry cat kibble. I went on Instagram and checked whether the M & Ms responded to my DM. There was no response in our group convo, but Madison had sent me a DM.

From: @madisonave
To: @maisywintersiscoming

OMG! How are you gonna live without your phone all summer?? I am crying for you. Miss you sm. ILY!!

The row of hearts and kissy face emojis only made me feel a little better. I knew the girls were all together at Mia's pool. But Madison was the only one who missed me enough to write back.

From @maisywintersiscoming
To: @madisonave

Miss you sm! Your post was sooooo cute! What R U guys doing?

From: @madisonave
To: @maisywintersiscoming

Hanging at Mia's pool. Everyone says hi, but Meghan says no one DMs anymore. Sry!

I had worked hard all year to hold my spot in the M & Ms. I made Dad buy the giant bag of Starbursts every time we went to Costco, then I would pick through it and bring all the pink and red ones for the girls. At lunch, I sat on the end of our cafeteria bench, near the garbage cans, because Meghan said the smell made her nauseous. I pick all the olives out of Mia's salads because she hates them so much she can't even stand the way they feel on her fingers. How was I going to hold my place in the group when I wouldn't be there to remind them how much they needed me?

To: @madisonave
From: @maisywintersiscoming

Tell everyone hi! Miss you guys sm!! ILY!!

I handed the laptop back to Dr. Beth, then backed toward the door. "Thanks. I have to get back to my cabin."

Dr. Beth didn't even look up from the rows of cat food bowls. "Laptop's here anytime you need it."

I had one hand on the doorknob, when Dr. Beth said, "About that question of yours."

I let go of the doorknob.

"Do you think your good reason justifies what you did?" She poured dry kibble into another bowl.

I thought about the first day of school when Bea saw me hanging out at the flagpole with the M & Ms. Her whole face had crumpled like when her hamster Fred had died. All I wanted to do was run over to her and fix things before it was too late. But that would mean telling Bea what was really going on, and I couldn't risk it, not just for me, but for Addy too. So, I had turned away from Bea's heartbroken face and didn't make eye contact with her again until I got stuck with her at camp.

I shook my head. "Not really."

Maybe Dr. Beth would say something important. But she just moved on to filling up the next cat food bowl.

"Why?" I asked.

She looked up and a few pieces of kibble landed on the floor. "Just wondering. I know you have to get back to your cabin now."

I went outside. I was supposed to wait for Ainsley to walk me back, but I just needed a few minutes by myself. There were too many people at camp, too many people judging me.

The dirt path smelled like mold and wet feet. It twisted and curved in so many different directions that I kept on walking in circles. Every part of the path looked exactly the same—worn down dirt lined with rows of gigantic trees. I kept hearing weird sounds like there were little animals all around me, but not the cute ones you see in Disney movies.

I sat down beside a huge tree stump and wondered what would happen if I just stayed in the woods until they sent a search party looking for me. Maybe I could hide in the haunted area. No one would think to look for me there. Then maybe Dad would finally take me seriously. But whenever they showed a search party in the movies, dogs were always leading the pack. That wouldn't work 'cause I'm terrified of dogs, especially big ones.

I thought therapy was supposed to make you feel better, but all it did was make me feel even worse about what I did to Bea. Meanwhile, it wasn't totally my fault. I couldn't help the fact that Bea is a genius. She was reading *Little Women* when I was still working my way through *Ivy and Bean,* and you can't hide something from someone that smart for too long.

Last summer, right before she left for camp, Bea came too close to figuring out my secret. The problem with Bea is that just knowing something isn't enough for her. She always has to fix things, and this is not a fixable situation. I didn't need her getting up in my business because that would only make things worse.

I couldn't tell Bea why I stopped being her friend, but maybe I could apologize for how I treated her without telling her about my mom.

Suddenly, I heard her voice, so I ducked low behind the stump so the girls wouldn't see me.

"Can you believe my own mom is the one who sold me out? She told Maisy's dad about camp!"

Um, I was the one Bea's mother sold out, not Bea. I debated blowing my cover just to correct her.

"Have you ever seen someone cry like that?" Hannah asked. "Not even the first graders pitch a fit about ziplining!"

"She only cares about herself," Bea said.

I *knew* Bea was only being fake nice to me earlier! Here I was feeling all guilty and ready to apologize and she was trash talking me.

"All those summers winning the tournament and someone who spent the last year being all Mean Girl on you is gonna keep us from getting the Cup?" Isa asked.

"Maybe Ainsley's right. Maybe we only know how to be friends with people when it's easy," Poppy said.

"That's not true!" said Bea. "You guys were all there for me that first summer when I was homesick and sad about my parents getting divorced."

I was the one who was there for her the rest of that school year when her parents were passing her back and forth for weekends and holidays. Where were these girls when she was crying about missing that first Thanksgiving with her mom? When her Dad bought a rotisserie chicken, cranberry sauce that was shaped like a can and jiggled on the plate, and a box of Stove Top Stuffing? He didn't even get the pumpkin pie right. I mean, who even knew you could buy frozen pumpkin pie?

"And Poppy got Nana Mary to donate to the scholarship fund when my mom got laid off so I could still come to camp," said Hannah.

"It's not us!" Isa cut in. "Maisy's the problem. She's only out for herself. That's why she dropped Bea to get popular and that's why she's never gonna try to help us win the Cup."

"I can't believe I let Ainsley make me feel bad," said Bea. "Ainsley wasn't there when Maisy ditched me out of nowhere. She didn't see what it was like for me to show up on the first day of sixth grade and have Maisy look right through me, as if we hadn't been best friends our whole lives."

Like it was my fault that she made no effort to fit in with *anyone else* at school? She left every summer and just expected me to sit home waiting for her to get back. That was fine every other summer when Mom was still Mom. She would take me for mani-pedis or clothes shopping or to the movies when Dad was at work and Addy was at gymnastics. But last summer, I needed to get out of the house, as far away from Mom as possible. It wasn't like I planned to join another friend group. It just happened since we all hung out at the Mapleton Country Club. One day, Madison complimented me on my navy and white floral bathing suit from Hollister and next thing I knew she had invited me to sit with them. It was just easier with them. We all hung out at the pool, or we went to Mia's house. I didn't have to worry about them coming to my house and asking too many questions. I didn't have to worry about them digging deep enough to figure out my secret.

"There's no way we're going to let her come in here and be friends with all of us," said Hannah.

"Not after the way she treated you," said Poppy. "She doesn't deserve our friendship."

"Don't worry, Bea. We'll make Maisy so miserable, they'll have to send her home," said Isa.

I waited for the girls to get a head start, then I followed them back to the cabin, leaving enough distance between us that I didn't have to listen to them bashing me the whole way. There was no way Dad was letting me come home. Not with the Mom situation. I was stuck here. All summer. With a bunk full of girls who hated me. If I was going to make it, I needed a plan.

BEA

Dear Dad,

Just wanted to let you know I'm all settled in at camp. I'm in the Sunflower Bunk with the same girls I bunk with every summer. It's always great to be reunited with them. This year, my old friend Maisy came to camp and she's in our bunk. She's a little behind in her skills, but we are going to work hard to get her ready for the tournament.

Hope you, Monica, and the kids are doing well. I'm sorry Monica got sick last month when I was scheduled to visit. Maybe I can come the last week of August when I'm back from camp? I would love to check out your new house. I know I've seen it on FaceTime, but that's not comparable to seeing it in person.

Hope you guys have a nice time at Disney! Take some pictures for me.

Love,
Bea

Last year, I forgot to write Dad till three weeks into camp and he gave Mom a hard time about it. So, I dashed off a quick letter, put it in the mail bin, then headed back to the bunk. Dad only likes to hear good things, especially about things he is paying for like camp, so I try to keep my communication with him light.

I got back to the cabin just in time for lights out, which is usually the most chaotic time in our bunk. Ainsley always comes up with an excuse to leave the cabin, like a mandatory counselor meeting or a trip to the nurse's cabin for calamine lotion for her nonexistent poison ivy. However, we all knew she was sneaking off to the boys' camp across the lake to hang out with the college boys who worked as counselors there, leaving us to our own devices long into the night. We usually talk nonstop at a loud enough decibel to drown out the buzzing chorus of crickets.

However, that night, we all climbed wordlessly in our bunks. It felt like we were playing the quiet game with much higher stakes than usual.

Next thing I knew, I was jerked awake by the rattling of my bunk. When I opened my eyes, I saw Maisy climbing down the bunk ladder. She's one of those people who gets up to pee a million times a night. When we had sleepovers, Mom used to remind her to stop drinking by six o'clock.

But Maisy didn't walk across the room to the bathroom. Instead, the floorboard squeaked like it does when Ainsley sneaks out, and the cabin door creaked open, which was weird because Maisy's afraid of the dark. I'm also quite certain she's even more scared of being in the woods at nightfall.

My eyes opened wider as they adjusted to the dark. The only reason Maisy would leave the cabin at night was to sneak away. This was just like that article I had read about campers who had bullied their bunkmate, forcing her to run away, and then she got attacked by a bear in the night. Poppy, Isa, Hannah, and I would never get into college because the admissions people would remember that viral news story about the camp Mean Girls who made their bunkmate so miserable that she sneaked off in the night and got eaten by a wild animal. I slid off my blankets and snuck out without stepping on the creaky floorboard or making the door squeak. It was up to me to save Maisy for the second time in one day.

Outside the cabin door, I looked around but didn't see Maisy anywhere. I whispered into the cold night air over the chattering of the crickets and cicadas, "Maisy? Where are you?"

I stepped off the porch and tried to figure out which direction she would consider the least frightening. I didn't anticipate her venturing into the woods alone because she would be terrified of the animals, but I also didn't think she would be dumb enough to go on the lit trail where someone would spot her.

"Maisy! Maisy!" I whispered a little louder this time.

I wasn't her biggest fan, but that didn't mean I wanted something to happen to her if she ran away.

"Maisy! Maisy!" I called as quietly as I could.

I heard a rustling sound and instantly regretted all those late nights reading Stephen King's *It* right before coming to camp.

"Maisy? Is that you?" I whispered.

"Bea?"

"Maisy? Where are you?"

"Behind you. At the art cabin." Maisy whimpered.

I spun around to face the cabin that was a few feet away from our bunk. Everyone called it the art cabin because that's what it had been back in the antiquated days when Poppy's Nana Mary was a camper. But over the years, as the camp became more serious about preparing the girls for the bunk tournaments, it was turned into a fitness center. Everyone, including the new girls like Maisy, still called it the art cabin.

"I'm around back," Maisy whispered. "On the porch."

Maisy was crouched on the porch railing with her back arched like a cat.

"What are you doing?" I whispered.

Maisy white knuckled the railing. "I was going to jump. But then I chickened out."

"You were going to kill yourself over the bunk tournament?"

Maisy's eyes widened. "Are you insane?" she whisper-yelled.

I tiptoed slowly to her with my arms stretched out like they do on TV shows when someone is about to jump off a bridge. "You're the one standing on a porch railing in the middle of the night and I'm the crazy person?"

Maisy rolled her eyes and shook her head, as if I was the unstable person in this situation. "I wasn't going to kill myself. I swear."

"Then what're you doing up there?" I asked in my most calm and soothing voice.

"Get me down, then I'll explain," Maisy hissed.

I was done with Maisy bossing me around. I folded my arms across my chest. "Tell me first."

She teetered on the edge of the railing as if she were hanging off a cliff. "I thought if I jumped off the railing, I would sprain my wrist or, even better, break my ankle."

"What? Why would you want to do that?"

Maisy put on her most dramatic face and tone of voice. "It's the only way out of here."

I couldn't help laughing. "We jump off that porch all the time. No one gets sent home for a skinned knee."

"It's not funny." Maisy's whispers were getting louder. "I can't go all summer living with a bunch of girls who hate me."

"Oooh, yeah." I resisted the urge to push her off. "I'd hate to be surrounded by people who hate me. I mean, that's really rough."

She looked down at the ground. She knew where I was going. "You could've made other friends."

"'Cause it's really easy? Like you can make friends here, right?" I turned away. Maisy could save herself this time.

"Bea, wait. Don't leave me," she pleaded.

I started walking away. It's not like she was on top of the Empire State Building.

"Please, Bea," she begged.

I turned back and looked her right in her hazel eyes. "Give me one reason why I should help you."

"I have a plan." Maisy stretched out the last word.

I raised an eyebrow. "I thought your plan was to jump off the porch."

"I have a new plan. A better one." There was a hint of desperation in her voice.

Maisy makes good plans. She always has. Once, she figured out we were wasting our time with a lemonade stand on my quiet cul-de-sac, and she came up with the idea to sell gluten-free, fat-free muffins on the commuter train platform instead. In one day we made enough money for a pile of glittery headbands, sequined skirts, and graphic tees from Justice. Looking back, those outfits were mortifyingly tacky, but at the time they felt like pure gold.

Maisy was steadying herself on the porch railing with two shaky hands.

"What's the plan?" I asked.

"If you make your friends like me, I'll try my best to help you guys win the tournament."

I laughed out loud—to be accurate, I guffawed. "That's your big plan?"

She wobbled a bit. "What's wrong with it?"

"You want me to get my friends to put up with the Maisy Show all summer in exchange for you," I made air quotes, "trying your best?"

"The Maisy Show?" She held her arms out like she was on a balance beam.

"You can't expect my friends to deal with all the Maisy drama all the time for the whole entire summer. And you can't expect me to make it all okay for you."

Maisy crouched to a squatting position. "I can't do this, Bea. I can't spend the whole summer here with my entire bunk hating me."

"Then go home," I said. "Call your mom and beg and plead. Say whatever you need to get your parents to come pick you up."

"Going home is not an option. You're my only hope at surviving camp this summer." Maisy breathed in so deeply that her whole rib cage moved underneath her pajama shirt. "Name your price."

What could Maisy offer me? I thought about what I really wanted, what I really needed. All I wanted was to feel at school like I did at camp. Some might call it popular; I didn't care what anyone called it. I just wanted to belong. But I knew Maisy's language.

I folded my arms across my chest. "I'll make you popular at camp if you make me popular at school."

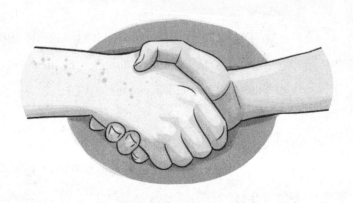

→·· CHAPTER SIX ··←

MAISY

I COULDN'T SLEEP BECAUSE AS SOON AS MY HEAD HIT THE PILLOW,
I started wondering how this whole pact thing was going to work.
The more I thought about it, the more questions I had that only Bea
could answer. After a while, I heard her get up, so I climbed down
from my bunk and followed her to the bathroom.

I could hear her peeing, then the toilet flushed and she opened
the door and jumped back.

"You scared me! What are you doing?" she hissed. Then she
looked down at my feet. "Why are you wearing sneakers? You're not
going to sneak out again, are you, because . . ."

"Calm down. I'm not going anywhere. I slept in my shoes." I
looked down at the expensive running sneakers Dad had bought me

just before I left. I should've known that was a clue he was sending me to a sporty camp. "They keep the bugs from touching my feet."

"What?" Bea wiped the sleep from her eyes. "I'm half asleep. What do you want?"

"I can't sleep. How's this pact gonna work?" I whispered.

She held her finger to her lips, then tiptoed to the bathroom door and pushed it closed slowly so it didn't make a sound.

"I'm going to make you fit in with my friend group at camp. When we go home, you're going to make me fit in with yours," Bea whispered, in a condescending way, as if I was the stupidest person on earth.

I swallowed hard. "You want to hang out with the M & Ms?"

"I don't just want to hang out with the M & Ms. I want to be a part of the group." Her tone of voice showed she knew she was the one with all the power in this situation.

"But you don't even like them," I said. "You think they're artificial, superficial, obsessed with popularity." I ticked each word off on my fingers.

Bea cut me off. "You know what I really don't like? Eating lunch alone in the library every day. You know what else I don't like? Going through a whole school day without anyone talking to me. Not. One. Single. Person," she hissed.

As much as I had tried to convince myself that she didn't mind being alone all the time, deep down I knew she was miserable. But there were some serious problems with her plan. The most obvious issue was that her name doesn't start with an *M*. Then there was the fact that I was the last girl in the group, and Meghan made sure to remind me of that on the daily. I mean, it wasn't like I really had the power to add on to the group when my spot was still kind of weak. Then there was the obvious problem—the M & Ms didn't like her. They thought Bea was a know-it-all, which was going to be pretty hard to prove wrong. But I had the whole summer to figure it all out.

I looked Bea in the eye. "It's a deal."

Bea reached out her hand. "Let's shake on it."

"Um, can you wash your hands first?"

She rolled her eyes. "This is going to be a long summer."

After I climbed back in bed, I must've fallen right to sleep, because next thing I knew the sun was shining in through the windows and I could hear the other girls moving around in their bunks. Bea had told me to pretend to stay asleep till she talked to the girls. So, I rolled to face the wall and snuggled deeper into my blankets. I was dying to braid my hair, but I stayed still as a statue so I wouldn't give myself up. The bedsprings creaked as Bea climbed out of the bottom bunk.

"Move over," Bea said. I could hear the mattress coils groan as she climbed into someone else's bunk, probably Hannah's.

Isa's Staten Island accent was strong first thing in the morning. "What time is it?"

"Too early for talking," moaned Hannah. "Ainsley's not back from her morning run yet."

"Especially because it's not like we have anything to train for because of a certain someone," Poppy whisper-yelled.

You know things are bad when the Poppys of the world are hating on you.

"Winning that tournament every summer is the only time I feel . . . like I'm in charge. Back home my mom and agent run my life." Poppy let out a loud sigh. "The Justice photo shoot made me the most popular girl in fourth grade. But this year, all the girls at school turned on me when I got the Abercrombie campaign."

No wonder I thought Poppy looked familiar. I probably had a shopping bag at home with her actual face on it.

"We lost all that power as soon as 'The Girl Who Is Afraid of Everything' moved into our bunk." Isa groaned.

"I can't stop thinking about what Ainsley said. Maybe we're the Mean Girls we all hate back home," Bea said.

Isa cut in, "Maisy gave up before she even started. All she cares about is herself."

The ironic thing is that Dad said one reason he was sending me to camp was so I could focus on myself. I had spent the whole last year worrying about Mom so much that I hadn't had much time to think about me.

"The only way to prove Ainsley wrong is by being nice to Maisy, whether she's good at rope climbing or not," said Bea. "What good is winning the Cup if we're as judgmental as all those people back home who drag us down?"

Hannah sounded suspicious, which helped prove her point that she didn't belong in that horrible math class. "I thought you hated Maisy."

"Yeah," Poppy jumped in. "You spent all year texting us about how materialistic she is . . . how fake . . . how all she cares about is being popular."

Bea acts all innocent, but she knows how to throw some shade.

"And how she spent the past year following the M & Ms," added Isa.

Seriously, the girl could cut deep with her words.

Bea cut in. "That was before she was part of our bunk."

Isa groaned. "The girl's phobias are going to keep us from winning the Cup. Why should we bother wasting our time on her?"

"That's my point," said Bea. "Maybe Ainsley was right about us."

"Don't say that. I already feel so guilty about the way we treated her yesterday," Poppy admitted.

Bea started talking faster. "Would you guys be friends with me if I wasn't such a good swimmer? Would we all be friends with Isa if she wasn't the faster runner at camp? Or Hannah, if she wasn't amazing at the ropes course? Or Poppy if she wasn't such a fast kayaker?"

"Of course we would all still be friends," said Hannah.

"There's only one way to prove that to ourselves," said Bea. "We give Maisy a chance."

I didn't realize I had been holding my breath until I let it out. *I needed this.* It was the only way not to think about what would be waiting for me back home at the end of the summer.

BEA

This past school year has been one of complete loneliness. I was the outsider in a sea of groups because tweens believe being unpopular is as contagious as the stomach flu. No one wants to catch being unpopular right before middle school. Things got so bad, I considered moving in with Dad to get a fresh start in a new school district. But the thought of leaving Mom behind made it hard to breathe. Even worse, Monica's kids are allergic to cats, so I'm not even allowed to bring Mr. Pebbles for a visit. Mom thinks that's just a cover for Monica, who doesn't want to get cat hair on her pristine furniture. Not to mention, when I brought up moving in with Dad casually at dinner, Monica gave Dad the "We'll talk about this later" look. The next day, he gave me a lecture about "not messing with things that work," like me living with Mom.

As much as I didn't want to trust Maisy, my destiny was now tied to hers. I was going to have to do everything in my power to make this pact work.

After breakfast, I took advantage of Ainsley getting pulled aside for a counselor meeting. As we left the dining cabin, I turned left at the birch tree with the peeling bark and headed down the rocky path.

"Where are you going?" Hannah asked.

Normally, we spent our post-breakfast free period poring through Poppy's fashion magazines. But I led us deep under the canopy of birch trees, where the air felt cool and damp. "We're not giving up on the ropes course."

Isa narrowed her eyes at me. "I thought we agreed to be nice to Maisy. Now you want us to torture her?"

I spoke in an octave deeper than I usually do because I read somewhere that doing that can give the illusion of confidence. "We're going to help Maisy conquer her fear."

Maisy wedged herself next to me on the path, which was really only wide enough for single-file walking, and hissed, "What if I don't want to conquer my fear?"

"You wanted me to help you fit in. This is how," I whispered back.

"Isn't there another way?" She was breaking into a sweat.

"This is it."

As soon as we got to the clearing that led to the ropes course, I stood up straight with my hands clasped so the girls would know I meant business. "We didn't give Maisy a chance yesterday."

Isa shook her head vehemently. "That's not true—"

"Not a real one," I cut in. "We all forgot it was her first time doing a ropes course. It's not like any of us aced it on our first try."

Poppy nodded, always ready to give someone a second, third, or even fourth chance. "Bea's right. You guys should've seen how bad I did at my first photo shoot."

Hannah picked up a helmet off the ground and handed it to Maisy. That was her way of saying she was in.

Maisy stared at the helmet. I gave her a look that said, "Take it or you're going to sabotage the pact."

Maisy put the helmet on. "You need to come with me, Bea."

I pulled on my own helmet and adjusted the chin strap. "That's the plan." I turned to the other girls. "And the rest of you guys need to be supportive, even if she has another nervous breakdown."

Isa shrugged in a passive-aggressive way. "It's not like we have a shot at the Cup otherwise."

I held out a rope harness for Maisy to step into. "Our only goal is to get across that zipline today."

"It makes sense to break it up into parts. That's how I learned algebra." Hannah pulled on a belaying harness. "I'll belay for you, and Isa will belay for Maisy."

"And I'll be here for moral support," said Poppy.

I pulled my rope harness tight. "Thanks, guys."

Maisy chattered as we walked to the tree. "What if I didn't put my helmet on right? Is it tight enough? If I'm not supposed to fall and I have people spotting me, why do I even need a helmet? Do people fall off? Is that a thing? Is that why we need helmets? And spotters? And harnesses?"

Maisy's nervous energy made the air around us thick. I unclicked her chin strap and swung the helmet around. "It was backward. But it's all set now and if it was on any tighter, your head would pop off."

Maisy put both hands on her helmet and looked satisfied when she wasn't able to jiggle it around. "Seriously, why do we need to wear helmets and harnesses if it's so safe?"

I leaned into her and kept my voice low. "You're never gonna be friends with these girls if you don't show them you're at least trying."

"Fine." Maisy sighed. "But remember, my life is in your hands."

I rolled my eyes. "You are so dramatic."

"Exactly. Which is why I should be at drama camp right now," Maisy said.

I slipped my feet into the plastic footholds and climbed to the first rung. "Come on. Right behind me."

I was shocked when she actually grabbed on to the plastic holds and stepped onto the tree. Clearly, she was as desperate as I was for this pact to work.

"You know you can climb the tree. You did it yesterday." I moved up to the next rung and felt Maisy close behind me.

"It's not the climbing that's scary, it's that tiny little platform." Her voice was shaky and breathless.

"You're not that big, and the platform isn't that small. There's plenty of room." I kept reaching hand over hand, foot over foot, with Maisy so close I could feel her breath on my shins.

"Come on, Maisy! You can do it!" yelled Poppy.

I pulled myself up and squatted down on the wooden platform. "All you have to do is climb up."

"Great job, Maisy!" Poppy yelled from right underneath the tree.

I put both of my hands on top of Maisy's as soon as she touched the platform. "I have you."

She pulled herself up, breathing super heavy, and flopped on the platform, looking just like that big trout that leapt onto the dock at my grandma's summer cottage that one time.

"That was the hard part! Ziplining doesn't require any upper body strength. All you have to do is jump!" yelled Hannah.

Maisy sat up and tried to catch her breath. "Jumping is the hard part."

She is the type of person who lays her clothes out the night before, even on the weekends. It was starting to make sense why ziplining would be scary for a control freak like her.

I grabbed the zipline bar. "We're going to jump together."

"Is it even meant for two people to go at once? What if we weigh too much and the zipline breaks?" She put a hand on her heaving chest. "Let me catch my breath."

I had learned over the years that you have to move quick with her. Extra time just makes her think of a hundred more reasons to be anxious.

I tried to hand her the bar, but she grabbed my legs and I could see how people got drowned by the person they were trying to save.

"This isn't going to work if you don't trust me." I kept my voice calm and measured.

Her voice was muffled with her face crammed against my legs. "It's not you I don't trust. It's the zipline, and the helmet, and the rope harness, and Isa, the girl who hates me but is supposed to save my life if I fall."

I pulled her up and grabbed her by the shoulders. I wanted to slap her across the face like you always see people do in the movies when someone acts insane, but Maisy bruises too easily. "Enough of this craziness."

I shoved the zipline bar at her and pressed her fingers around it. I wrapped my left hand over hers and my right hand over the bar and jumped.

CHAPTER SEVEN

MAISY

DON'T TELL BEA, BUT ZIPLINING WASN'T AS SCARY AS I THOUGHT.
It felt kind of good to be soaring through the trees, far away from
the drama back home.

We flew into the platform on the other side of the field super
hard, then bounced back. It was scary to have my feet dangling in
the air, but Bea kept her hands wrapped around mine super tight.
That's the thing with Bea, I still felt safe with her, even though we
weren't friends anymore.

The girls below were yelling and cheering, and it felt so much
better than when they were hating on me yesterday.

Bea's voice was calm, like when she used to help me study for
math. "Now all you have to do is get back on the platform. I'm going

to have to let go of your hand for a second to get up there first. Then I can help you."

The last thing I wanted was for Bea to let go of me.

"Okay, on the count of three I'm letting go. Nod if that's okay," she said.

It took everything I had to nod slowly, up and down.

"One . . . two . . . three." Bea lifted her hand and reached for the platform.

Don't look down, don't look down, I repeated in my head, while Bea pulled herself up. She reached for me, then I realized reaching out for her would mean letting go of the bar, which was the one thing keeping me from falling to my death, okay, besides the rope harness and Isa belaying me. But still, you could see how scary this would be, right?

"Come on, Maisy! You can do it!" yelled Poppy.

"You're doing great, Maisy!" cheered Hannah.

Bea's voice cut through my fear. "I've got you, Maisy." She sounded just like she did that time she tried to teach me how to ride my bike. That didn't work out so well, but at least she never said she was holding on to the back and then let go like Dad did.

I let go of the bar with my right hand and reached out to Bea. She wrapped her hand around mine. "Now gimme the other hand."

I don't know what got into me, but instead of freaking out and crying, I let go with the other hand and grabbed on to Bea. Before I knew it, she had pulled me up onto the platform.

It felt so good to have my feet on something solid.

"This platform is so much bigger than the other one," I said.

Bea shook her head. "Nope. They're the exact same size."

"Are you sure?"

Her red curls were flying out of her helmet in all sorts of crazy directions. "You just feel safe, so you're realizing it's not as small as you thought it was."

Hannah, Isa, and Poppy were all waiting down at the bottom with high fives and cheers. A few hours in and Bea was already holding up her end of the pact. I was going to have to start figuring out how I would hold my end up when we got back to Mapleton. I didn't have anywhere near as much power over the M & Ms as Bea had with the Sunflower girls.

"There you guys are!" shouted Ainsley. "It's swim time. You girls go to the usual spot and wait for me. I'm going to walk Maisy to Minnow Pond for her lesson."

"Make sure you bring your water wings," said Hannah.

I swallowed hard, certain that Ainsley's announcement had taken away whatever street cred I had just earned. But then I looked at Hannah and she was smiling at me, letting me in on the joke, so I could laugh at myself with the other girls. I made sure to laugh in a nice way, which was the smart thing to do because Bea gave me a tiny nod.

As I followed Ainsley down the dirt path toward Minnow Pond, I noticed one thing: I was taller than every other single camper who ran past us—by a lot. When you're short like me, you always notice anyone else who is smaller.

"What's with all the little kids?" I asked.

"Minnow Pond is at the other end of camp, where all the mini campers stay," Ainsley said.

I groaned. "I thought it was humiliating when I failed the swim test, but it just keeps getting worse."

She cracked her gum as she walked. "You think this is bad? When I was your age, I begged my mom to sign me up for gymnastics. The class was seven hundred bucks nonrefundable. So, my mom and step-dad made me promise I would go to every single class, no matter what."

I nodded. "I get it. My dad says he could've bought a brand-new Porsche with the money he's spent at my sister's gym."

Ainsley blew a super big bubble and popped it between her lips. "I didn't really think it through before I promised. First of all, I didn't think about the dress code. Who wants to walk around in a leotard when you're going through puberty?"

"That sucks."

The rocky path led straight to Minnow Pond. "There was no beginner class for kids my age. So, there I was, this five-foot-ten sixth grader in a class full of super tiny kids who had been doing gymnastics since preschool, but just weren't quite good enough for the team.

You should've seen me towering over them all on the tumble track while they were flipping away."

"Let me guess. Your mom wouldn't let you quit because she already paid for it," I said.

Ainsley walked with bare feet and didn't even cringe when she hit a jagged stone or a bug crawled on her foot. "I knew better than to even ask. I had to spend the next fourteen weeks in class with these kids. I thought I was going to die of embarrassment when my crush showed up on family day to watch his baby sister."

I cringed. "Oooh, that's rough."

"It was." She nodded. "But then the next school year, I made the track team. On the first day, the jumps coach asked if anyone had gymnastics experience. I raised my hand even though his idea of experience probably wasn't a fourteen-week class with a bunch of little kids. But I was the only one who raised my hand, so he put me on pole vault."

"That's cool."

She nodded again. "It was even more cool when I became the pole vault state champ junior year and got a track scholarship to U of Miami."

I sighed. "You made your point. I'll give the swim lessons a chance. Even though I don't see how learning to swim is ever going to help me later in life. It's not like I'll ever get good enough to earn a swimming scholarship."

Ainsley looked at me wide-eyed. "Ever thought about going on vacation one day and being able to swim in the ocean? Like Hawaii or the Bahamas or even Miami?"

"Nope."

She shook her head. "You are one strange kid."

BEA

Dear Bea,

I miss you like crazy already! So does Mr. Pebbles. He keeps forgetting you're gone and scratches at your bedroom door until I open it and show him you aren't there. He's very bossy when you're away. He's been demanding ice cubes in his water bowl and back scratches while we watch Netflix.

I thought Dr. Winters was just trying to make polite conversation about your summer plans when I bumped into him at Stop and Shop. I never thought he would send Maisy to Camp Amelia! Drama camp, I could see—but adventure camp? Not in a million years. I am so sorry!!!

I know how awful Maisy was to you. BUT there's a reason why a girl who's scared of her own shadow got shipped off to adventure camp for the summer. Things aren't like you remember at Maisy's house. This is one of those times in life when you are being called on to be the bigger person. A hard feat, but something I know I raised you to do.

I love you more than anything. I'm counting down the days till you get back home and we have our Gilmore Girls and pepperoni pizza binge-fest!

Love always,
Mom

P.S. You're the best daughter ever! XOXO

P.P.S. I am actually going on a blind date this week. Keep your fingers crossed that he doesn't show up two hours late, floss his teeth at the table, or order filet mignon and stick me with the bill like my last few blind dates.

Mom is not a cryptic person. In fact, she's whatever the antonym of *cryptic* is. She always says it like it is, whether you have kale in your teeth, your haircut didn't turn out like the magazine picture, or you shouldn't even attempt the magazine picture haircut in the first place. I had no idea what Mom meant about Maisy's house being different, but she didn't need to encourage me to be nice to Maisy. If being nice to Maisy was my ticket to belonging, then it was worth the steep price of admission.

To her credit, Maisy has put a lot of effort into getting to know the girls over the past few days. She spent hours during the craft block making friendship bracelets with Hannah and teaching Poppy how to do double dutch braids. But these surface niceties were only getting her so far. She was going to have to work harder to become a real Sunflower Bunk girl instead of someone the girls were just being polite to. And if I wanted to be a part of the M & Ms when we got back to Mapleton, I needed to make Maisy a genuine part of our bunk.

I had figured out how to get around the fact that my name doesn't start with an *M*. I was thinking maybe we could say my middle name is Mackenzie or Morgan. If it took changing my name to be seen again, I was all in. It's not like I even like the M & Ms. But my babysitter Lauren filled me in on how middle school works.

First of all, there are monthly teen centers, which are basically school dances with different themes. Lauren showed me pictures from the Wild West night and told me all about it. All of her friends texted each other to come up with coordinating outfits. They wore matching bandanas, jean shorts, straw cowgirl hats, and pigtails. They got ready together at one girl's house so they could help each other get their hair and makeup right. The key to dressing up for a theme night is matching a group of people so you don't stand out on your own. For example, the last thing you want to do is show up to an Out of This World theme night dressed as a character from L. M. Maverick's novel of the same name when everyone else is dressed up like aliens. This is definitely something I would do without a group to lead me down the right path.

Then there's the four-day trip to Boston the seventh graders take every spring. Students pick their roommates, and Lauren said there's always one room filled with the random kids who no one wants to room with. Everyone knows who gets put in that room, and according to my current social status, I was sure to end up there, along with Isabelle Barnes, who eats her own ear wax, Lissie Stemple, who still plays with Barbies, and Rachel Gotwinn, who cries every time she gets called on in class.

Being a part of the M & Ms would guarantee me a place in a group for all of the awkward herd mentality experiences of middle school. Mapleton School's version of Mean Girls was my only means of survival. I needed to make this pact work.

Ainsley waited for lights out and sneaked out to the boys' camp as usual. She was on track to be on her second boyfriend by the second week of camp.

Maisy sat on the opposite side of the cabin from the other girls. I wasn't used to her being so quiet. At school, she couldn't get through a class without being reprimanded for talking with one of the M & Ms.

I jumped off my bunk and yelled, "Girls' night!"

Maisy wrapped a braid around her head like a crown so she looked like a music festival princess and asked, "How is that different from every other night here?"

Hannah tossed a bag of marshmallows at her. "S'mores!"

I grabbed a box of cinnamon graham crackers and mini Hershey's bars from under my bunk. "Grab the hair dryer, Isa."

"What do we need a hair dryer for?" Maisy asked.

Isa plugged the dryer in the outlet above Ainsley's bunk. "Roasting marshmallows."

Hannah used Ainsley's bunk as a table and set out a paper plate. Next, she broke the graham crackers apart and put them in neat rows on the plate. Then she added one square of chocolate and one marshmallow on top of each one. "We used to roast these over an actual fire in the woods."

Poppy jumped in, "But we stopped because Bea's cousin Teddy became a wildfire fireman and he . . ."

Maisy stared at me. "Teddy, who used to play Grand Theft Auto for hours a day, is a fireman? Mind blown."

At moments like this, the sting of being left behind was almost too much to bear. If we had been friends for the past year, Maisy would have known this and so many other things about me.

"For six months now," I said, trying to keep the edge from my voice.

Isa pointed the hair dryer at the plate at a diagonal so she could heat up a few s'mores at a time.

Maisy stood over her and watched. "Can you get cancer from the stuff blowing out of the hair dryer?"

Hannah laughed. "You are so funny, Maisy."

Meanwhile, I gave Maisy a look that said, "Cut the crazy talk."

Then I added, "Hannah, you should let Maisy do a side french braid on you. It would look so good with your blue tips."

"Can you, Maisy?" Hannah asked.

Maisy pulled out the only chair inside our bunk. "Sure. Sit here so I can reach."

Hannah sat down and Maisy's fingers flew through her hair as she pulled strands into a complicated pattern.

Poppy moved the dial and adjusted the antenna on our old purple boom box as she tried to get past the static to actual music. It had been around since Poppy's mom was in our cabin back in the eighties. We could've brought a newer one, but there was something magical about that old purple radio. It always seemed to play the perfect songs.

Poppy found the local station, the one that played mostly current music. We all sang along to Taylor Swift and talked about how much better her older albums were.

Isa turned off the hair dryer when the marshmallows had deflated into soft white clouds over the softened Hershey's squares and walked around the room with the plate.

Luckily, Maisy was smart enough to know that turning down Isa's s'mores was not a good move, even if she was creeped out by the hair dryer germs all over her food. She twisted the last strand of Hannah's hair and wrapped a clear plastic rubber band around it. Then she grabbed a s'more and took a bite.

A bit of graham cracker flew from Maisy's mouth. "This is amazing!"

Isa smiled. "Thanks. I'm making another batch."

If Isa could smile at Maisy, maybe there was hope for me with the M & Ms. Maybe all it took was a nudge from someone within the group to make the others more likely to open themselves up to an outsider.

Hannah stood by the mirror and ran her fingers over her braids, the twisted brown and blue strands of hair. "Maisy, you're a genius."

"It's so easy," Maisy said. "I'll teach you."

"Thanks!" Hannah said.

Maisy turned to me. "OMG! Bea! Remember when I taught your dad how to do your hair?"

"After he . . . after he . . . ." I was laughing so hard, I couldn't catch my breath.

Maisy jumped in, "Used sandwich bag ties in your pigtails instead of rubber bands!"

"He didn't!" shrieked Hannah.

"Oh, yes, he did," said Maisy. "On class picture day!"

The cabin filled with our laughter.

"Bea doesn't have to worry about that anymore now that Monica's there full-time," said Poppy.

"Who's Monica?" Maisy asked.

"Her dad's live-in girlfriend," Isa shouted over the hair dryer.

Maisy's eyes widened. "Do you like her?"

I shrugged. "I can't tell yet. I don't know her well enough to have an opinion of her."

"She moved in with your dad and she's practically a stranger to you?" Maisy asked.

"Bea hasn't even seen their new house yet," said Isa, in what sounded like a "we are her real friends so we know these things" tone.

"And she has two daughters," added Poppy. "Peyton's a year older than Bea and Vivi's a year younger."

Maisy looked at me with the same expression she wore when I won the Three Rivers short story contest and Dad mixed up the days and missed the award ceremony. "Oh, Bea. That sucks."

I swallowed hard. "He signed up to coach Vivi's soccer team."

"Did you remind him about when we played in the Pee Wee league and he didn't show up to one single game because he didn't want to bump into your mother on the sidelines?" Maisy asked.

"That wouldn't fit with Bea's nonconfrontational ways," Hannah said.

Isa passed around the second batch of s'mores and everyone grabbed one.

"Giving my dad a list of all the times he didn't show up won't make him feel more inclined to be there for me now," I said.

"Yeah, but then you'll only ever have a surface-level relationship with him," Maisy said.

"I realized that's all some people are capable of," I said, hoping she would catch my pointed reference.

The song switched and Maisy shrieked, "OMG!"

I almost choked on my s'more. The song that at one time had been our best friend anthem was playing. We won the third-grade talent show dancing to this song. Back then, I was so proud to be up on that stage with Maisy. I didn't care about being popular. I had my best friend and that was all that mattered.

After Maisy ghosted me, Mom knew to change the station on the car radio whenever it came on. This was probably the first time in a year I had heard more than the opening notes.

"Come on, Bea!" Maisy ran to the center of the cabin and started doing our dance routine.

I didn't want to listen to the song, let alone dance around the cabin to it. But Isa was looking at me and the whole key to this pact was winning Isa over. So I got up and danced.

I remembered the moves like it was yesterday because Maisy made me practice over and over again until we got it perfect. Being in the spotlight with Maisy was so bright, it was only when I stood in her shadow that things went dark. Dancing with her in the middle of the cabin made me remember what it was like to be in her light.

Suddenly, the window by Ainsley's bed flew open. We stopped mid-move, like we were in a game of Freeze Dance.

Maisy grabbed my hand just as a huge swarm of crickets landed on the floor and filled the cabin with a deafening roar. The cricket army moved across the wooden planks closer to us.

Maisy screamed like she was in a horror movie and scrambled up the ladder to the top bunk while the other girls and I ran toward the window just in time to see the Dandelion girls sprinting away through the woods.

The crickets weren't the only gift they had bestowed on us. There was an old white sheet fastened to the porch rails. Purple dripping paint spelled out "LOSERS!"

CHAPTER EIGHT

MAISY

I LEANED DOWN AND PUT MY EAR TO THE FLOORBOARD. THE CHIRP was so loud it sounded like there was a cricket in my ear.

"Here. I think it's under here," I said. I could be brave because there was a lot of wood between me and that cricket.

"Which means we're never getting it out." Bea groaned.

"I haven't slept in two days," said Hannah. "The chirping's driving me insane."

Bea dug the palms of her hands into her forehead. "I feel like these crickets have taken up residence in my brain."

Isa jabbed a metal comb into the floorboard and groaned when it didn't budge. "We gotta give those Dandelion girls credit for a crazy good prank."

"Can't believe we haven't gotten revenge yet," moaned Poppy.

"That's because we're all too sleep deprived to come up with an effective countermove," said Bea.

"Why do the Dandelion girls hate you guys so much?" I asked.

"You know, we didn't always hate each other," said Poppy. "We actually all started out in one big bunk together."

"Yeah," Hannah jumped in. "First-year campers are in double cabins, with eight campers instead of four. You don't compete in the tournament the first year. You just get used to going to camp and learn how to do all the events."

"They weren't so bad back then," said Bea. "The A twins already knew how to kayak because they live on a lake. So, they taught us all the basics. Tinka and Isa were both fast runners even back then, so they would run all over camp together, pretending that they were training for the Cup, like the big girls. And back before Kaya started her Instagram beauty account, she was just like any other girl who's into Lip Smackers and Bath & Body Works."

"What changed?" I asked.

"We became each other's biggest competitors," said Isa. "Every summer, the tournament comes down to us versus the Dandelion girls, and I guess they're just sick of losing."

I thought about Bea and me and how we had gone from best friends to practically strangers overnight, and I could see how that could happen. Which meant that the M & Ms could forget all about me while I was at this stupid camp.

"They're not the same girls we went to camp with that first summer. They play dirty and we need to come up with a good prank to let them know we're not playing games," said Bea.

"What if we Saran Wrap the toilet seats in their cabin?" I asked, glad Bea was focusing on how her other former friends turned on her instead of the many ways she thinks I wronged her.

Isa shook her head. "Been there, done that, when we were junior campers."

"Shaving cream bomb?" suggested Poppy.

"They get covered in shaving cream, then take a shower. We need something bigger than that," said Hannah.

"It's been raining all day," said Isa. "You'd think we would've come up with a prank by now since we got nothing better to do."

I may suck at swimming and climbing ropes, and maybe I don't even know how to kayak, but I'm good at coming up with a good prank. Addy and I played pranks on our cousins every summer when we visited them at their cabin in Maine. Maybe if I came up with the perfect revenge prank, my bunkmates would give me a real chance. I needed them to stop being nice to me just as a favor to Bea. I needed them to really make me a part of the group.

Ainsley suddenly jumped off her bunk and pulled on a yellow raincoat. "Phone block!"

All the girls grabbed their bright primary-colored raincoats and ran to the door. Standing together, they looked like a vinyl rainbow.

I stayed right where I was.

"Come on, Maisy." Ainsley pulled her hood over her head. "You don't want to wait 'til next week to call home."

"My dad's probably doing surgery now," I said. "Maybe I should just stay here. I bet I could come up with a really good prank if I have some alone time."

Ainsley wasn't giving up that easy. "You won't know if you're dad's hung up in surgery unless you try. Besides, I'm not allowed to leave you alone in the cabin."

There was no way I was calling Dad. He was just gonna want to talk about *her* anyway.

"Why don't you call your mom instead?" Poppy asked.

I grabbed my Lululemon rain jacket, another guilt gift from Dad. "I totally forgot. I have an appointment with Dr. Beth."

Bea stared at me, in that lie detector way of hers, so I pretended to have problems hitching the zipper up.

"I thought she could help me get over my fear of the ropes course," I said.

I could still feel Bea's eyes burning into the back of my neck, so I added, "I don't want to be the reason you lose the Cup."

I've learned over the past week that all you have to do is mention the Cup and everything else is forgotten.

Isa raised her eyebrows. "Gotta give you credit for being a team player."

Dr. Beth didn't look surprised when I showed up, dripping water all over her office floor. She tucked her wild gray hair behind one ear and said, "Hungry?"

I spotted a Taco Bell takeout bag, so I nodded.

"Perfect timing. You can split my tacos with me," she said.

She popped the plastic top off a supersized to-go cup and dumped half the bright orange soda into one mug, and half into another. Then she handed me the hot pink mug that said *She believed she could, so she did.*

If only life were that easy.

Dr. Beth pointed to the giant pillows on the office floor. "Take-out is meant to be had while being as cozy as possible."

There was a calico cat snuggled up on one of the floor pillows. Without looking, Dr. Beth sat down on the pillow without smooshing the cat. Her white mug said *Today will be awesome* in glittery gold paint. She was serious about keeping her mug game on point.

"I'm so glad you're back again, Maisy."

"I don't really have anything to talk about." I sat down on the only non-cat-covered pillow and took a sip from my mug. The fizzing bubbles from the orange soda tickled my nose and woke up my mouth. "Unless you know any good camp pranks."

"I see things haven't changed much since I was a camper." Dr. Beth opened the takeout bag while a black cat crawled into her lap. The calico cat hissed, but then they both settled in, one on each of Dr. Beth's legs. The cabin was silent except for the low purring of the cats and the rain tapping on the roof.

She pulled a taco from the bag and handed it to me. I took my time unwrapping it. I would have to eat it really slowly if I wanted to wait out the hour-long phone block. I could tell Dr. Beth was going to try to make me talk since she didn't hand me the laptop this time. Silence makes me really uncomfortable, but not as much as talking about my mom.

"I'm only here because I don't want to call home," I blurted out.

Dr. Beth fished a melted-down ice cube from her mug and held it out on her fingertip until the black cat licked it off. Then she reached back in her mug with the cat saliva finger and got another ice cube for the other cat. I tried my best not to gag.

She pulled a packet of hot sauce from the bag and squirted it all over her taco. Then she took a big bite.

She smiled like it was the best taco ever and said, "Now that is a taco worthy of an entry in my gratitude journal."

"You don't look like someone who eats fast food," I said, trying to keep the conversation on her so she wouldn't start asking me questions about my life.

"You mean, I look like I live on tofu and kale, right?" Her eyebrows raised.

"Kind of, yeah," I mumbled.

"My husband, Jerry, and I were serious vegans for twenty years. We grew our own vegetables and bought our dried beans and tofu from the local co-op. I even made our almond milk from scratch, which, let me tell you, takes a very long time."

She took another bite of her taco and kept talking with her mouth full. "Anyway, one day, I woke up and all I wanted was a big, fat cheeseburger. I tried to distract myself with meditation and yoga, but the craving wouldn't go away. I went out that very day and got myself a Big Mac with supersized fries and a great big chocolate shake. It was the best damn cheeseburger I've ever had. So, when I'm home with Jerry, I eat lentils and kale and all that vegan stuff. But when I'm at work, I live on takeout. I figure all the junk I eat here gets canceled out by the health food at home."

I wasn't sure what to say, so I took a bite of my taco, which was amazing.

Dr. Beth laughed. "Sorry, I just gave you a big dose of TMI. Want to tell me how you ended up here again?"

"I didn't want to call home, plus it's raining out. So, I don't really have anywhere to go," I said.

Dr. Beth didn't even flinch when a gray cat curled up on her shoulder. She just kept sipping her soda, like she didn't have cats hanging all over her. "Back when I went to camp here, I loved to kayak, even though I tipped over all the time. I would even sneak out my kayak on days like this when it was raining cats and dogs."

I rolled my eyes. "Thank God I failed the swim test. I don't have to go anywhere near those death traps."

"Something tells me you're not a fan of the ropes course either," said Dr. Beth.

"I would rather take a math test every day for the rest of my life than do the ropes course ever again," I said.

She laughed and her whole body shook, cats and all. "How the heck did a girl like you end up at adventure camp?"

"It was the only camp that wasn't sold out when my dad decided to send me away a few weeks ago. Now, I can see why," I groaned.

Dr. Beth handed me another taco. "I have a feeling your dad is going to be hearing about sending you to this camp for many years to come."

"My mom used to be in charge of all those things. She had this huge color-coded calendar in our kitchen. Red for Dad, blue for Mom, pink for Addy, and purple for me. Dad loved checking the calendar every morning before he left for work to see what everyone's day was going to be like. He used to say that Mom's calendar was even more organized than his surgery schedule."

"Wow. Sounds like a lot of work to keep everything running that smoothly at home. Do you think she ever got tired of overseeing every-one and everything?" Dr. Beth asked.

I don't know what it was about this fast-food-eating hippie cat lady, but something made me want to talk to her. Maybe it was because she didn't know me from back home. Or maybe it was because Mom's secret was burning in my chest.

I took a deep breath. "It all started two years ago when my mom forgot to pick me up from play rehearsal."

———·———

I must've done a good job talking, because Dr. Beth handed me her laptop when I finally shut up twenty minutes later. It felt pretty good getting some things off my chest.

The first thing I did was check Instagram. The M & Ms were back at Mia's pool, this time with Mia's brother Tim and his crew, who were all two years older than us.

Of course, Madeline was sitting super close to Mia's brother. Madeline is so boy crazy she doesn't even care that Tim's room always smells like dirty socks and his mother still needs to remind him to brush his teeth before school. Madison had captioned the post with more emojis I didn't get. This one said, *mustard in yo eye,* with a barfing emoji, a poop emoji, and a cheeseburger emoji.

It was hard to comment without using emojis, which feel safer than words because they can mean more than one thing. It's a lot easier to mess up with actual words.

I commented, *Miss you guys sm! XOXO* Then, I realized the guys might think I was talking to them, so I deleted it and then commented, *Looks like fun!* I added a smiley face using a colon and a parenthesis.

Bea is not an emoji kind of girl. She believes in words that are written out all the way with the right letters and correct spelling. She used to hate when I texted her *ILY SM!* I don't know why she thinks she's going to fit in with this crew. Looking at Insta was just making me more anxious about my end of the pact, so I moved on to email.

From: addyflips@gmail.com
To: dramagirl@gmail.com
Subject: Re: Hiiiiiiiiii!

Hi Maisy,

Can't believe you emailed me already. You didn't write me once when I was away training last summer. You must really hate camp!

Dad said they're making you take swim lessons. OMG!!! I cannot even picture that! I've never even seen you get your hair wet at the pool. But that means you can swim with me at the lake next time we visit Grandma.

I am more sore than I've ever been in my entire life. I swear, even my hair hurts. I am super close to nailing my front tuck-round off-back handspring-back layout on floor. Coach Rutherford is going to talk to Dad about homeschooling me this year so I can train full-time. You are going to be sooooo jelly when I don't have to go to school.

XOXO
Addy

P.S. Do you think Mom's okay?

From: dramagirl@gmail.com
To: addyflips@gmail.com
Subject: Re: Hiiiiiiiii!

Hi Addy!

Camp is the worst. The Dandelion Bunk girls pranked us by filling our whole cabin with crickets!!! It was seriously the grossest thing I have ever seen in my life. Luckily, I sleep in the top bunk because apparently crickets don't fly.

I know you're probs shocked I'm emailing again. I mean, it's not like writing is my thing. But I'm at Dr. Beth's cabin (she's the camp therapist) and she said I could spend the end of our session writing to you.

Dr. Beth is a legit hippie. She showed me a picture of herself from the 60's when she was at a protest with Martin Luther King Jr. It was hanging on the wall next to a picture of her from the D.C. Women's March. She looks exactly the same in both pics and I even think she's wearing the same flare jeans in both. But her hair is A LOT grayer now.

I know you are also probs shocked that I've been meeting with a therapist. Remember that woman with the nasty coffee breath and non-ironically ugly Jack-o'-lantern sweater? The one who kept calling our parents Mom and Dad like she was their kid. OMG! How creepy was that? I know we SWORE we would never talk to a therapist again, but it felt good to talk to Dr. Beth. I told her about Mom. Things that only you and me know, things we haven't even told Dad. I thought it would feel bad to talk about it. But this year, it's felt kind of like I've had a huge ball of yarn, like the ones Grandma knits with, stuck in my chest, making it hard to breathe. Talking to Dr. Beth made me feel like the ball was unraveling. So when we stopped talking, that big ball was still there, but it was smaller and I felt like I could breathe better.

Anyway, I thought you would want to know that talking about Mom isn't as bad as we thought it would be. So maybe when we get back to Mapleton we can find someone to talk to together? Just not the Halloween sweater lady. LOL!

XOXO
Maisy

P.S. I am going to be so pissed when you don't have to go to school and I do. You better get me front-row seats at the Olympics one day.

P.P.S. Don't waste your summer worrying about Mom.

From: dramagirl@gmail.com
To: docwinters@yahoo.com
Subject: Supplies Request

Hi Dad,

Camp still sucks because it's filled with everything I'm scared of, bugs, bears, and other wild animals that make creepy sounds at night. Even Minnow Pond where I take swim lessons with the babies is scary because it's filled with slimy seaweed and fish that try to nibble my toes.

Can you send me water shoes so my feet don't have to touch all the gross stuff on the bottom of the lake? My swim teacher thinks I will have an easier time if I'm not so worried about what my feet are touching. Can you also send me some friendship bracelet supplies? I need lots of different embroidery thread, a pack of large safety pins, and beads. I also need some hairstyling supplies, like tiny clear rubber bands, gel, and hairspray. If you go in old orders on Amazon, you can find all the good stuff. My bunkmate Hannah has been teaching me how to make bracelets and I'm teaching her how to do hair. It's one of the only fun things about camp.

Maisy

P.S. Is Mom okay? I don't really care. I'm just checking for Addy.

BEA

I held the phone to my ear, and, as soon as I heard Mom's voice, I felt like I was home. I pictured her tucked into the corner of our gray couch with Mr. Pebbles purring in her lap. She probably had her wild red hair slicked into a top knot and was wearing a flowy summer work dress that had long sleeves to cover her tattoos. She was certain to be on her third cup of coffee already.

"Mom!" I yelled into the phone.

"I miss you sooooo much!" Mom squealed.

"Me too! Have you been feeding Mr. Pebbles twice a day?"

Mom was quiet for a second. "I knew I was forgetting something."

"Very funny," I said.

She lowered her voice. "How's it going with Maisy?"

"You don't have to whisper."

But she kept her voice low. "I know she can't hear us through the phone, but it still feels weird talking about someone who is inches away from you."

"She skipped the phone block," I said.

"Oh," said Mom in a normal volume voice.

"Remember when I first went to camp and Mrs. Winters acted like you were handing me off to a pack of wolves? Then she emailed you all those child development articles about how shipping me off to camp could cause abandonment issues into adulthood."

Mom laughed. "I forgot about the intensity of Mrs. Winters and her emails. I used to get anxious just reading the subject lines."

"When did Maisy's mom suddenly decide camp was a good parenting strategy? And when did Dr. Winters start taking care of things like camp registration?" I asked.

Mom sighed. "The Winters family's really going through it right now."

"Going through what exactly?" I asked.

"Let's just say they're in a transitional period," Mom said.

I rolled my eyes. "Maisy said her parents weren't getting a divorce. I should've known she was lying."

I could hear Mr. Pebbles purring. He does that when he hears my voice through the phone.

"Some things are more complicated than divorce," Mom said.

I thought about when Dad first left and I felt an ache in my chest every time I looked at his empty dining room chair. He forgot his Yankees T-shirt and I slept in it every single night for two years straight. I thought about how he missed the Girl Scouts Father-Daughter dance because he was fighting with Mom about child support. Dr. Winters let me tag along with him and Maisy. He even bought me a pink rose corsage. But it did little to take away the sting of being stood up by my own father.

"More complicated than divorce?" I asked.

"Oh, honey, there are far worse things." Mom sighed. "Be kind to Maisy."

"You're not gonna tell me what's going on?"

I wondered if Mrs. Winters was sick. The last time I saw her she looked emaciated, but I thought she was juice cleansing too much and doubling up on spin and barre classes like the other Mapleton stay-at-home moms. I didn't have to worry about Mom doing that because the only exercise she had time for was her Saturday morning spin class with the Single Squad.

"I just heard a great quote on my spiritual fulfillment blog." Mom paused for dramatic effect before continuing. "Holding on to anger is like drinking poison and expecting the other person to die. You get what that means, right?"

I knew from experience this conversation wasn't going anywhere until I gave into Mom's quote of the day lesson. For someone so Zen, she gets quite agitated when I don't participate in her little chats. "It means holding on to my anger and not forgiving someone only hurts me."

I could feel Mom smiling through the phone. "Exactly. I feel bad, like I didn't steer you in the right direction. I never discouraged you from staying angry at Maisy. But maybe you were meant to forgive her and move on. I mean, what're the odds that she would end up in the same cabin as you?"

In case you haven't figured it out, Mom's a big believer in "signs." When I was a baby, she hated her website design job. One morning, she was supposed to be working on a project, but she kept getting distracted by the falling snow outside the window. A real estate agent came along and stuck a For Sale sign up in the yard across the street and Mom took that as a literal and figurative sign to sell houses. The next day, she resigned from her job and signed up for an online realtor course. Thirteen years later, she still loves selling homes.

"Maybe it's time to let go of the past," Mom continued.

I desperately wanted to tell her about the pact. I wasn't exaggerating when I called her my best friend. Not telling her about the pact made me feel like a liar.

But Isa, Poppy, and Hannah were all within earshot, and the pact would be over if they knew about it. Deep down, though, I knew that wasn't the only reason. Because if I really wanted Mom to know about the pact, I could write about it in her next letter. The truth was, I didn't want Mom to talk me out of it.

"Maybe just try to have fun together," she said.

I thought of the dance party in our cabin. "We're actually kind of having fun. Like we used to."

"Try focusing on her good qualities that made you guys friends the first time around. Come at this with an open heart," Mom said.

But if Maisy didn't follow through with the pact, then this whole summer would be a waste. I didn't know how I would make it through another school year being invisible. "Okay, but if you're wrong about her . . ."

"If I'm wrong, then at least you'll know you did the right thing," Mom said.

I swallowed hard. "Yeah, I'm doing the right thing. Now tell me what's going on with you. What happened with the blind date?"

This time it sounded like Mom was the one swallowing hard. "Well, it turns out the date wasn't as blind as I thought it was."

"What does that mean?"

"I knew my date and it turns out you do, too," said Mom.

"OMG! Was it the coffee guy from Caffeine Addict? The one with all the tattoos?" I asked. "You guys would look so cute together."

Mom laughed. "Not even close."

I wracked my brain for another guy we both knew. "The mechanic from the gas station who always cleans your windows when we gas up?"

"Oh, he is just the sweetest. But, no. This is going to be a little weird for you."

"Oh, no. Who is he?" I asked.

"Gavin Pembrook, your—"

"My fourth-grade math teacher," I finished for her. "I'm guessing the date was a flop since he wears a bowtie and gives detention to people who chew gum. I can't believe someone set you up with him. How gross!"

I waited for Mom to laugh with me, but she was strangely quiet for almost a full minute. Then she said, "Bea, I like him. Quite a bit."

"But he teaches math. He's all about rigidness and conformity and you get tarot readings and Reiki when life gets crazy."

"What can I say?" she said. "Sometimes opposites attract."

"Polar opposites, in this case," I said.

"I'm sure when you get to know him outside of the classroom, you'll see he's not that rigid when he doesn't have to keep thirty kids under control."

I felt a weird buzzing in my head. "You must really like him. I've never met one of your boyfriends."

"That's because I've never really gotten past a date or two with anyone," she said. "We still have quite a while until you're back home from camp. If I'm still dating him, then I would love for you to get to know him better. But I didn't want to keep anything from you in the meantime, since we always tell each other everything."

"Um, okay," I said. "Phone block's over."

"Love you!" said Mom.

"Love you, too!" I hung up the phone and joined the other girls. We stepped out of the phone cabin and saw the sun shine through the spaces between the dripping branches. The storm had passed.

Ainsley stayed behind to call her boyfriend because having multiple camp boyfriends wasn't enough, she had to have one back home, too.

I didn't tell the girls about Mom's date because they would ask me a million questions that I wasn't ready to think about yet. As happy as I was for Mom, I wasn't sure I was ready for my old math teacher to be hanging out at my house on a regular basis.

"What if we put Crystal Light Fruit Punch mix in the Dandelion Bunk's showerhead? It would look like the scene in Carrie when they dump blood on her head," I said.

"I need a minute to recover from talking to my mom before I can think about pranks. My mom is obsessed with soccer," said Isa.

"What else is new?" said Hannah. "Your mom's been talking about you becoming a professional soccer player for as long as we've known you."

Isa kicked little pebbles on the path as she walked. "She was harassing me about keeping my skills up while I'm here."

Hannah rolled her eyes. "Did you tell your mom you wake up an hour early every day to train?"

"And that you spend every quiet time block and every free block conditioning and doing training drills from the list your coach sent you with?" I added.

"I did. But you know how crazy she gets. We better win this

Cup. She's already planning to put it on my college application," Isa said. "You know, to show I haven't been wasting my summers just having fun or anything."

Poppy cleared her throat like she always does when she has a big announcement.

"I talked to my mom about the Maisy situation," she said.

"What does that mean?" I asked.

Poppy waited for the Buttercup Bunk girls to walk past, then lowered her voice. "I know this is drastic, but Mom said she could get Maisy switched out of our bunk if we want."

"What?" I said. "How?"

"Mom and Nana Mary are big donors," said Poppy.

I suddenly had a really weird feeling in the pit of my stomach. If this was the first day of camp, I would've jumped at the chance to get Maisy out of my bunk. But that was before the pact.

"I don't know." Hannah stopped walking. "Maisy's really not that bad. We've been making friendship bracelets together."

"Is having someone to make bracelets with worth losing the Cup over?" Isa asked.

I felt another twinge in my stomach.

"Dr. Beth will definitely cure Maisy of her fear of the ropes course," I said. "Remember how she helped Hannah when she was scared of the dark when we were junior campers?"

Hannah laughed. "Thank God for Dr. Beth. I was driving you guys crazy every night when you wanted to turn the lights out. If anyone can help Maisy, it's her."

"Do you really think Dr. Beth can get Maisy over her fear in time? She's terrified of the easiest part of the course. How are we gonna get her to cross the spider web?" asked Isa.

"Trust me, if anyone can get Maisy across the ropes, I can. I've known her practically my whole life. I get how she thinks, and I always know what to say to calm her down," I said.

"I can't stop thinking about what Bea said about us not being the Mean Girls we hate back home," said Hannah.

Meanwhile, all I wanted was for Maisy to make me friends with those Mean Girls back home. I suddenly felt like a hypocrite of epic proportions.

"What did you tell your mother?" asked Isa.

Poppy sighed. "I told her to wait 'til we all talked about it. I have special permission to use the camp office phone whenever I want. So, I can call her anytime with the answer." She took a deep breath. "Uh, there's one more thing. We can switch Maisy to whatever bunk we want."

"Are your mom and Nana Mary in some Camp Amelia mafia we don't know about?" Isa asked.

Poppy looked down at the ground, which she always did when she was embarrassed about how rich she was. "Nana Mary just donated money to renovate all the cabins."

Isa smirked. "You're not talking about just a new paint job, are you?"

"New roofs, porches, and furniture," Poppy mumbled.

"That means we could stick Maisy in the Dandelion Bunk and be guaranteed a win," I said half to myself.

"This is our fifth summer working toward the Cup. Why give it up for one person?" Isa asked.

"Who says we're giving it up?" asked Hannah. "We might be giving up a definite win, but keeping Maisy doesn't necessarily mean a definite loss either."

"What do you think, Bea?" Poppy asked.

All the girls turned to me and waited for my answer.

> ·· CHAPTER NINE ··

MAISY

I OPENED DR. BETH'S DOOR AND SAW THE RAIN HAD STOPPED. THE
sun was shining, and, for the first time, I felt like maybe things might
be okay when I got home at the end of the summer.

Technically, Ainsley was supposed to walk me back from these
sessions, but I think she was using the time to meet up with a counselor from the boys' camp across the lake. I was glad to have some
time by myself. Dr. Beth asked lots of questions. She said they're the
type of questions you don't have to answer right away. She gave me
lots to think about.

I cut through the haunted woods on my way back because I knew
no one else would be there. It looked exactly like the regular woods
except the path was a mess of weeds and really long grass. I pulled

my athletic socks high because—ticks. I might not be scared of ghosts, but ticks are gross and carry Lyme disease.

When I got back to the bunk, the girls were hanging out on the porch making friendship bracelets—the one camp thing I'm good at.

Hannah jumped to her feet. She didn't even care that she just dropped her friendship bracelet in the middle of a crazy hard stitch. "Did Dr. Beth make you better?"

I stopped with one foot on the porch step and one still on the grass. How did Hannah know what Dr. Beth and I talked about? I thought therapy sessions were confidential. I should've known better than to trust a therapist who lives on food that comes in a paper bag.

"Are you still scared of the ropes course?" asked Isa.

I am the only person who would forget her own cover story. I smiled and used my most "I'm sorry" sounding voice. "Dr. Beth said it's going to take more than one session."

Isa groaned. "Is it going to take more than five weeks?"

"Does Dr. Beth know how to hypnotize people?" asked Poppy. "That's how Father quit smoking."

I blinked hard and fast, trying to hold back my tears. I might as well give up fitting in with these girls.

All of a sudden, Bea grabbed my hand and pulled me up the porch steps. "Maisy figured out our revenge prank. Right, Mais?"

Bea squeezed my hand and gave me a look that said, "Make something up."

"Maisy comes up with the best pranks. One time she . . ." Bea started. Then she went on and on about a prank I pulled on our third-grade math tutor to get us out of learning long division. I could tell she was stretching the story out to give me time to come up with a plan. I was beginning to realize that not speaking to Bea for a year wasn't going to take away the fact that I knew her better than my own sister.

I ran ideas through my mind while Bea hyped up my pranking skills. But her playing me up as the best prankster ever was really putting the pressure on.

When she stopped talking, I opened the cabin door and waved the girls toward me. "Come on, so no one hears."

I walked as slowly as I could to give myself an extra second or two to come up with a plan. Then I paced back and forth to get the creative juices flowing while the girls grabbed Pop Tarts and Capri Suns from under Hannah's bunk.

Finally, when everyone was all settled and the only sounds were the crinkling of drink pouches, I clapped my hands together. Maybe making friendship bracelets wasn't the only camp thing I was good at. Some of my best plans come to me when I am the most desperate.

"We're gonna need three tape recorders and an old Camp Amelia uniform," I said. "Like the ones in those really old black-and-white pictures hanging in the dining hall."

"You may as well add backstage passes to Taylor Swift while you're at it," said Isa, balancing a soccer ball on her knee.

"Seriously. It's not like we have Amazon Prime here," added Poppy.

"Or a time machine," mumbled Hannah through her straw.

"Obviously, you guys used to have art here since there's an art cabin. There must be an old drama or music cabin somewhere," I said.

"OMG!" shouted Hannah. "Yes, there is one."

"Yeah, we just forgot all about it since none of us are musically inclined," Bea added.

"I bet there are tape recorders in there," I said. "Don't just grab the tape recorders. Make sure there are tapes in them. And working batteries."

"There are ancient camp uniforms stacked away in the storage cabin behind the square. What size do we need?" asked Bea.

I looked at my bunkmates' curious faces. "Small enough to fit me. I am going to play my best role yet." I paused for dramatic effect. "The ghost of Camp Amelia."

BEA

I should've offered to play the ghost. After all, I had been the resident ghost of Mapleton Elementary School for the past year. But Maisy was perfect for the part, which she had to be, because pulling off this prank was the only way to convince the girls to keep her in our bunk. There was no way I could hold up my end of the pact if they kicked her out.

I was becoming obsessed with the idea of having a friend group at school like I had at camp. I don't consider myself an anxious person, especially not compared to someone like Maisy. But I woke up every school day with a pit in my stomach, the kind of pit that couldn't be cured by antacid, a good breakfast, or even one of Mom's pep talks. The more invisible I became to the other kids, the more I felt like I had lost my place in the world. There is nothing worse than waking up every morning and feeling like you don't matter to anybody but your mom. Being invisible in elementary school was bad enough, but I imagined being a nobody in middle school would be a fresh new hell. I needed to make this work, so I ran around with the girls until we came up with all of the items on Maisy's scavenger hunt list.

Years starring in plays and musicals had turned Maisy into a highly skilled makeup artist. Her tan face was transformed to a sickly white—close to my shade, but minus the freckles. She had swooped dark circles under her eyes and contoured her makeup to create a perfect hollow in each cheek. She had also shaded her lips with dark gray eyeliner to add to the corpse-like effect.

The ancient Camp Amelia uniform Hannah had dug up was a perfect fit. It looked like an old-fashioned Girl Scout uniform, except it was cardinal red rather than Girl Scout green. The thick cotton was cuffed into short sleeves and pleated in stiff accordion folds in the skirt. The waist was cinched with an ancient leather belt and the dress was topped off with a gray and red striped kerchief. There was even a matching red felt beret.

Poppy clasped her hands together. "Maisy! You look just like the girls did back when Nana Mary went here!"

Isa wrinkled her nose. "I didn't know Nana Mary went to camp with a bunch of ghouls."

Poppy playfully smacked Isa's arm.

Hannah tied red ribbons on the ends of Maisy's braids. "There. Now you have the full effect."

Isa walked around Maisy like she was looking at a wax museum figure. "I can't believe girls had to dress like this back then."

"Only for camp ceremonies and visiting day," Poppy said. "Nana Mary said they spent the rest of the time running around in shorts they stole from the boys' camp laundry line."

Maisy slid a bobby pin into the side of the beret. "Are you sure they overheard you guys talking?"

"Positive," I said. "We waited until we knew they were behind us on the path to the lake. Then we talked about sneaking out tonight and meeting boys near the haunted woods."

"How do we know they'll take the bait?" asked Poppy.

Maisy slid another bobby pin on her hat, then moved it back and forth to make sure it was secure. "Because boys," she said.

All the girls nodded in agreement. This was the first time I had seen the confident Maisy since we arrived at camp. We were finally doing something she was an expert in—tricking people.

"Okay, does everyone know what to do?" she asked.

"Yes!" we all said in unison.

"Let's go scare the crap out of those Dandelion girls!" shouted Maisy.

Ainsley was so desperate for face time with her latest guy, she started making her way to the boys' camp right after dinner. We waited until all of the surrounding cabins had gone dark, then walked quickly and quietly on the path that would lead us from our bunk to the haunted woods. It was quiet except for the buzzing symphony of the cicadas and the nonstop chirps of the crickets. The full moon served double duty, both as a light source and to add to the horror movie vibe that we were setting out to create.

When we got to the haunted woods, Maisy positioned Isa, Poppy, and Hannah on the perimeter spaced about three feet apart from each other. They were more than happy with their stations since they weren't technically in the haunted woods and they were close enough to each other in case the real Amelia ghost made an appearance.

The girls had been shocked that the "Girl Who Is Afraid of Everything" wasn't scared of the one actual scary place at camp. But being friends with Maisy all those years taught me that anxious people can surprise you sometimes with their bravery.

I automatically stopped as soon as we got to the row of rocks that divided the regular footpath from the haunted one. I felt a breeze on the back of my neck and involuntary shivers went up my spine and sent my teeth into chatters. Now I knew what Maisy felt like on the ropes course.

Maisy reached out and grabbed my hand. "It's okay. I've got you."

Holding Maisy's hand actually did make me feel protected, even though she's so much smaller than me. Her confidence was contagious.

The high grass scratched my calves as she pulled me deeper into the woods. I heard the swishing of bushes as the other three girls arranged themselves in their positions.

Maisy stopped when we got to a gnarled oak tree. "Look. There's a face in the tree."

I smoothed my hand over the knots and twists in the bark that did indeed form what looked like a face. You would think an old tree with a face would creep Maisy out.

But she held her hand there for a second and said, "It's almost like you're meant to tell the tree your secrets."

Maybe it was her ghostly makeup, but she looked sad. Not the kind of sad when you find out you failed a math test. More like the deeper sadness when something bad is going on that is much bigger than you. Not for the first time I wondered what was going on at her house.

Maisy reached behind the tree and pulled out an old rope swing with a seat made from a wooden plank.

"There's nothing scarier than a ghost girl on a swing," she whispered, and climbed onto the seat.

"You look like you belong on *American Horror Story*," I said.

"That's exactly what I was going for." She smiled. "When we get the signal, give me a good push and stay down so no one can see you."

I ducked behind the tree as Maisy sat stoically on the swing. She didn't talk, she just sat there waiting. She looked so scary sitting there that I had to repeatedly remind myself she wasn't a real ghost.

The minutes ticked by as we waited for the Dandelion girls to show up. It felt awkward sitting there with nothing to say to the girl who had known me better than anyone else for practically my entire life. The silence was killing me.

Finally, I couldn't take it anymore. I whispered, "My mom has a boyfriend."

"Go, Heather!" Maisy whispered. "But why don't you sound like this is a good thing?"

"It's not the fact that she's dating, it's *who* she's dating," I said.

"Who is it?"

I scrunched up my face. "I'll give you a hint. He wears bowties with matching socks and gives detention for chewing gum in class."

"Your mom is dating Mr. Pembrook?" she asked. "OMG! I would never think to put those two together. He's so straight edge, and she's so . . . not."

"I never thought my mom would date someone who has every single holiday-themed bowtie you can imagine. Remember his Groundhog's Day one?"

Maisy laughed. "With the matching socks sticking out of the bottom of his too-short pants?"

"Does he seem like the kind of guy who would date a tarot-card-reading, tattooed single mom?" I asked.

"Maybe he's a different guy when he's not at school," Maisy said. "Those dorky socks could be covering up full leg tattoos."

I looked at her, and we both shook our heads at the same time.

Maisy's tone turned serious. "Does he make your mom happy?"

"You know my mom. She would rather stay home and reread one of the Harry Potter books for the hundredth time than go on a second date with someone if they didn't make her happy," I said.

"Then it's maybe worth her dating the dorky math teacher. Because unhappy moms have a way of making the whole family miserable," Maisy said.

I turned this over in my mind, the first bit of insight into what might be going on at Maisy's house, but then there was a rustling in the bushes, and we heard the Dandelion girls' voices. I had forgotten for a moment the real reason we were here.

"Could they have picked a creepier spot?" Tinka asked. "What guys are gonna want to hang here?"

"They're already gonna scare away the guys with their ugly faces," said one of the A twins.

I prayed Isa didn't jump out of her hiding spot. I gave Maisy a hard push and she swung through the air.

"What time did they say?" asked Kaya. "I feel like they should be here already."

"Who cares when the Sunflower girls get here? The guys will take one look at us and it'll be all over for them," said Tinka.

"Shhhhhh," said one of the A twins. "Did you hear that?"

"What? Did we hear what?" Kaya's voice rose. "What did you hear?"

"OMG . . . OMG . . . OMG! I told you we shouldn't come!" shouted Tinka.

Maisy pumped her legs harder so she swung high enough to be seen over the tall grass and weeds. Her braids swung in the slight breeze, but her hat stayed in place because of all those bobby pins.

I could practically hear arms being grabbed. "Who is that?" yelled one of the A twins.

"What the . . . !" Kaya shrieked.

"OMG! Is that a ghost?" Tinka squealed.

Maisy's perfect soprano voice broke through the crickets and

146

cicadas to the tune of "On Top of Old Smokey" in a high, reedy rendition fitting for a horror movie.

> *The place to disc-o-o-o-over, your hopes*
> *and your dreams.*
> *Camp Am-e-e-e-e-e-lia, become part of*
> *the team.*
> *You'll count d-o-o-o-own the days till you*
> *attend,*
> *Camp Ame-e-e-e-elia, you'll find friends to*
> *the end.*

My mouth dropped open. I couldn't believe Maisy had learned our camp song. Even I was terrified and I *knew* she wasn't a real ghost. The Dandelion girls had to be scared out of their minds.

If you listened close enough, you could hear the click of all three tape recorders on cue. Suddenly the woods were filled with the sound of a swarm of bees flitting and flying around, as if someone had tilted over an entire hive of honeybees. I found myself swatting at my ears even though I knew there weren't any actual bees.

The Dandelion girls ducked and swatted at their faces, arms, and legs. Their piercing screams were so loud, you could barely hear the bees.

Maisy kept swinging, back and forth, and whispered, just loud enough for them to hear, "Don't mess with the Sunflower girls!"

All four of the Dandelion Bunk girls ran through the woods,

with Tinka yards ahead of the pack, the sound of their screams trailing behind them.

I ran over to the other girls.

"OMG! I am going to pee my pants," said Poppy, clutching her stomach and hunching over laughing.

"Did you see the looks on their faces?" I asked. "I thought Tinka was going to have a heart attack!"

"That was the best prank ever!" said Isa.

"We never could've pulled that off without Maisy," I said.

"No way we could've done that without her," Hannah agreed. "That was sick!"

"So." I folded my arms. "Does that mean we can keep Maisy in our bunk?"

No one answered. They just looked at each other, then at the ground.

Maisy ran toward us, her braids whipping behind her. Even with the ghost makeup, she looked like the old Maisy, hopeful and eager to make me happy. At moments like these, I had to remind myself that the past year really had happened.

Her words came out in a jumbled rush. "How did I do? Did you guys like the prank? Was it scary enough? I think Kaya peed her pants!"

The girls kept their eyes to the ground and my heart sank. I realized it was over. I was going to remain the ghost of Mapleton School.

But then, Isa looked up and said, "That was seriously the best prank ever, Maisy. Glad you're in our bunk."

I didn't realize I had been holding my breath until just then. Maisy was in. I'd done it. And when we got back to school, I wouldn't be alone.

CHAPTER TEN

MAISY

To: dramagirl@gmail.com
From: docwinters@yahoo.com
Subject: Supplies shipped

Hi Mini,

Grandma thought I might be lonely with you girls gone, so she's staying with me for a few weeks. She came to Michaels to help me pick out your friendship bracelet supplies. She was convinced Michaels would have better quality thread than Amazon. You know she doesn't trust Amazon ever since the time she thought she ordered a dollhouse, and they shipped her a doghouse. I still crack up every time I think of that! She refuses to acknowledge it was time for a stronger pair of readers. That was a long-winded way of saying everything you could possibly need to make bracelets this summer is on its way to you. We also got you the requested hair-styling supplies and water shoes at Target. Grandma can't believe how tiny your feet are! According to her, I was born with size 12 feet.

We sent everything overnight, so you should get this asap. Email me to let me know it arrived.

Grandma wanted me to remind you to eat enough. Consider that your reminder :). Don't worry about Mom. I just talked to her last night and she sounded really good. How are the swim lessons?

Love,
Dad

To: docwinters@yahoo.com
From: dramagirl@gmail.com
Subject: Re: Supplies shipped

Hi Dad,

OMG! You sent enough supplies for Hannah and me to open up our own ETSY store. You and Grandma did a great job picking things out. I love the glittery thread and the silver beads, especially the ones shaped like dragonflies. Tell Grandma it was a good idea to go to Michaels.

Swimming lessons aren't that bad. I thought it would be annoying to take lessons with the little kids, but they idolize me. They seriously think I am the coolest person they have ever met. They are so freaking cute too. This little girl named Hillary lost both of her front teeth, so she has a lisp. She calls me Maithy and it is so adorable I can't take it. Wish I had my phone so I could video her to show you and Addy how cute she is.

Thanks for letting me know Mom is okay. Don't tell her I was asking about her. I only wanted to make sure she was okay for Addy, so don't get any ideas about me writing to her.

XOXO
Maisy

To: addyflips@gmail.com
From: dramagirl@gmail.com
Subject: Mom's Fine

Hi Addy,

Dad said Mom is doing good. Don't waste any more of your summer worrying about her. We already spent way too much time stressed out because of her. Just focus on your gymnastics and have fun.

Is Dad really going to let you homeschool? I've seriously never met anyone more serious about school than Dad. Remember the time I got a B- on that math test? I thought he was going to lose his mind.

XOXO
Maisy

From: @maisywintersiscoming
To: @madisonave

Miss you sm!! Camp still sucks. Counting down the days till I'm back home. ILY!

From: @madisonave
To: @maisywintersiscoming

Meghan's being mean to me again. I didn't even do anything wrong. She keeps making faces at everything I say and whispering to the other girls right in front of me. Wish you were here.

I was the last one added to the M & Ms, which was bad enough, but Madison didn't have it much better. She's been in the group since the beginning, but only because she and Meghan were family friends. Meghan's mom and Madison's mom grew up together in Mapleton, and they've been best friends for pretty much their whole lives. So, the moms decided back when they were both pregnant at the same time that their girls would be best friends too. Since the moms never asked the girls if they actually wanted to be friends, Meghan reminded Madison all the time that she's a pity friend. I think being a pity friend is way worse than being the new friend. Holding up my end of the pact was going to be even harder if my best friend in the M & Ms was having trouble with her spot.

To: @madisonave
From: @maisywintersiscoming

Meghan always does this, then she gets bored of being mean after a few days. Just smile and be nice and pretend not to notice. Whatever you do, DON'T get in a fight with her about it. It will just make drama for you with the other girls. Miss you sm!! ILY!!

I yawned as I handed the laptop back to Dr. Beth.

"I heard you guys running past my cabin last night," she said. "It was after eleven. No wonder you're so tired this morning."

"We got the Dandelion girls back," I said. "But that's not why I'm so tired."

Dr. Beth leaned in so close I could feel the steam rising off her giant mug of tea. "Then, why have you been yawning nonstop?"

"Besides the fact that you made me meet with you before breakfast today . . . I've had the same nightmare every night since I got here," I said. "I'm back from camp and my mom comes home. She runs right over to Dad and Addy and gives them super big hugs and tells them how much she loves them. But she can't see me. I keep calling her name and waving my arms at her. But no matter how loud I yell, or how close I get to her, I'm invisible to her," I said.

"Hmmm," Dr. Beth said. "It's interesting that you're the only person that she can't see. Why do you think that is?"

"How should I know?" I shrugged. "Didn't they teach you how to analyze dreams in therapy school?"

Dr. Beth leaned back in her floor pillow. "Unfortunately, Princeton didn't offer dream analyzing in the curriculum. But, if you ask me, I would say to try to think about what makes you different from your dad and Addy when it comes to your mom."

I didn't have to think that hard. "They forgave her already and I'm still really mad at her."

She nodded slowly. "I see."

"And I don't think I'm ever not going to be mad at her," I said.

Dr. Beth took a long sip of tea. "Looks like we have a lot to talk about today."

———•———

"BZZZZZZZ. BZZZZZZZ," we all said, as we walked past the Dandelion Bunk an hour later on our way to the dining hall.

Ainsley narrowed her eyes. "I'm not sure what that means and I have a feeling I'm better off that way."

"You said we should bond with Maisy," said Isa. She was walking and bouncing a soccer ball on alternating knees the whole way.

"True. Just make sure that bonding doesn't get us all kicked out of camp," Ainsley said.

Can I just say the best thing about camp is the dining cabin? Bath & Body Works could make loads of money bottling up the pancake and syrup smell coming from the building every morning.

"The usual?" asked Mary Anne, my favorite camp cook. She kind of reminds me of my grandma because she wears her readers on a fancy chain around her neck, she always has perfectly painted nails, and she's always trying to fatten me up.

"I love having a usual!" I held out my plate while she loaded it up with the fluffiest blueberry pancakes in the universe with a thick, melty slab of butter on top. Then she piled on three slices of bacon.

"If only my grandkids had the same attitude when they visit. They think all food needs to come frozen, prepackaged, and filled with enough chemicals to make it last till the next century," she said, passing me a glass of orange juice.

I laughed. "Maybe you should trade grandkids with my grandma, because that's exactly how she eats, too. Her famous lasagna is actually frozen Stouffer's."

Mary Anne laughed a big belly laugh as I headed to sit down. The dining hall was noisy, but in a good way, like everyone was really happy to hang out with each other. When the cafeteria is loud like that at school, it's usually from the boys getting too rowdy and doing stupid things like that annoying water bottle flipping trick. When the M & Ms are noisy at school, it's because we're trying to show off how popular we are.

I sat down with the Sunflower Bunk girls at the table we shared with the Tulip Bunk. It was easy to spot our table because Hannah was wearing an orange velour romper with thick white stripes down the side, and yellow polka dot sneakers. Of course, Isa was wearing her usual outfit that made her look like a professional soccer player, and Poppy was wearing bright turquoise Lilly Pulitzer shorts with a white polo shirt. Bea wore the same Camp Amelia T-shirt and athletic shorts she had slept in the night before. I was going to have to work on her clothes when we got back to Mapleton. The M & Ms had high standards about personal appearance, and Bea's lack of outfit planning and personal grooming was going to be a serious issue. It takes her two minutes to get ready in the morning, which is about fifty-eight minutes less than it should.

"Let's play two truths and a lie," said Hannah, through a mouthful of waffle.

"I'll go first," Ainsley said. She was eating her usual egg white omelet with steamed broccoli and mushrooms. Mary Anne always made special "athlete food" to help her stay in shape for when she got back to school.

"I went to prom with my cousin. I eat a box of Mike and Ikes before every meet. I was a competitive gymnast," Ainsley said, before winking at me. "What's the lie?"

"The cousin thing," said Poppy.

Isa chewed on her nail. "I think the cousin thing was a trick. There is no way you eat a box of Mike and Ikes before a meet."

Ainsley winked at me again. "Maisy, what do you think?"

"The gymnastics thing is the lie," I said, keeping my eyes on my pancake stack so I didn't give anything away.

"What?" said Bea. "It has to be the cousin thing."

"Maisy's right," said Ainsley.

"How did you do that?" asked Poppy, eyes wide.

"Maisy's good at reading people," said Ainsley, then she winked at me.

"Ew! You took your own cousin to the prom?!" shrieked Hannah.

"Technically," Ainsley said, "my step-uncle Mark married my date's mom a week before prom."

"That doesn't count," said Poppy.

"Your turn, Maisy," said Bea.

I had spent so long lying for Mom that it was hard to come up with two truths. Even my reason for coming to camp was one big lie. But I put a smile on my face and played along.

BEA

Hi Mom!

Sorry I was awkward when you told me about Mr. Pembrook. It's just hard to get past the whole math teacher façade. I think I would've been less shocked if you told me you were dating Mr. Miller, the drama teacher, or Mr. Lansing, the environmental arts teacher—someone who doesn't adhere to societal norms. But I guess the whole bowtie-wearing thing makes Mr. Pembrook a little alternative in his own way. At least he's an elementary school teacher, so I don't have to worry about any awkwardness bumping into him in the hallways. Not sure what would be more uncomfortable—bumping into him if you guys break up or bumping into him if you're an actual couple. Just wanted to say to you what I should've said on the phone. You deserve to be happy even if it's with my old math teacher.

I miss you so much! Can't wait for our weekend-long Gilmore Girls marathon! Notice I said weekend-long. I've decided that our traditional twenty-four-hour binge-fest must be extended to a full forty-eight hours in order for us to stretch our stomachs to full capacity. I'm thinking pizza the first night, and bacon cheeseburgers and curly fries the second night, with lots of Pop Tarts, ice cream, and donuts in between. That would truly be a Gilmore-inspired feast! Of course, we will also get Mr. Pebbles a few cans of his favorite tuna so he can indulge with us.

Thanks so much for the s'mores bars. The girls and I polished them off in one sitting. They were even better than Nana Mary's famous chocolate chip cookies. Thanks also for the rest of the care package items. I can't wait to dig into *The Perks of Being a Wallflower*, but I've been falling asleep as soon as my head hits the pillow every night. We've been training so hard for the tournament that every muscle in my body is fatigued.

I hope you are using this six-week hiatus from being a mom to have fun with the Single Squad and to see if you really like Mr. Pembrook. Seriously, I know my year of loserdom cost you your social life too. No matter how hard you tried to hide it, I know how many times you turned down plans with your friends because you didn't want to leave me. But you don't have to worry about that happening anymore. I have it all figured out. Next school year is going to be different. You aren't going to have to worry about me anymore.

Love your #1/only daughter,
Bea

P.S. I mailed Dad's letter the first day of camp. Haven't heard from him yet. Do you think I got his new address right?

Isa bumped the cabin door open with her hip. She had a soccer ball under one arm and was chugging water. Her sweaty hair was thrown in a ponytail, but quite a few little curls had escaped and were sticking to her forehead.

She looked around the room, then asked, "Where's Maisy?"

Poppy looked up from perfect hospital corners. Luckily, her maid had taught her the right way to make a bed, and Poppy had bestowed her wisdom on us, because we always passed bunk inspection with flying colors.

"With Dr. Beth," she said, smoothing her thousand-count Egyptian cotton sheets.

Isa stowed her soccer ball in the corner of the room. "When do you guys think these sessions are gonna kick in?"

"It's too late to kick her out of our bunk," I jumped in. "We all agreed she could stay."

I had lied to Mom in my letter. I hadn't been falling asleep right away every night. I had been staying up late imagining what it would be like to finally be a part of a group at school.

"Whoa. Slow your roll, Bea. No one said anything about kicking her out," said Hannah. "We already said she could stay."

Isa turned to face me. "What's the deal, Bea?"

I focused on pulling the corners of my own bunk sheets tight and kept my face down because being dishonest always makes me flush bright red, which of course my friends know about.

"You're acting really weird," said Poppy.

"I'm not being weird" I said. "And there's no deal. It's too late to switch her to another bunk. We especially couldn't move her to the Dandelion Bunk after that ingenious prank."

"None of us said anything about kicking her out. She's actually cooler than we thought she would be. I mean, that prank—" Hannah started.

"Best prank ever!" Poppy cut in.

Isa narrowed her eyes at me. "You went from hating her and trying to get her pawned off on any other bunk than ours to sticking up for her and expecting us all to be her friend. You gonna tell us what's going on?"

I ran to the window to make sure Maisy wasn't coming. Then I turned to the girls. "You have to promise not to tell Maisy I told you."

The girls all trained their eyes on me.

"You can trust us," said Poppy.

They all nodded and murmured in unison that I could trust them.

I took a deep breath and looked them all in the eyes.

"Maisy's going through a hard time at home," I said. Telling them at least part of the truth would make me feel better, right? In fact, it made me feel even worse. I was exposing a secret about Maisy for my own personal gain that she didn't even know I was aware of.

"Hope it's not as bad as when my mom got laid off. That was the worst," said Hannah.

"Are her parents getting divorced?" Poppy asked. "I wish mine would."

I bit my bottom lip. "I'm not quite sure *exactly* what's happening. My mom said it was worse than divorce."

Poppy wrinkled her nose. "What does that mean?"

I shrugged. "I don't know. But whatever it is seems pretty bad. Which makes everything else seem trivial, you know?"

Hannah shook her head. "You are such a good person, Bea. I don't know if I would be able to forgive someone who ghosted me."

But I didn't feel like a good person. I felt like a liar of epic proportions.

"Thanks for trusting us enough to tell us," said Poppy. "We won't say anything."

Isa bounced her ball off the cabin wall. "Of course Bea told us. We tell each other everything."

This was the moment—if I didn't come clean now, I knew I never would. But when I willed the words to come out, my mouth wouldn't cooperate.

Poppy waved us over to the window. "Looks like the Dandelion girls are pissed about the prank. They've got Maisy surrounded."

I always told Mom that she looked for signs to support whatever decision she wanted to make. If she was thinking about cutting her hair, she would see a Facebook story about fall hairstyles and take it as a sign that she was meant to go for a radical new look. Now here I was, taking the Dandelion girls' interruption as a sign that I wasn't meant to confess.

Hannah headed to the door. "We need to go save Maisy before those girls eat her for breakfast."

Isa grabbed her arm, saying, "At least give the kid a chance to defend herself so we don't humiliate her."

We all leaned into the window to watch Maisy try to stand up for herself, ready to jump in when necessary.

Tinka, with her arms folded across her chest, towered over Maisy. "Well, if it isn't the Camp Amelia ghost."

Maisy gave her a blank stare. "The what?" she said, playing dumb. "I didn't know camp was haunted."

"Should we check to see if she's real?" asked one of the A twins.

The other girls nodded vigorously. The A twin poked Maisy in the arm.

I waited for Maisy to flinch, but she held her ground.

Kaya poked Maisy's other arm. "Guess she's real."

"Unlike those boobs of yours," said Maisy.

Kaya smoothed down her shirt over her heavily padded bra.

"Whoa! Maisy knows how to give it back!" said Hannah.

Kaya took a step toward Maisy, and Isa was out the door. We all followed.

"Back off!" said Hannah.

Tinka rolled her eyes. "We aren't dumb enough to hurt Maisy. She's more good to us all in one piece than she is injured. After all, she's the one who's going to cost you the Cup."

Kaya shoved Maisy toward us. "Good luck teaching this girl the ropes."

The A twins laughed. One of them said, "Literally."

I pulled Maisy away from them and swallowed hard. I needed to get Maisy through that ropes course, or I would have spent the summer lying to my only real friends for nothing.

⇢·· CHAPTER ELEVEN ··⇠

MAISY

From: @madisonave
To: @maisywintersiscoming

You were right!! Meghan's being nice again. ILY!!

From: @maisywintersiscoming
To: @madisonave

Yay!! It sucks when Meghan's mean to you. With me gone you probs felt all alone. Even when I'm there it's 2 against 3.

From: @madisonave
To: @maisywintersiscoming

I know! It's always me and you, then Meghan, Madeline, and Mia are all teamed up together.

From: @maisywintersiscoming
To: @madisonave

You are so right!!! Wish we could fix it.

From: @madisonave
To: @maisywintersiscoming

Me too :(

From: @maisywintersiscoming
To: @madisonave

Maybe we can . . .

"BZZZZZZ," we all said as we passed the Dandelion cabin a few days later.

"OMG! It's still funny," said Hannah.

"It's not gonna be funny when they kick our butts at the tournament," said Isa.

"Stop stressing," said Poppy. "All this extra conditioning is going to give us a huge advantage."

We spent most afternoons in the art cabin, which is really the gym, aka the place where I threatened to jump off the porch. It's a little embarrassing now when Bea and the girls jump off the railings like it's no big deal.

Five minutes later, Bea's face was so close to mine I could smell the pepperoni from her pizza at lunch. "Don't give up."

I groaned. "Ugh, I can't do this."

Bea flicked her wrist and looked at her watch. "Thirty more seconds to go."

My arms were on fire. "You said that thirty seconds ago."

Bea tapped her watch. "Holding a two-minute plank is the secret to the ropes course."

I wanted to groan but didn't have the energy. I also wanted to tell her the secret to the ropes course was not being scared, but talking required even more energy than groaning.

What felt like a million years later, Bea finally stopped her timer and jumped up. "Two minutes! Great job!"

"Nice!" Hannah called from across the room where she was doing push-ups with Isa.

"Next up is partner crunches!" Bea actually sounded excited about this next kind of torture.

She locked her ankles with mine and we had to do sit-ups while passing a five-pound ball back and forth to each other.

Bea reached for the ball. "What's the plan?"

I laid back down. I knew exactly what she was talking about, but I needed a few extra seconds to think. "What plan?"

"For when we go back to school?" Bea whispered, as she passed me back the ball.

"For starters, you need some new clothes." That was a no-brainer.

"What's wrong with my clothes?" Bea hissed.

"You need to dress like you actually care."

"You need to come shopping with me then." Bea wasn't even out of breath from passing the weight back and forth. "You're much better at picking out clothes than I am."

It was starting to hit me that this really was going to be a thing when we got back. I was going to have to convince the M & Ms to hang out with Bea. "I don't understand you. You always hated the M & Ms."

Bea practically threw the ball at me. "I hate being invisible even more."

The ball felt like a hundred pounds of guilt. "What are you talking about? We've been going to school with the same people since preschool. Everyone knows who you are."

Bea narrowed her eyes as I handed her the ball. "How many graduation parties did you go to this year?"

The alpha moms had gotten together at the beginning of the year and decided everyone should space their graduation parties throughout the year so that there wouldn't be any scheduling conflicts or venue double-bookings at the end of the school year. It was easier to count the new dresses I had bought than to remember whose party I was invited to. I was still counting when Bea interrupted, "How many?"

I wasn't done dress counting, so I estimated, "Thirty." I sat up and reached for the ball.

Bea looked me in the eyes and held the ball for an extra second before asking, "Did you see me at any of them?"

I hadn't thought about it before, but, if I had, I would've assumed Bea was somewhere in the crowd.

"What about David Mosko . . ."

"No."

"Becky Smithson . . ."

Bea tossed the ball a little harder at me this time. "I wasn't invited to any. Not one . . . single . . . party."

Not getting invited to an elementary school graduation party in Mapleton is a huge deal. The parties are usually at the Mapleton Lake Club or the Pemberton Golf Club, which is one town over. Both places are big enough to hold our whole grade, so pretty much everyone gets invited. Even the kids who are considered losers got invited because their moms are friends with the mom of the kid who was throwing the party. But Bea's mom only hung out with the other single working moms in town, who didn't have time to network with the Lululemon crowd.

So I did what people do when they feel guilty. I turned the situation around.

"You could've made other friends," I said.

Bea held the weight ball for a minute before handing it over. "I always had you. I never figured out how to make new friends."

I thought about the time we learned about India's caste system and Madeline started calling the unpopular kids Untouchables. Then there was the time I bought mac and cheese for lunch and Mia made me throw it out because "we don't eat fat people food in public." The worst was when Stephen Shipley asked out Meghan, and Mia videoed it and posted it on her Snapchat story, including the part where Meghan said no.

"Did you ever think you might not like the M & Ms? They're not like your crew here," I said.

"I know what I have here is special and that the M & Ms are nothing like my friends here. That's pretty obvious."

"It's not just that they're different than the Sunflower girls. It's hard work to get in the group and stay in the group. I've been in the M & Ms for a year and I still have to work really hard to hold my spot," I said.

"You think I care about working hard to get in the group?" Bea put the ball down. "I can't spend my life alone anymore. I can't spend day after day with people looking right through me. I can't sit home on a Saturday night seeing everyone else's Snapchat stories of parties I'll never be invited to. I can't go through entire school days without having an actual conversation with anyone. Hanging out with the M & Ms is infinitely better than spending another school year alone."

I was starting to realize that Bea had a lot more at stake than I did. We would be out of camp by the end of the summer, but Bea was stuck going to school with people who ignored her for the next six years if I didn't hold up my end of the pact. Because if she couldn't find a friend group in middle school, she was going to be in the same sucky situation for high school.

I took the weighted ball from Bea's hands and said, "You can count on me."

Bea practically whispered, "I counted on you before, and look where that got me. Alone. Not just at school, but when I really needed to talk to someone about Dad's Instant-Family. You abandoned me."

Bea looked at me with that same crumpled up face she had on the first day of school, and I knew I should tell her why I did what I did. I still didn't know what things were going to be like when I got home from camp, but it was time for me to apologize. I grabbed Bea's hands and squeezed them. "I am so sorry about how horrible I treated you last year. I promise things are going to be different when we get back to Mapleton. You really can count on me this time."

"I hope so," Bea said.

BEA

"Hurry up!" I shouted. "We don't want to be late for the bonfire."

"Hold on. Maisy has to finish my braids," Hannah said. Her idea of bonfire attire was a denim overall dress with a rainbow-striped shirt, knee-high athletic socks with red stripes at the top, and generic Keds that were covered in red cherries.

"I need to finish my makeup," Poppy said. She was applying nude lipstick to her already natural-hued makeup that made it look like she was barefaced. She looked like she had stepped right out of the pages of the J. Crew catalog in her simple white sundress with gold sandals.

Even Isa had dressed for the occasion. She had traded her typical soccer clothes for a black T-shirt dress with black-and-white Adidas Gazelles. Instead of pulling her hair into her everyday ponytail, she let her thick black hair dry in natural waves. She dribbled her soccer ball while she waited.

"How does it fit, Bea?" asked Maisy through a mouthful of bobby pins.

"Perfect," I said as I twirled around to show off the blue and white checkered dress with the ruffled sleeves I had borrowed from Maisy.

"I told you it would. We're close enough to the same size that you can borrow some of my clothes for back to school," said Maisy.

"Bea doesn't care about clothes," said Isa. "Not like you do."

What Isa didn't know was that I now cared about anything that would make me be seen at school.

"Middle school is different," said Maisy. "Everyone cares about clothes in middle school."

"Not me," said Isa. "As long as my clothes are comfortable and I can play soccer in them, they work for me." She bounced the ball on her knee as she headed to the door. "Let's go."

It was easy for Isa not to care about things like clothes. Four of Isa's soccer teammates went to school with her. They carpooled to school and practice. She never had to worry about being alone.

"Wait," said Maisy. "Bug spray!"

Maisy pulled out her jumbo-sized bottle of bug spray and ran around the cabin spraying everyone while lecturing about Lyme disease and unsightly mosquito bite scars. I thought the other girls would be annoyed at her anxious ways, but they all laughed and thanked her as she sprayed them.

As the girls got to know Maisy, they were starting to like her little quirks, so maybe the M & Ms would get used to mine.

"Don't forget your bonfire item," Poppy said.

Every year, we had to bring something to camp that was symbolic of something that was holding us back in some way. Then we toss it in the fire. Last year Poppy brought her actual modeling agency contract and her mother was livid when she found out. But then it got the wheels turning in her momager head, and she helped Poppy sign with an even better agency where she is much happier.

Ainsley ran in the door, still sweaty from her evening run. "Everyone ready?" she asked as she ran to her bed.

We all assured her we were ready, and she pulled out an old shoebox from under her bed. "Let's roll," she said.

As soon as we stepped outside the cabin, we could smell the familiar smoky bonfire smell mixed with the aroma of barbequed hamburgers and hot dogs. We followed groups of girls along the trails that led to the open field where the bonfire crackled. One girl was carrying a math book, and all I could think of was how sad it was for a book to burn, even if it was a geometry book. I couldn't wait to see what my bunkmates brought this summer.

"Food first," said Hannah.

She led the way to tables piled with foil-wrapped burgers and hot dogs and Mary Anne's legendary grilled corn on the cob drizzled with garlic butter. Camp Amelia is usually a soda-free zone, but an exception was made on bonfire night. We grabbed stacks of food and grape sodas and walked through the crowds of girls until we found a spot that wasn't too smoky.

We ate quietly except for the occasional exclamations about the delicious food and the sound of us chugging our soda. Twenty minutes later we were all leaning back, rubbing our bellies, and complaining about how full we were.

"I wish Mary Anne could move in with me and cook like this all the time," said Isa. "I come home from practice and my mom has a green smoothie and broiled fish with baked sweet potato waiting for me. Every. Single. Night."

"I would take that over chicken nuggets or frozen pizza," said Hannah. "My mom doesn't even cook them in the oven. She microwaves everything until it's rubbery and gross."

"Are you guys ready for the ceremonial burning, because I am," I said.

I looked around the bonfire and saw small groups like ours with girls pulling things out and talking about them before they threw them in the pit. I hoped everyone followed the "safe to burn" rules. The smell was awful that time a girl burned her Barbie doll.

"I'll go first," said Ainsley.

She held up her shoebox, which looked like it had once housed special pole-vaulting sneakers. Then she cleared her throat in a dramatic way.

"I am no longer bound by the label of Ted's crazy ex-girlfriend. I have moved on. No more stalking his Facebook and Instagram. No more calling him from a blocked number. No more accidentally on purpose bumping into him on campus."

Ainsley took the lid off the box and dumped the contents into the fire. Greeting cards, movie ticket stubs, photos, and handwritten notes poured out of the box. Ainsley took a deep breath and smiled as she watched her memories burn.

"You're up next, Hannah," she said, as she tossed the empty shoebox into the fire.

Hannah pulled out a manila folder. "This is my original educational evaluation that labeled me as dyslexic."

"Wait!" Poppy said. "Remember what happened when I burned my contract? My mom wouldn't talk to me for days."

"Relax, it's a copy," said Hannah. "I may be dyslexic, but I'm not stupid." Then she covered her mouth. "OMG! I am so sorry, Poppy. I didn't mean . . ."

We all laughed really hard.

Hannah clutched the folder while she stood up. "I am no longer bound by the label dyslexic. I am not a dyslexic person. I am a person with dyslexia. My learning disability does not define me. I am a good friend, a strong athlete, and I have the best fashion sense of anyone I know."

We all clapped as she dropped the folder into the fire with a flourish so it opened and the papers fell out and turned black. Then she sat down with a huge grin on her face. "Who's up next?"

Poppy raised her hand. "I am, if that's okay with you guys."

We all nodded encouragingly. Poppy stood up and showed us all a paper shopping bag. It was the Abercrombie bag with her face on it. Someone must've said something funny at the shoot because the photographer caught her mid-laugh. Poppy has the most beautiful smile when she laughs because it lights up her whole face. The reason she was such a great model was that she wasn't scared to show the world who she really was on the inside. That was something I didn't know if I would ever learn how to do outside of camp.

Poppy held the shopping bag up. "I am no longer bound by the label of model. I am so much more than that. I am a good friend, a strong student, and an empowered young woman. Being a model is a small part of who I am, and I need to start reminding people of that when they judge me. If I want to empower other girls, I need to start with myself."

It was weird to see her beautiful blond hair and white teeth turn black and then eventually float away in crisps of burned paper, but the ear-to-ear smile on Poppy's real face was wonderful to see.

Isa stood up next. She held up the stack of college brochures her mother had mailed her and fanned them out so we could see the pictures of grassy quads and ivy-covered stone buildings. "I am no longer bound by the label of soccer college recruit. I love soccer and I want to play it in college and on a professional team after that. But I'm only in middle school, so I don't want to talk about my future soccer career every single day of my life. When I get back home, I'm going to threaten to quit if my mom doesn't stop harassing me about my playing, lecturing me about college, and coaching me from the sidelines."

Isa dropped the brochures in the fire and then clapped her hands together.

I stood up next and held up my sixth-grade yearbook. The yearbook that represented the worst school year of my life. I cleared my throat. "I am no longer bound by the label of invisible. I am not going to spend another school year walking the halls alone, eating lunch with only the company of a book, and sitting home watching everyone else's social lives on Snapchat. No more sitting on the sidelines for me. I am going to put myself out there this year."

I didn't say anything about the pact and how it was going to fix everything for me, so the other girls probably just thought I was going to work on getting my confidence up. They smiled at me as I dropped my yearbook in the fire. Then Maisy reached out her hand and squeezed mine, and I knew everything was going to be okay.

"Your turn, Maisy," said Hannah.

Maisy stood up holding a stack of letters in her shaky hands. I recognized her mom's handwriting right away. When we were little, Mrs. Winters was the one who wrote out all of my birthday cards. She always scribed the same message: *Wishing you a year ahead full of wonderful new adventures and lots of love.* When we were older, she would write out grocery lists: EGGS, ALMOND MILK, GLUTEN-FREE BREAD, GOAT CHEESE and send us to the farmer's market on Saturday mornings with a pocketful of cash. She always gave us extra so we could buy cookies from our favorite bakery stand.

Maisy fanned the letters out in her small hands. There were ten crisp envelopes and two that looked like they had been pulled from a garbage can—all unopened. All with Maisy's mom's handwriting on them, and when I leaned in close I could see a return address in Minnesota.

She blinked a bunch of times, which she always does when she's trying not to cry. "I am no longer . . ." she stopped. Then she took a deep breath. "Can I start again?"

"Yes," said Ainsley. "Take all the time you need. We're here for you."

We all nodded in agreement. I wondered if Maisy was finally going to open up about why she ended up at Camp Amelia.

Maisy kept blinking, but it wasn't helping. Tears streamed down her face. Her legs were shaking along with her voice. "I am no longer bound by the label of forgiver. I've forgiven way more times than anyone should have to and I just can't do it anymore. I'm not a bad person just because I need more time to get over things. No one can take away my anger. I am going to stay mad as long as I want. I'm not like Dad and Addy. There are some things that saying sorry doesn't fix."

Maisy dropped the letters in the fire one by one with tears spilling down her face and silent sobs wracking her body. When she sat down, we all surrounded her. I wrapped her in a hug and rubbed her back. "It's okay, Maisy. It's all going to be okay."

While the other campers were laughing and dancing around the fire, we tuned out everyone else and stayed with Maisy. She didn't tell us what was going on at home. We didn't find out how she ended up at camp, why her mother was in Minnesota, or why she was so angry at her. But we did show her that we were there for her.

As I was hugging her, I couldn't push down the feelings of anger that were fighting the part of me that was sad for her. If she hadn't left me behind, I would've been there for her just like I had been for practically her whole life.

>--- CHAPTER TWELVE ---<
MAISY

From: @madisonave
To: @maisywintersiscoming

Hello . . . Where you been? You drop a bomb about fixing things with the M & Ms, then go MIA???

From: @maisywintersiscoming
To: @madisonave

Sorry!!! Camp has been crazy busy. We need to add our own girl to the M & Ms. Someone who would always be on our side. So when Meghan's being mean to you, we won't feel ganged up on.

From: @madisonave
To: @maisywintersiscoming

OMG!! Best idea ever!!!! What about Missy Edwards? She is looking much better since she started going to the dermatologist. Or Medford

Richards? She's kind of annoying, but her mom owns that clothing shop on Woodward and can get us all discounts.

From: @maisywintersiscoming
To: @madisonave

Maybe we should do something crazy and pick a girl who doesn't have an M name.

"We've been running around camp for weeks and you guys are finally showing me the actual race course?" I said.

Poppy smiled. "We needed to focus on getting you comfortable with the ropes course. Relax, this is going to be easy in comparison."

"Especially since you've been running and doing conditioning all summer," added Isa.

Of course, Poppy and Isa thought the run would be easy. These sporty girls think anything athletic is easy. But I had to admit, this was the only part of the tournament that didn't scare me. Running is just putting one foot in front of the other, and that's what I had been doing for the past two years.

Ainsley stood in the center of the field. She was wearing running clothes and had her hair pulled back like she meant business. She was even wearing a whistle around her neck.

She held up a stopwatch. "I'm timing this run, so we can see where we're at. We're doing the full two miles, so try your best to run your race pace."

Isa turned to me. "Run like you're chasing those nasty Dandelion girls in your ghost costume."

Hannah tugged on my arm. "Think about something that makes you really mad. That's what pushes me on a long run."

"You guys better not even think about walking in the woods because I'll be right behind you!" Ainsley yelled.

She blew the whistle, and Isa and Hannah took the lead across the grass.

I didn't know what running two miles at race pace felt like because I had never done it before. But I took Hannah's advice. It wasn't hard to make myself mad enough to run fast.

I took off after the girls and thought about the time Mom was supposed to pick me up at Madison's house and never showed. Madison's mom ended up driving me home, but I was locked out because Mom was passed out inside. I pretended I was going to let myself in the back door, but because it was locked, I was stuck waiting in the backyard until Addy got dropped off after practice. It was a freezing cold February night, so it took hours for my hands and feet to get the feeling back. I really thought I had frostbite, but I couldn't ask Dad what he thought because that would mean telling him about Mom.

I stuck close behind Isa across the edge of the field into the opening in the woods.

"Pace yourself, Maisy," called Ainsley.

Like I knew how to pace myself.

Then there was the time Mom promised to bake Irish soda bread for my social studies unit on Ireland. I didn't believe she would actually make it, but there it was sitting on the dining room table the morning the project was due. When Mr. DeSouza bit into a piece, he gagged and spat it out right away. He said, "You were supposed to make *Irish soda bread,* Maisy, not Irish Spring soap bread." The whole class laughed, and Mr. DeSouza kept it as a running joke for the rest of the semester.

My feet slapped the dirt. I thought about that last day before Mom left. I knew things were bad because Dad took the day off from work on a surgery day. All I had ever heard growing up was how he couldn't miss a surgery day, even if that meant skipping my chorus concert or the elementary school holiday breakfast or my dance club performance. Dad missed more things than he made it to. It never used to bother me because Mom came to everything. But when Mom stopped showing up, it really sucked.

When I had woken up that morning, Dad was sitting on the chair across from my bed with his head in his hands. He was still wearing his scrubs from the night before, even though he *never* wore his scrubs home because—germs.

I focused on pumping my legs up and down and breathing in and out as I flew through the woods.

I thought about how Dad had swept my hair off my forehead and said, "I am so sorry, Maisy."

Dad, who never cried because he had to keep it together when giving patients bad news, started to tear up. It was literally the first time in my life I had seen him cry. "I could've lost all three of you last night. All because I kept my head in the sand."

I didn't know what he meant about the sand, but it was making me really uncomfortable to see him cry. His nose was dripping and he didn't even notice.

"I thought Mom was doing better. I thought she was going to meetings. Why didn't you girls tell me?"

The words got caught in my throat before they tumbled out. "Addy and I saw a movie where the kids got put in a foster home because their mom was taking pills. We didn't want to get taken away."

Dad hugged me so tight I felt like I couldn't breathe. "I would never send you away."

But then a few days later, Mom was in rehab and Dad sent me here.

"Go, Maisy!" called Isa, when I passed her on the trail.

I could hear Isa's feet crunching in the leaves as she followed me. I hoped I was going the right way because I was the one leading the pack. I guess running angry really does help.

The trail opened up into a wide field with bright red tape marking the rest of the path. Ainsley was waiting there with her stopwatch.

I kept running until I passed Ainsley. Then I collapsed on the grass. As I panted and gasped for air, I felt like my bad memories were pushing their way outside of my body.

Ainsley held up her stopwatch and screamed, "Eleven minutes, twenty seconds!!! That's a camp record!"

BEA

Hey kiddo,

Sounds like camp is going well. Glad you got put in the same bunk with your friends. Good luck training for the tournament!

We had a great time at Disney World. We got fast passes so we could ride Space Mountain, Thunder Mountain Railroad, and Splash Mountain all in a row. Peyton and Vivi got a little motion sick by the third roller coaster, but they both said it was worth it. The girls got really into taking artsy pictures around the park. Monica posted them all on Instagram. You can catch up when you're back in the digital world. Too bad you're at camp all summer. We would've loved to have you join us.

Looking forward to you visiting the new house. We're going to be at Monica's parents the first weekend you're back from camp, and the girls have their first travel tennis tournament of the season the weekend after that, but maybe you can come the Sunday after that? I'll check in with your mom and Monica when it gets closer to the date.

Enjoy the rest of camp! Monica says to remember your sunblock.

Love,

Dad, Monica, and the girls

Dear Dad,

I'm so happy to hear that you guys had such a great time at Disney! Can't wait to see the pictures. I bet Peyton and Vivi took some really cool shots. I'll take a look on Instagram as soon as I have phone access again.

I would love to visit the first weekend you are free. Just let me know when it works best for you. I know how busy you guys are!

Sorry for the short letter, but we are super busy getting ready for the camp tournament. Give my love to everyone.

Love,

Bea

I took Hannah's advice and ran mad. I thought about how I wasn't just invisible at school. I was invisible at Dad's house, too.

Dad started dating Monica two years ago, after she ran out of gas right in front of his car dealership. It may sound like a Hallmark movie, but I wouldn't be surprised if Monica drove around and around until she ran out of gas, hoping some unsuspecting Prince Charming would save her. That person just happened to be my dad.

Monica always makes this cheesy joke that she came as a "package deal" with her daughters Peyton, who's a year older than me, and Vivi, who's a year younger than me. The first time I met them, Dad called us "his girls." As if a few months of dating their mom had made her daughters as important to him as I was.

"The girls" each have their own rooms in the new house. This is knowledge that I've gathered from our FaceTime chat, because I haven't been to the new house yet, even though they moved in six months ago. Dad says it's because we haven't been able to coordinate our schedules. Meanwhile, I've been free every weekend because I have no friends in Mapleton. Dad and "his girls" are the ones who've been busy. Peyton has a room with a window seat covered in purple and white floral fabric that matches her bedspread and curtains. Vivi's room has a custom-made loft bed with a homework nook under it complete with a desk hutch and swivel chair.

Meanwhile, I don't have my own room in my own Dad's house. He thought I would fall for it when he designated the finished basement as "my own personal space." As if the pullout couch made it a real bedroom. I don't see a washer and dryer in Peyton's or Vivi's rooms. Monica loves to pretend that relegating me to the basement is a high honor instead of the stereotypical banishment of the biological child in favor of the step-children—a tale as old as time. But the more he shows me that I'm not important, that I don't matter, the more I want him to see me, and the more I want to be a real part of his life.

Running angry really did make me run faster. Poppy and I brought up the back of the pack. We're fast compared to a lot of other girls at camp, but not as fast as Isa, Hannah, and, apparently, Maisy.

When we got to the finish line, the girls were jumping up and down and cheering for her . . . a sight I never expected to see.

Maisy broke away from them and ran to me. "I'm a runner, Bea! Who knew I would actually be good at something?"

The irony is that Maisy is talented at a lot of things. She's an amazing singer with a broad range who can also play any song on the guitar and piano. She taught herself how to play both instruments from YouTube, the same way she learned how to do every hairstyle imaginable. Part of me was glad that camp humbled Maisy, but the other part of me felt bad that going to Camp Amelia broke her confidence. Because I know better than anyone else what that feels like.

Ainsley blew her whistle.

I realized I hadn't seen Maisy smile like that since she got here. In fact, I couldn't remember the last time I'd seen her smile like that—a real smile. Sure, she was always laughing with the M & Ms when I saw them at school, but her smile looked fake, like those cardboard cutouts of smiles on sticks you find in photo booths.

"You know what this means, girls?" asked Ainsley.

Poppy put both hands on top of her head. "We still have a chance at the Cup!"

Isa paced back and forth like she always did when she was working something out in her head. "Tinka and I take turns winning the run. With Maisy, we'll have a definite shot at that first spot, which might secure us enough points to bring in the win!"

Hannah smoothed down her perfect french braids, which of course were done by Maisy. "As long as you can get across the ropes course, Maisy."

"Unless I pass the swim test. Then I just need to complete the swim. Right, Ainsley?" Maisy turned toward Ainsley with a look of sheer desperation on her face.

Ainsley laughed. "You have a better chance at winning the lottery."

CHAPTER THIRTEEN

MAISY

To: docwinters@yahoo.com
From: dramagirl@gmail.com
Subject: Guess what????

Hi Dad,

Apparently I'm like a superstar runner! I beat the camp record on my first try. Our counselor Ainsley, who goes to college on a track scholarship, told me I should try out for cross-country in the fall. I might do it, as long as I can still find time for drama and voice stuff.

I'm definitely not a superstar swimmer, not even in the baby group. But I can put my head in the water and blow bubbles now! My swim coach says you have to start somewhere.

My bunkmates turned out to be pretty nice. You know how Grandma always says, "I can be a bit much, and that takes some getting used to"? I think they're getting used to me.

Guess what? Bea and I are friends again. At first it was kind of out of necessity, but now I kinda like hanging out with her. Just don't say I told you so. . . .

So I'm doing kind of okay. That doesn't mean I want you shipping me off to adventure camp next summer, so don't get any crazy ideas. But I'm doing all right. I've been talking to Dr. Beth and she said she would give you the name of a good therapist back home. I know I said I would NEVER go to therapy, but that was before I met Dr. Beth. She said she could give you the name of someone for you too, you know, if you need to talk.

If you're still feeling guilty about shipping me off to boot camp for the summer, Bath & Body Works or LUSH products would help. . . . And maybe some cookies from Insomnia. Make sure you send enough for the whole bunk. These girls eat A LOT!

Love you and miss you,
Mini

From: docwinters@yahoo.com
To: dramagirl@gmail.com
Subject: Re: Guess what????

Hi Mini,

Wow! Congrats on the running superstardom. I'm not surprised at all. Mom and I used to have the hardest time keeping up with you when you were little. We always had to worry about Addy climbing out of the Pack and Play because she was so strong, but we always had to worry about you running off at Target because you were the fastest toddler in history. You LOVED to run through the aisles! I wanted to get you one of those kiddie leashes, but Mom put her foot down about that.

Your swimming coach is right. You have to start somewhere. I didn't just wake up one day knowing how to do surgery. There were lots of little steps on the way, like high school science classes, pre-med classes, medical school, you get the point. The people who get somewhere in life are the ones who are willing to take all those little steps on the way.

I'm glad Dr. Beth is helping you. She already emailed me with the name of a few therapists back home. She also sent me a link to Taco Bell coupons for something called Taco Tuesday??

Love you,
Dad

From: @madisonave
To: @maisywintersiscoming

Won't it be weird if the new girl doesn't have an M name?

From: @maisywintersiscoming
To: @madisonave

It's like being fashion-forward . . . knowing the trend before it even happens.

From: @madisonave
To: @maisywintersiscoming

??? I don't get it.

From: @maisywintersiscoming
To: @madisonave

Having a group where everyone's name starts with the same letter is so babyish. We need to mix it up for middle school or the 8th graders will make fun of us.

From: @madisonave
To: @maisywintersiscoming

Ooooooh. Now I get it!!!

———•———

Things I Know About the M & Ms

1. When Madison borrows something, you're never getting it back, even if your name's written in black Sharpie on the tag.

2. When Madeline finds out who your crush is, she'll say she's liked him forever and you're copying her.

3. Mia can't figure anything out without calling her mother. She even calls her every day at lunch to ask what she should eat.

4. Meghan never gives photo creds on Instagram but calls out anyone who posts one of her pics without giving her credit.

Things the M & Ms Know About Me

1. I have to buy my bras at Justice.

2. I'm scared of everything.

3. My sister's a superstar gymnast.

4. Dad's a doctor—speaking of which, it really creeps me out when Madeline says he looks hot in his scrubs, like the guys on *Grey's Anatomy*.

What the M & Ms Don't Know About Me

1. My mom is a drug addict.

Things the Sunflower Girls Know About Each Other

1. EVERYTHING

Poppy texted all the Sunflower girls as soon as she got her period. They knew Hannah's dad was downsized last year and that she was at camp on scholarship, a scholarship Poppy's Nana Mary helped pay for. They also knew about Hannah's dyslexia and that Poppy's parents weren't divorced, but sleep in separate bedrooms in super-faraway wings of their gigantic mansion. They know Isa's dad isn't her biological dad, even though he treats her like he is. They know that Bea's dad is living with a needy woman named Monica and that he spends more time with her daughters than with Bea. These girls don't believe in secrets. Neither do the M & Ms, but in a totally different way. They don't believe in secrets because they can't keep their mouths shut. I could never confide in them the way that Bea does with the Sunflower girls.

It was kind of weird to be around girls who were so close to each other on such an intense level. But it was also nice to have them not really hating me anymore. At first, I thought I just cared about fitting in, but I was starting to realize I genuinely liked hanging out with them, even Bea.

But once the girls realized we had a shot at the Cup, the pressure was back on. If I had known that was gonna happen, I might not have run so fast.

Bea gave my safety harness a tug. "You're finally ready for the hard part of the course!"

I shuddered. "I don't think I'm ever gonna be ready for the spider web. Look how high up it goes!"

Bea squeezed my hands. "Once you get up to the top platform, you'll be done with the course. You can do this."

"But the space between each rope is huge! What if I fall right through?" I asked.

Bea took one look at my face and said, "Isa's never fallen and neither will you."

I pulled at the rope attached to me and looked at how the web had six rows between me and the next platform.

Bea looked me in the eyes. "And, yes, your rope is long enough. You are so ready for this. I am here for you. Now do you trust me?"

"Will you go first? And wait for me? And go super slow?" I asked.

Bea nodded and her bright red curls bounced from underneath her helmet. "Yes to all of that."

"Should we recheck our helmets? Do you think they loosened up while we were ziplining?"

Bea put both hands on top of my helmet, then yanked on my chin strap. "Feels perfect."

"What about my rope harness? I feel like I could just slip through the leg holes."

Bea tugged on the ropes around my waist. "All good."

I gave another tug just to be sure.

Bea started climbing. "Quit stalling," she called and moved up the web just enough to make room for me.

My arms and legs stretched as far as they could go as soon as I tried to climb up the web. When Bea moved, the whole web started swaying with her.

I clutched the rope tight and tried to stay as still as I could to stop my body from moving. "Wait! Stop! You're shaking the whole thing!"

Bea's voice was calm. "You have to get used to that feeling. During the competition, we'll both be crossing the web at the same time. It might feel kind of weird, but every time you feel the ropes move, it will mean I'm right up here with you."

I felt that tingling feeling in my fingers and pounding in my chest that happens right before I have a panic attack, but I thought about what Dr. Beth told me. She said to focus on breathing in and out. So I breathed in while I counted to ten in my mind, then I breathed out for ten. I did this until my heart stopped feeling like it would jump out of my chest.

I wish I could bring Dr. Beth back to Mapleton with me, but she would never leave all her cats behind. Apparently, she lives on a farm not far from camp with all of her cats and her husband, Jerry, during the school year. She said we can FaceTime, but it won't be the same as packing her in my suitcase and bringing her home.

I moved up to the next row. Now I only had five more to go.

"You can do it, Maisy!" Isa shouted from where she was belaying below.

Hannah called, "Come on, Maisy! You can do it!"

But it still felt nice to have them all sticking by me. No matter what. I've never once felt like that with the M & Ms. I've always been one wrong haircut, one bad outfit, or one wrong comment away from being dropped. With these girls, all they wanted was for me to try my best, which made me want to try harder. I didn't want to let them down, not because I was scared they would drop me from the group, but because I wanted them to be proud of me.

I tried to ignore the way my body was shaking and swaying on the ropes as I moved up to the next row. But this row was even higher than the last one and, as much as my arms wanted to reach for the next level of rope, my brain wouldn't let them. All I could do was picture myself falling to my death.

"Come on, Maisy!" shouted Bea. "I know you can do this. You are so close!"

The other girls were shouting from underneath us, but I couldn't hear them over the ringing in my ears.

"I can't do it!" I yelled.

I started climbing back down, ready for Bea to give me a lecture about giving up when I was so close to finishing. But I just couldn't do it. I could feel my face heat up with the shame of letting Bea down again.

I could feel the ropes move back and forth as Bea made her way next to me. I looked at her, ready to take whatever she gave me.

But she put her hand on mine. "You came so close this time. The closest you ever have."

I bit my lower lip and pushed the tears back. "But I didn't make it to the top. What if I can't do it at the tournament? What if I let you guys down?"

Bea moved down a rung, ready to help me get back down to the ground. "I know you can do it at the tournament. You almost did it today. You'll get it during the tournament when the adrenaline is pumping and we have a Dandelion girl coming behind us. I believe in you."

I really hoped I could do it the day of the tournament because the guilt of letting Bea down would be too much to handle.

BEA

Dear Bea,

I'm missing you like crazy. But I've been keeping busy working and hanging out with the Single Squad. Frank at Pizza Amore groans every time he sees us coming because we hit his all-you-can-eat salad buffet hard after spin class. Last time we went, he tried to hide the breadsticks from us, but Nicole busted him. You don't want to get between Nicole and her post-workout carb loading.

I'm sure you are waiting on the Mr. Pembrook update. . . . I think I finally found someone as obsessed with Harry Potter as I am! We spent the weekend binge watching all the movies. Gavin even made Harry Potter–themed food. We had pumpkin juice, Hogwarts Acceptance Letter puff pastries, Hagrid's steak and kidney pie, without the steak because Gavin is vegan, which was great as long as I ate around the kidney beans, and butterbeer cupcakes for dessert. We agree on all the important things: *Harry Potter and the Chamber of Secrets* is the worst book/movie of the series and *Harry Potter and the Goblet of Fire* in the best, Professor Snape is a hero, and Gryffindor all the way!

I finally sold the Cherrybrook Lane house! You know the blue one with the big turret and gingerbread trim? That means you and I can take a nice trip for spring break this year. We can stay in one of those all-inclusive resorts where you can order unlimited Shirley Temples and swim with the dolphins like we've always wanted! When you get home, we can go online and pick out a resort together.

I know I already said it, but I miss you sooooo much! Counting down the days till you come home. Brilliant idea to extend our Gilmore Girls marathon to a full forty-eight hours. I will make sure to have my leggings with the stretched-out waist ready!

Love you more than anything,

Mom

P.S. Mr. Pebbles is getting a little spoiled. Now he likes alkaline water in his water bowl and he will only eat the fancy organic cat food.

I looked around the cabin and all of the girls were keeping themselves entertained during our "reading and writing block." Poppy was writing a letter to Gwyneth, her best friend from back home. Isa was practicing a new soccer move, even though Ainsley had been getting on her case about playing in the cabin. Maisy was busy making team bracelets with Hannah for the tournament. They had figured out how to make a Sunflower design on each bracelet and they were working hard to finish on time for us to wear them to the competition.

I closed Mom's letter and tried to calm the thoughts that were swirling in my brain. It was one thing for Mom to go on a blind date with Mr. Pembrook, it was an entirely different matter to spend the weekend together bonding over Mom's favorite book/movie series in the entire world. If this was what anxiety feels like, I couldn't imagine dealing with it every day like Maisy.

Maisy looked up at me and asked, "They're still together?"

I put the letter on my bunk shelf. "They just spent the weekend together having a Harry Potter marathon."

"Who's still together?" Hannah asked.

"My mom's dating our old math teacher," I said.

"Isn't that a good thing?" Poppy asked. "Haven't you been trying to get her to start dating again?"

"Seriously," said Hannah. "Your poor mom's been single for as long as we've known you."

"Yeah, but I didn't expect her to end up with a guy who wears holiday-themed bowties and gives detention for gum chewing," I said.

"He can't give you detention if he isn't your teacher anymore," Isa said.

Maisy put down her friendship bracelet. "I always liked him, aside from the whole detention thing. He was really patient when I had trouble with a math unit, and he always explained things to me without making me feel dumb."

"I'm not saying he isn't a nice guy, but he isn't someone I expected my mom to end up with," I said.

Hannah groaned. "I wouldn't want my mom dating my old math teacher."

"Agreed," said Poppy. "School and home are supposed to be two different worlds. It's creepy when they collide."

"At least he's an elementary school teacher," said Hannah. "Could you imagine if your mom's boyfriend was your middle school teacher?"

"Blech! Our school campus is so small, though, that the middle school is connected to the elementary school," I said. "This year is going to suck."

Maisy raised her eyes to me. "Don't worry, Bea. You're going to have a great year, even with the Pembrook situation. I'll make sure of that."

I had a feeling this pact was going to be the one thing keeping me sane when I got home from camp.

CHAPTER FOURTEEN

MAISY

From: @maisywintersiscoming
To: @madisonave

We need the other girls to think adding a new girl without an M name is their idea. The key is Mia. If you can convince her, the other girls will follow. So start dropping hints about it, until she thinks it's her idea.

From: @madisonave
To: @maisywintersiscoming

You're a genius!!

Mary Anne handed me a plate filled with fluffy blueberry pancakes with a pat of melty butter on top of the stack. "Here's your usual."

"Thanks!" I said and put the warm dish of food on my cold stainless-steel tray.

"What's your bunk doing for the talent show?" Mary Anne asked, handing me a mini-pitcher of real maple syrup.

"Talent show?" I grabbed a chilled glass of OJ and put it on my tray. "What talent show?"

Mary Anne started scooping scrambled eggs onto a plate for Ella Ray from the Rose Bunk. "We have one every year. The bunks all perform. They do skits, dance routines, someone usually sings."

Ella Ray grabbed a bagel and a chocolate milk. "It's tonight. But your bunk never does it," she said.

"There's always a first time for everything," I said, quoting Dr. Beth, who thinks this applies to just about everything in life. Never been on a ropes course? "There's a first time for everything." Never been in the deep end of the water? "Well, there's a first time for everything." You get the picture.

"Thanks for the heads-up, Mary Anne," I said.

Mary Anne gave me a little nod to let me know she was rooting for me.

"What's this I hear about a talent show?" I practically shrieked as soon as I sat down with the Sunflower girls. I slammed my plate down so hard that one of my pancakes landed on the table.

Isa waved her hand as if she was swatting a fly. "We never do it."

I picked my runaway pancake off the table and stuck it back on my plate, then poured lots of syrup all over the stack. "What do you mean you never do it?"

Hannah looked up from her overflowing bowl of raisin spice oatmeal. "We have no hope of winning, so why bother?"

I whipped my head around to face Bea. "Why bother? Did she seriously just say 'why bother'?"

Bea shrugged. "We're usually so focused on getting ready for the tournament that we don't want to waste time rehearsing for the talent show."

"Not to mention, we're really not that talented," added Poppy, through a mouthful of scrambled eggs.

I couldn't believe what I was hearing. "A talent show isn't about winning." I waved a piece of bacon at them. "Not everything in life is about winning."

"Tell that to the Dandelion girls," said Hannah. "They'll never let us live it down if they beat us."

"Who cares about the Dandelion girls?" I said. "The one cool thing about this camp is the talent show. We are not missing it!" I pounded my fist on the table and everyone's juice glass rattled. All the girls, including the campers at the next two tables, stared at me like I had lost my mind.

"Do you seriously care this much about the talent show?" Poppy asked.

"I did kick some serious butt on the race course, and I am so close to getting through the spider web! We can afford one day of fun, can't we?" I pressed. I clasped my hands together like I was praying, which it kind of felt like I was. "Pleeeeeeease?"

Bea sighed and looked at the other girls. "Well . . ."

I clapped my hands together. "OMG! This is going to be so much fun! What're you guys good at—besides tournament stuff?"

Poppy looked up at the dining hall ceiling. "I'm good at modeling, but I don't think that's really talent show kind of stuff."

"I'm good at soccer," said Isa. "But also not really talent show stuff."

I swallowed a huge bite of pancake and washed it down with Bea's OJ since mine had a fly floating in it. "Don't worry, guys, we'll figure it out. Raise your hand if you can sing."

I raised my hand, but everyone else just looked at each other.

Hannah started to raise her hand, then put it back down. "My singing's more like 'sing in the shower when no one's around' kind of singing."

"Can anyone play a musical instrument?" I asked.

"I played the recorder back in third grade," said Poppy.

Hannah rolled her eyes. "I had to drop clarinet because it conflicted with resource room."

"I had to drop violin because I never had any time to practice," said Isa.

I tried my best not to look hopeless. For a bunch of sporty girls, they really didn't know how to do regular things. "Does anyone have a really good comedy act?"

The girls laughed so hard that Isa almost choked on her toast.

"Know any magic tricks?" I asked.

No one even bothered to answer that one.

"Give me a minute. I'll come up with something," I said.

I spent the rest of breakfast chowing down while running through ideas in my head. I tuned out all the chatter around me and brainstormed.

When all of my pancakes and bacon were gone, and I had worked my way through Bea's plate of toast, I finally got my stroke of genius. "I've got it! We're going to do a dance number with Isa in the starring role."

"That's not gonna work because I have no rhythm. Like, literally no rhythm," said Isa.

"Ah, but you can play soccer," I said.

Everyone looked at me like I was sitting in the dining cabin in my underwear. Everyone except for Bea, who always trusted my plans.

BEA

Maisy grabbed my arm and asked, "Is that girl really gonna do the cups song from *Pitch Perfect*?"

Hannah rolled her eyes. "Lisa Turner does it every . . . single . . . year."

Lisa sat in the middle of the square, which served double duty as our Talent Night stage. She ceremoniously waved a red Solo plastic cup in front of her before beginning. As she sang the song with the accompanying movements, I ran through our choreographed routine in my mind. Maisy had ingeniously taken the same exact eight count that we had used for our talent show routine at school and put it together for the camp routine. It was crucial for me to get it right because I would be standing in front of Poppy so that she could look on, while Maisy would be modeling the moves for Hannah.

As soon as Lisa finished her song, Maisy broke through the dull applause with her own boisterous clapping and cheers.

"I can see why she does that every year," she said. "She was amazing!"

Isa smacked Maisy in the arm. "You're cheering for the wrong team."

Maisy rubbed her arm. "Ow! Tonight's not about competition."

Hannah smirked. "Good thing 'cause we have no shot at winning."

Bailey stepped onto the middle of the court. "Let's all have a big round of applause for Lisa." She started clapping and a bored smattering of claps spread through the crowd.

"Great job, Lisa, um, really . . . perfecting that act," Bailey said enthusiastically. "Next up are the Sunflower Girls, who are making their Camp Amelia Talent Night debut!"

We all reluctantly stood up while Maisy practically ran to the stage. She had asked Isa for a list of all the other soccer players at camp. Then she knocked on all their cabin doors until she had scavenged four matching pairs of black soccer shorts, four black headbands, black soccer cleats in the right size for each of us, shin guards, and knee-high black-and-white soccer socks. She even found semi-matching white soccer tees for all of us. Then she styled everyone's hair in matching double dutch braids. Isa was "starring" as the goalie. So she made sure to stand out in a neon green goalie shirt with matching padded goalie gloves.

At first, I was shocked the Dandelion girls didn't boo us off the stage, but then I realized that was to Maisy's credit because she had cheered for them during their ten-minute mixed martial arts demo, which included Tinka flipping one of the counselors, the A twins breaking boards with their hands, and Kaya doing a spinning back kick.

"Come on, girls," Maisy said, in an exaggerated cheerleader voice. "Put it in." She put her hand out and waited for us all to pile our hands on top of hers. "Sunflower girls, on three!"

We all pumped our hands with her for three counts and then threw them in the air while shouting "Sunflower girls!" I felt simultaneously cheesy and proud.

I waited for the first beats of "Jump Around" by House of Pain. Admittedly, it's a dated hip-hop song, but we were relegated to whatever mixed tapes we could dig up in the music cabin.

As soon as the song started, Maisy and I led Hannah and Poppy in the first set of eight counts that we would repeat over and over again until the song ended. As we went through the eight count, we moved across the grass so it looked like we were playing soccer. While we danced, Isa lifted the ball with her feet and did trick after trick. The entire time we were dancing, she moved the ball seamlessly from foot to foot, then up in the air, and around her body without letting the ball touch the ground once. Every time the audience thought she had shown them every trick imaginable, she pulled out another one.

I messed up a move or two, but it didn't matter, because we were having so much fun. When I got on stage, I couldn't wait for it to be over, but when the song ended I was sorry it did. Maisy grabbed our hands and led us in a bow. I extended my bow for just a second longer than necessary just to hold on to that moment.

When we sat back down in the audience, I actually enjoyed watching the other bunks perform. Maisy was right; not everything at camp should be about the tournament.

At the end of the night, when the paper plate awards were being handed out, we all gripped hands like we were on the cast of some reality dance show. Even Isa looked excited at the prospect of being awarded a superlative that was the equivalent of a participation trophy.

Bailey cleared her throat. "And the award for most creative choreography goes to . . . the Sunflower Bunk."

Maisy turned to us all with a look of pure delight on her face. "OMG! We won an award!"

"Go on, Maisy," said Isa. "You can accept it for us. You did all the choreography."

Maisy shook her head. Even though every other bunk had sent up only one representative for their award, Maisy wouldn't accept the award on her own. "We're all going up."

We all did the mandatory grumble as we followed Maisy to the stage. But when we got up there, we all got caught up in the participation trophy victory with Maisy and smiled and slow-waved to the crowd as if we were winners of a beauty pageant.

CHAPTER FIFTEEN

MAISY

From: @maisywintersiscoming
To: @madisonave

Did you drop hints about adding a non M girl to the group?

From: @madisonave
To: @maisywintersiscoming

Tried to, but Meghan's being mean again. She planned a sleepover with just Madeline and Mia and then only invited me after her mom found out. Too scared to bring up a new girl when I feel like Meghan wants to get rid of me :(

From: @maisywintersiscoming
To: @madisonave

Sorry Meghan's being mean again. Don't worry. I'll be home soon. Miss you!!

I still wasn't used to how cold and damp it was in the mornings, especially in Dr. Beth's cabin. I snuggled into a floor pillow and pulled my sweatshirt over my legs. Okay, it was actually Isa's shirt. Who would've thought I would ever be borrowing clothes from Isa?

"And then we hung up the paper plate award over our bunk door," I said. "Everyone said I should keep it since I was the choreographer, but I told Isa to bring it home since her soccer skills rocked the show."

Dr. Beth smiled. "From what you've told me before, she's going to be on a professional team one day."

I nodded. "For sure. Oh, and we had another running practice. Guess what? Turns out I'm not just freakishly fast when I'm thinking mad mom thoughts. I'm fast all the time!"

Of course Dr. Beth asked, "How does that make you feel?"

I need to find a sparkly mug that says *How does that make you feel?* for her collection. I'm totally gonna order one on Amazon for her when I get back to civilization. But unlike the school guidance counselor, Dr. Beth made me want to answer her questions.

"Like I'm not dragging my bunk down. Like we might actually have a chance at winning this thing. Like I might care about the Cup and these girls," I said.

"Including Bea?" she asked. She didn't swat away the gray kitten who was chewing on her braid.

I threaded yellow string on Poppy's bracelet. Hannah and I were determined to have the Sunflower bracelets ready for the tournament so I was working on them every spare minute. "It's easier to be friends with her here, away from home. At camp, it's as if nothing bad ever happened between us."

"You guys are in what's called the honeymoon stage." Dr. Beth scratched the orange and white cat on her belly till she purred. "Couples have an amazing time on their honeymoon because they're away from all the everyday stress like bills, jobs, family, friends. When they get home, they have to get used to life together in the real world."

I pulled green thread into the yellow to start building the Sunflower stalk. "I get it. It's easier for us to be friends here at camp, away from the Mapleton drama."

Figuring out how to get the M & Ms to accept Bea when we got back home was keeping me up at night—all right, not that late because all the crazy workouts really tired me out. But I did worry about it for the two minutes and thirty seconds after my head hit the pillow, before I fell asleep.

"One thing you can reflect on is how you can include Bea in your life back home," Dr. Beth said. "Think about how you can make her part of your life, like she did for you here at camp."

I swear sometimes it's like Dr. Beth is reading my mind.

"Think it through and we can talk more about it next session. There's something else we have to talk about today." Dr. Beth tossed me a Milky Way bar from her emergency chocolate stash. "Here, kid. You're gonna need this."

No matter how much time I spent hanging around my bunk-mates, I would never be that girl you can expect to catch things. "You're freaking me out," I said.

Dr. Beth grabbed the chocolate bar from the floor and handed it to me. "I know talking in circles makes you anxious, so I'm going to tell it to you straight. Your mom wants to make amends."

My heart started beating superfast and my hands were instantly sweaty. "Mom's here? At camp?"

"No, honey. She wants to have a phone conference," Dr. Beth said.

Sour heartburn collected at the back of my throat. "What if I don't want to talk to her?"

Dr. Beth stared at me the way she does when she thinks I can answer my own question.

I let out a big breath. "You think I should talk to her."

Dr. Beth scooted back on her floor pillow to make room for her latest stray, a calico cat with an attitude. "Talking to her on the phone, here with me, might make you less stressed about seeing your mom at the end of the summer."

"I bet she's only calling me because she has to. It's probably part of her program."

"What makes you say that?" Dr. Beth asked.

I rolled my eyes. "She only went to rehab because Dad made her. He threatened to divorce her if she didn't."

"Most addicts end up in rehab because someone made them or because they've gotten in trouble. But sometimes once they're in a program, and they have a chance to sober up, they want to get better," Dr. Beth said.

"Do you know how many times she told Dad she wanted to get better? He fell for it. Every. Single. Time."

Dr. Beth nodded. "It can be really hard to trust someone after they've lied to you."

"Then why should I give her another chance?" I asked.

Dr. Beth sighed. "Because camp is almost over, and so is your mom's treatment. I won't be with you when she comes home. But I'm here now. So let me help you get through this first step."

BEA

As usual, while the girls and I called home, Maisy spent the phone block meeting with Dr. Beth. When we got back to the cabin, Maisy sat in one of the rocking chairs, her normally tan face looking as pale as when she played the Camp Amelia ghost. Maisy's a dweller who lets all her worries and emotion well up until there's a big tornado inside her. And there was definitely a storm brewing inside her.

I sat down in the rocking chair next to her. "Mr. Pembrook's clearly in it for the long haul."

Maisy stared off into the trees across from our cabin. "Really?" she said, in a dull tone.

I kept talking to see if I could snap her out of it. "They're going to a Harry Potter convention in Hartford this weekend. In matching costumes. Mr. Pembrook is dressing up as Dumbledore and Mom is dressing up as Professor McGonagall."

"Don't tell anyone, but Dr. Beth lets me use her laptop when I see her. I'll go on your mom's Facebook next time I'm there and I'll report back to you," Maisy said. "Can't wait to see the pictures she posts."

"No wonder you go there all the time. Mom said I can get to know him better if they're still dating at the end of the summer."

Maisy turned to me and asked, "Why are you making your freaked-out face?"

"This is the first time she's talked about introducing me to a guy," I said. "She's never really gotten past a second date with anyone before."

Maisy twisted her face into a serious expression. "How do you feel about that?"

I laughed. "You've been hanging out with Dr. Beth too much."

Maisy smiled. "I know! It's contagious. But seriously, it's been just you and your mom for such a long time. Maybe that's why you're obsessing about who she's dating. You know, because it's going to be weird for you."

I looked up at the puffs of white clouds moving across the bright blue sky. "I think it will be good for us. I love being so close to Mom, but sometimes it's hard being just the two of us. All the pressure is on me to make my mom happy. It would be nice to have someone else around. Even if it's our old math teacher. I think I can even get past the bowties if he makes her happy."

Maisy nodded. "Your mom's cool. She deserves a good guy. She deserves to be happy."

That was the thing about breaking up after a long friendship. You have all these shared memories with each other's family. I'll never forget the time Dr. Winters helped me with my science fair project on DNA. He helped me make a double helix out of mini marshmallows and Twizzlers. Then there was the time he stitched up that five-inch gash on my leg when Mom was waiting for her new health insurance to kick in. He even gave me antibiotics that he said were free samples, but Mom suspected he paid for them out of his own pocket because they came in a prescription bottle with my name on it from CVS. I'll always remember those Cookie Monster cookies Mrs. Winters made whenever I slept over because she knew I liked them. She always undercooked them just a little bit so they would be soft in the middle just the way I liked them. One Halloween she made me a My Little Pony costume from scratch because Mom was in the middle of closing three big deals at once and Maisy and I wanted to be Pinkie Pie and Rainbow Dash. And

I know Maisy remembers how Mom taught her how to do her first french braid. No matter how many times Mom tried to teach me, I couldn't figure it out. But Maisy picked it up on her first try. Mom and Maisy spent hours watching YouTube hairstyling videos together and trying out the intricate styles on me. And then there were all those times Maisy was anxious about something on a sleepover and Mom would make her chamomile tea and sit with her till she felt better. Mom always had a way of talking Maisy out of her nervousness. I guess you could say Maisy and I have more good history than bad.

"I missed this," I said. "I missed us this year."

Maisy breathed in so deep, I could see her chest move. "I did, too."

"It felt like someone died," I said.

Maisy turned to me. "I really am sorry, Bea. I was just wrapped up in my own stuff."

"What stuff could you be dealing with? You're friends with the most popular girls in school. You're always surrounded by people. You never have to be alone," I said.

"Sometimes things aren't what they seem. Being a part of the M & Ms is a lot harder than it looks. I always have to worry about looking the right way and saying the right things. It's not like it was with us," she said.

"Then why did you leave me behind?" I asked.

The girls ran out on the porch with Isa in the lead, interrupting our moment. They were all wearing their best bikinis instead of the sporty one pieces we usually wore.

"Ainsley said we can jump off Whistler's Rock today!" Poppy said.

"That's the rock . . ." I started to explain to Maisy.

"On the website, in the picture where everyone's jumping off a cliff into the river below," finished Maisy. "I've had nightmares about jumping off that rock. You guys can go without me. Thank you very much."

"You might change your mind when we get there . . . Whistler's Rock connects the boys' and girls' camps," said Hannah.

Maisy shrugged. "Seeing cute guys isn't gonna get me to jump off that giant cliff."

We had spent the past five weeks doing all of the things that Maisy was terrified of, all the things she would've never done on her own. Since arriving at Camp Amelia, Maisy was forced out of her comfort zone on a daily basis. She had spent every day proving herself to the girls.

"I'll hang out with Maisy. You guys go ahead," I said.

"But you love Whistler's Rock!" said Poppy, with an incredulous look on her face. "You always say it's your favorite thing about camp."

Hannah wrinkled her nose. "You guys sure you don't want to come?"

I waved my hand at them. "Go ahead. We're fine."

We watched the girls run off into the woods in a haze of Bath & Body Works and bug spray. I grabbed Maisy's hand. "Follow me."

The old Maisy would've asked limitless questions. Where are we going? What should I wear? Will there be bugs? But this time, Maisy followed silently behind me as I ran on the overgrown path to the red cabin that was nestled under a weeping willow tree.

I pushed open the door and motioned for Maisy to follow me inside.

Maisy groaned. "Please tell me we're not doing more conditioning. I just can't. I need a . . ."

She spotted the acoustic guitar in the corner of the deserted music cabin. She ran over and sat on the dirty wooden floor next to it. Then she cradled the guitar in her arms as if it was a newborn baby.

"Can I play it?" she asked.

I smiled at her. "That's why we're here. Play that Taylor Swift song."

Maisy strummed and sang our old favorite song that she used to play every afternoon at her house before we started homework. She would insist to her mother that it was the best way to warm up her brain. My voice isn't good enough to sing in public, but since it was just the two of us in the cabin, I let loose and sang along like it was karaoke night at Pizza Amore.

When the song ended, Maisy switched to playing Johnny Cash's version of "Hurt" and her sadness filled the room. I didn't know what was going on with Maisy. I didn't know why her father forced her to go to camp for the first time at twelve years old, or what she had to forgive her mother for. I didn't know why she woke up one day and decided not to be my friend. But I suddenly and completely understood that Maisy was sad in a way that I had luckily never been. I sat there with her while she played, and I became a witness to her sorrow. I had the strong sense that's what she needed: someone to see that she was hurting, even if she didn't disclose the source of her pain. So I sat there while she played one depressing song after another. When my back got tired from sitting on the hardwood floor, I lay down next to her. I stayed with her, the way I wish she had stayed with me last year. Gradually, as she played, I felt that distance between us close, that space that had opened up like a chasm last summer.

She abruptly stopped playing in the middle of a Beatles song, and the cabin was suddenly quiet. She put the guitar back in the corner of the room and the twang of the strings hitting the wall echoed through the room. She turned back to me.

She breathed out and gave me a small smile. "Thank you, Bea. You're the only person I could do that with."

That's when I knew we were going to be okay, and at the end of the summer, we would still be friends, and I would be part of the

M & Ms with her. Maybe they would even come up with a cool new name for the group since I wasn't an *M*. Or they would give me a nickname that started with an *M*. I didn't really care. As long as I belonged. As long as I wasn't alone when we went back to school. As long as I didn't lose Maisy again.

CHAPTER SIXTEEN

MAISY

From: @madisonave
To: @maisywintersiscoming

Miss you too! Can't wait till you get home! Things have been a little better with the girls. ILY!

From: @maisywintersiscoming
To: @madisonave

Glad things are better. Can't wait till I get home too. ILY!!

From: @madisonave
To: @maisywintersiscoming

Good news!!! I found a twenty in the lint thingy in the dryer. So I paid Tim to tell Mia that girls in his grade were making fun of us for all having M names.

From: @maisywintersiscoming
To: @madisonave

OMG!!! Did she believe him?????

From: @madisonave
To: @maisywintersiscoming

YES!! She told us all as soon as Tim told her. Meghan is so dumb.
She started talking about changing our names. Then I said all we
had to do was add a new girl to change things up. They all thought it
was the best idea ever!! Now we have to figure out who the new girl
should be.

From: @maisywintersiscoming
To: @madisonave

Leave it to me. I will have our new girl by the time I get home from
camp.

Dr. Beth handed me a mug with a picture of a yoga lady, and
fancy cursive that said, *Smile, Breathe, Be Brave.* Then she curled up
on a floor pillow with Fozzy Bear, a chocolate-brown cat who had
gotten very fat since she found Dr. Beth.

I groaned and said, "As if I could just smile and then all of a
sudden I would be brave."

"Drink up," said Dr. Beth. "It's my homemade tea and herb
blend. It can stop a panic attack in its tracks, or in this case before
it even starts."

"Too late for that," I said.

My fingers were tingly, my mouth was dry, my hands were sweaty, and I was somehow freezing cold and burning hot at the exact same time. The tea smelled like skunk and garlic. But I was desperate to get my act together before the Mom call, so I tried it.

"It tastes much better than it smells," I said. "Kind of like licorice mixed with honey." I took another sip. "With a kick of cayenne pepper."

Dr. Beth laughed. "You've come a long way this summer. Not every camper I've handed that tea to has been brave enough to take a sip."

"When does this stuff kick in?" I asked. "My fingers are all tingly and my heart feels like it's beating out of my chest."

"The tea will help. But you also need to give in to the overwhelm. A panic attack is what happens when you resist whatever it is you're scared of. Just let yourself feel it," Dr. Beth said, while she rubbed Fozzy Bear's belly.

I put the mug on the table so I could pace across the cabin, because if I didn't move, I was going to lose my mind. "I don't want to feel these things. I'm not ready. I don't know if I'll ever be ready to talk to Mom," I said.

Dr. Beth jumped up from her floor pillow, and Fozzy Bear gave her the stink eye as she walked across the room to me. She grabbed both of my hands in hers. "Look at me," she said.

My hands were shaking so badly that Dr. Beth's thick silver rings kept knocking into each other while she held on to me. But I didn't want to look at her. I just wanted to be back in my cabin, making friendship bracelets in my new world that didn't have Mom in it.

"You have a choice, Maisy. If you don't want to talk to your mother today, you don't have to," Dr. Beth said.

"I can't do this!" I looked up at Dr. Beth. "I'm not ready to forgive her. I'm still too mad."

Dr. Beth kept her warm hands on mine and I hoped her calm energy was contagious. "This isn't some TV show where everything gets wrapped up in thirty minutes," she said. "Forgiveness isn't something that can be scheduled and it doesn't happen in one conversation. It happens on your own terms in your own time."

I dropped Dr. Beth's hands and asked, "Then why do I have to talk to her today? Why can't I wait till she gets home?"

Now Dr. Beth was the one taking a deep breath. "Because the longer you put off talking to your mom, the harder it will be. I'm here with you right now, so let me help you."

I collapsed onto a floor pillow and grabbed my tea. I was going to need it.

"We have a minute or so until that phone rings. Let's use it. What are you nervous about specifically?" asked Dr. Beth.

Dr. Beth's all about naming your fears to get power over them, but it was something that was still kind of hard for me.

"What if she's the same? What if she isn't any better?" I asked, then I took a long sip of tea.

"That's a valid concern. But my guess is that her therapist wouldn't have set up this phone call with you if she wasn't doing at least marginally better."

"You don't know Mom. She's a really good liar," I said.

"But you know her. If you think she's faking it, we can talk about it after you get off the phone."

"What should I say?" I asked.

Dr. Beth put her cell phone in between us and a gray kitten started pawing at it. "You could start with hi."

It felt good to laugh out the knot in my chest. "Then what?" I asked.

Dr. Beth reached out and smoothed down my hair. "Say whatever's in your heart. And when you don't have anything to say, just listen."

My hands got that tingly feeling again as soon as the phone rang.

"Are you ready?" asked Dr. Beth.

I nodded and she leaned over Fozzy Bear and put the call on speaker.

Dad's voice was rough and raspy like it always sounds when he hasn't gotten enough sleep. Usually, it's from doing a late surgery, but I can guess the same thing that kept me up all night kept him up, too. "How's camp, honey?" he asked.

I swallowed back the lump in my throat and the words came tumbling out because talking to Dad about camp was easier than talking to Mom. "My bunk just won the talent show for best choreography and I can get through the ropes course without having a panic attack. Thanks for the water shoes. I've been doing much better at my swim lessons now that I don't have to worry about touching the slimy seaweed on the bottom of the lake."

Dad cleared his throat, but his voice still sounded rumbly. "I am so proud of you, Maisy. I knew you would make it work."

I closed my eyes and held on to Dad's words. He never says things like that. At least not to me.

"You're not going to believe this, but I can kind of swim now."

Dad whistled through his teeth. "No way? You mean you actually get your hair wet and everything?"

"Yeah. But don't get too excited. I only passed the shallow water test," I said.

"That's amazing, Maisy. We need to go to the pool as soon as you get back so you can show me," Dad said.

"I've been getting really good at making friendship bracelets. I sent one to Addy and made a matching one for me," I said. "I sent her an actual letter with the bracelet."

"I bet that made her very happy," Dad said.

A man's voice cut in. I could tell right away that he's one of those people who talks differently to kids than he does to adults. "Hi, Maisy. I'm Dr. Robbins, your mother's therapist."

I took a deep breath and Dr. Beth gave me one of her super-sized encouraging smiles.

"Your mom is really looking forward to talking to you," Dr. Robbins said, in a sing-songy way, as if I was a kindergartner.

Even after all the tea I just drank, my mouth was suddenly so dry that my teeth were sticking to the inside of my mouth. I tried to talk, but nothing came out.

"Maisy?" Mom's voice filled the cabin and my whole body started shaking from head to toe.

Dr. Beth put her hand on her chest and inhaled in a deep and exaggerated way to remind me about my breathing. I tried to breathe in, but the air felt trapped in my chest.

Mom's voice sounded different, more awake than she had been in a long time. "I miss you, Addy, and Dad so much. But I'm working really hard to get healthy so I can come back home."

I looked at Dr. Beth in a panicky way, then I pressed the mute button. "I don't know what to say."

Dr. Beth looked at me with her therapist's game face on. "Speak your truth. This is your chance."

Mom kept talking. "Maisy, I'm different now. You'll see when we're all back home together."

"You spent *two years* lying every single day! You lied to me, Addy, Dad, your friends, our teachers, Addy's coaches. Why would I believe *anything* you say?" I cried.

Dr. Robbins cut in. "Maisy, let's hear your mother out. Let's try listening without judgment."

Dr. Beth jumped in. "I think it's important for us to hear Maisy out and validate her viewpoint as well."

"Everything is always about how Mom feels! Dr. Beth is the only one who cares how I feel," I cried.

Mom's voice was quiet, but firm. "I care, Maisy. I just need the chance to tell you how sorry I am for the things I did when I was sick."

"Sick? That's what we're calling it?" I shrieked.

Mom sighed. "I know it doesn't seem like I'm sick . . ."

I cut her off. "Kyle Madson's mom is sick. She has breast cancer and is going through chemo. She lost all her hair and has to wear a wig."

"I know this isn't the same thing, but . . ." started Mom.

I kept my voice steady and calm. "I get that you acted crazy when you were on the pills. I can even kind of understand that time you smacked me in the face for flushing your pills down the toilet."

Dr. Beth sucked in her breath. She scooted in closer to me and wrapped her arm around me in a side hug.

Dad's voice cut in. He sounded like he was begging. "Kristen, is that true? Please tell me that's not true."

I rolled my eyes. Why was Dad asking Mom if it was true? She's the one with the lying habit, not me.

Dr. Robbins interrupted again, this time using his voice meant for adults. "Eddy and Kristen, we can have our own breakout session after this call to dig in deeper to issues like this."

Mom made kind of a strangled crying sound, then said, "Oh, Maisy."

I broke away from Dr. Beth's grip and cut Mom off. "There were moments in the day when you were sober. Like when you woke up in the morning and the high from the night before had worn off. Or halfway through the day when your buzz was gone. You were sober in those moments when you chose to take the next round of pills. How could you do that to me and Addy? How could you do that to Dad? How could you do that to yourself?"

Mom's voice was high-pitched and desperate. "I wasn't ever truly sober then. Not like I am now. I've been clean the whole time I've been here, but back then . . ."

"You could've killed Addy and me. If we hadn't hit that barrier, we all would've landed in the river!" I shouted.

Mom whispered. "That was my rock bottom. That's what made me realize I needed help."

All of a sudden, I was brought back to that night, when I knew Mom was too out of it to pick Addy up from gymnastics. I couldn't stop her, and I was stupid enough to think that if I went for the ride

I could keep Addy safe.

"I can't do this," I whispered to Dr. Beth, and sprinted outside before she could stop me.

BEA

Nana Mary's famous chocolate chip oatmeal cookies had finally arrived. She only makes them once a summer, when she's able to talk the nursing home staff into letting her use the stove. Nana Mary studied baking at Le Cordon Bleu, so her gastronomical skills are unrivaled. Poppy has a strict "everyone must be in attendance to dive into the cookies" rule, ever since the time she busted Isa and Hannah gorging on them while we were stuck on laundry duty.

Poppy held up the accompanying note from Nana Mary. "OMG, I finally got through to her. She actually used Fair Trade chocolate this year."

"Maybe there's hope for getting her to go to the next women's march with you," said Hannah.

"Let's not get too crazy," said Poppy.

"You guys load up on milk from the dining cabin. I'll get Maisy," I said, as I hopped down the porch steps. I took off for the therapy cabin. I was certain Maisy would rather dine on Nana Mary's culinary masterpieces than talk about her fear of the ropes course for the hundredth time.

The quickest way to Dr. Beth's cabin is through the haunted woods, which didn't seem so haunted after our prank. But as I neared the site of our prank, I heard a rustling behind me that made me stop in my tracks. A cold shiver ran through me as I slowly turned around.

There was a girl swinging through the air, her brown hair flowing in the wind as she pumped her legs, taking herself high into the leaves. I jumped back and shrieked at the top of my lungs.

I almost fainted with relief when the girl turned to face me and I realized it was Maisy.

"You just scared the living daylights out of me!" I shouted. "What are you doing out here? Aren't you supposed to be with Dr. Beth?"

Maisy jumped off the swing and shouted, "Can't I ever be alone at this stupid camp without someone sneaking up on me? Are you spying on me?"

Maisy's nose was red and her cheeks were wet. As she walked toward me, she threw her hair up in a bun that didn't look intentionally messy. Her legs were spattered with mud and her arms had tiny scratches on them as if she had been running through the woods.

"Why would I spy on you?" I took a step closer to Maisy and asked, "Are you okay?"

"Why do you care?" asked Maisy. "It's not like we're really friends," she spit the words out, like razor blades shooting from her tongue.

I felt a sinking in my stomach as I asked, "Why would you say that? What's going on with you? You were fine thirty minutes ago."

Maisy crossed her arms. "Come on. No one's here. It's just us in the middle of the woods. You don't have to pretend to be my friend."

"What are you talking about? Where is this coming from? I thought we were . . . I mean, I thought . . ." I stuttered.

"I hate you and your stupid friends and this stupid camp!" Maisy yelled through the trees.

I shook my head back and forth. "You don't mean that."

"Don't pretend like this wasn't about the pact the whole time. I used you and you used me. But the secret all along was that I used you worse." Maisy lowered her voice, so it sounded even meaner. "Did you really think you would suddenly become popular when we got back to Mapleton?"

I could feel my face crumpling as I blinked back tears. "But you said . . ."

"I would have said *anything* to make it through this horrible camp. That doesn't mean the M & Ms would've accepted you when we got back. Because you are still Bea, the biggest loser at our school."

Before I could answer, Maisy took off running through the woods and I was all alone, in the one place where I had never felt alone before.

I was used to spending days by myself at school, feeling like I had no footing in the world. Now that feeling had followed me to camp.

I always thought my place in my school world was connected to Maisy, that our symbiotic relationship was the key to shedding my invisibility cloak. She was the one who made me invisible and she would be the one who would make me seen again. But Maisy was right. I was still the same old Bea. That wasn't going to change even if Maisy pretended to be my friend.

When I got back to the bunk, sweaty and short of breath, Isa, Hannah, and Poppy were sitting on the floor with a plate of Nana Mary's cookies and little cartons of milk spread out on Hannah's favorite throw blanket. The cabin smelled like warm cookies and everyone looked content, like things were before Maisy came to camp and messed everything up.

"Where's Maisy?" Hannah asked.

I scarfed down a cookie like a rabid dog. "Which version of her?" I said, and little cookie crumbs flew from my mouth.

"What?" Poppy asked. "I don't get it."

Hannah put her milk carton back down on the floor mid-chug and wiped the back of her mouth with her sleeve. "Are you okay?"

Isa motioned for me to sit, but I shook my head. I felt like my homemade volcano after I added the vinegar to the baking soda and it started bubbling over. I couldn't get too close to the other girls or I might explode all over them.

The words tasted bitter as they came out of my mouth. "She was never going to go through with it. She played me all summer."

Isa jumped to her feet. "Maisy's dropping out of the competition?"

"Oh no!" I put both hands on top of my head. "I didn't even think about that."

Hannah waved her hands in the air. "I'm totally confused. If you're not talking about the competition, what *are* you talking about?"

"Yeah," said Poppy. "What're you talking about?"

Cookie bits flew out of my mouth as the words tumbled out. "Maisy and I were never really friends. I thought we were, maybe not at first, but, at some point, I thought we were friends again, real friends, like I am with you guys. She even apologized for what she did to me last year. But it was all about the pact this whole time."

Isa put her hands on my shoulders and gently pushed me toward the floor till I sat down. "It's hard to figure out what you're talking about when you walk back and forth like that."

"Yeah, it's really distracting," said Hannah. "And I'm already lost in this conversation."

I took a deep breath and covered my face with my hands. This was going to be mortifying enough without seeing the looks on the girls' faces. "Um. Maisy and I. Um. We uh. We made a popularity pact."

Hannah scrunched up her face. "A what?"

I peeked out from between my fingers and mumbled, "She promised to make me popular at school if I made her popular at camp."

Poppy blinked her wide eyes at me. "What?"

"Why?" asked Isa. "I mean, I get what's in it for you, but what was in it for her?"

I kept my face covered. "She couldn't stand having everyone in her bunk hate her."

Poppy breathed out hard. "And you didn't tell us?"

I uncovered my face but kept my eyes on the floor. "You don't know how many times I wanted to tell you but couldn't. It was part of the pact. Maisy said she would only hold up her end of the bargain if I didn't tell anyone."

Isa scrunched up her forehead until a deep crease appeared between her eyes. "You tricked us into being friends with Maisy?"

Poppy's voice was quiet. "How could you lie to us? We tell each other everything." She took a deep breath. "Even the things that make us look bad."

"I hung out with her all summer!" said Hannah. "I thought we were friends. I even told her all about how Carter and I went out for two days before he dumped me for Ashley Brewer."

"I hated lying to all of you," I started. "But I had no choice. Not if I wanted the pact to work."

"We had the chance to get her out of our bunk. You were the one who convinced us to keep her!" yelled Isa.

"Was that all about the pact?" Hannah stretched out the words as if she couldn't bear to think them, let alone say them out loud.

"Did you convince us to keep her, just so you could be popular back at school?"

Shame burned the tips of my ears. I croaked out one word: "Yes."

"We're stuck with her now! We're gonna lose the Cup and it's all because of your stupid pact," Isa yelled.

"Four years of winning the tournament down the drain," said Hannah.

Poppy stood up and held up her hands. "We've also had all of these years being friends with Bea, so let's hear her out."

I flashed Poppy a grateful smile. "At first, I thought it was fake, that Maisy and I were just playing our parts. I was helping her out, and she was going to help me when we got back home. But then, along the way, it seemed like Maisy became my friend again. I thought she was genuinely friends with all of us. When I told you guys to keep her because of the pact, a small part of me thought she was really going to try for us."

"Maybe she really was our friend," said Hannah. "She wouldn't have made the pact with you if she didn't want to be friends with all of us in the first place."

"She didn't care about being friends. People like Maisy need a group. They don't know how to survive on their own," said Isa. "Just like baby animals."

I grabbed another cookie, but my mouth was too dry to taste it. "I can't believe I fell for it."

"Why would you make a pact with the one person who showed you that you shouldn't trust her?" asked Hannah.

"Make us understand," said Poppy.

All the tears that had been buried inside of me came out in one big blubbering, snotty mess. "I was desperate! I can't take another school year being alone all the time. You don't know what it's like to be invisible! I could go a whole school day without one single person talking to me, except, of course, Mrs. Shingles, the librarian, and Mr. Cadence, my homeroom teacher. I sometimes wonder if they're just nice to me because they feel bad for me. I just can't do it anymore!"

I covered my face with my hands again and let it all out. All the tears that had been stuck inside of me for the past year.

Then I felt a hand on my back.

"Oh, Bea. I wish we all went to school together," said Poppy.

"But we don't," I cried. "All I want at school is what we have here. I just want to find my people back home."

Poppy turned to the others and asked. "We can understand that. Can't we?"

Isa sighed. "Why do you girls always have to make it so hard to stay mad?"

>>··CHAPTER SEVENTEEN··>>
MAISY

I RAN SO FAST THROUGH THE WOODS MY LUNGS WERE ON FIRE.
Of course Mom had her doctors fooled. She had Dad fooled all
along. Dad works all the time, so he had no clue how bad things got.
Or maybe he really didn't want to know. Even when we bumped
into Zoe's mom in the frozen food aisle of the supermarket and
she slipped up and mentioned about not carpooling anymore
and then got really uncomfortable when she realized Dad had
no idea.

Zoe's mom sucks, too, because as soon as she realized Mom
was out of it on one of her drop-offs, she told all the other carpool
moms and even the gym moms who didn't carpool with Addy. But
the one person she didn't tell was Dad. So Addy got stuck in the
car with Mom six days a week driving to and from the gym in rush

hour traffic. I would get so worried about them, I would track Addy's iPhone to make sure they got to the gym all right.

I thought I hated Dad for sending me here, but I'm starting to realize that none of this is his fault. I had done a really good job covering for Mom. Too good of a job.

I didn't stop running until I found myself back at Dr. Beth's cabin. I wasn't planning on going there. It's just where my legs took me.

Dr. Beth was sitting on the porch with a bowl of chocolate bars in her lap and four cats, including Fozzy Bear, stretched out around her soaking up the sun. In the sunlight, you could see that her red Camp Amelia T-shirt was covered in cat hair. She tossed me a Snickers. "I knew you'd be back."

The Snickers bar landed at my feet. I grabbed it and sat down on the porch in the only spot that didn't have a cat. I peeled back the wrapper and took a big bite of chocolate. "Mom wasn't always like this. She did homework with Addy and me every day after school. She was my Daisy troop leader, Addy's team mom, and the head drama mama for all my plays. She made dinner for us every night and always had clean laundry folded on our beds when we got home from school. She even sorted it into little piles so all we had to do was put everything in the right drawers. She waited up for Dad to get home from work every night, still in her nice clothes and makeup from the day, no matter what time it was. She was the perfect mom. Everyone said so."

"Must've been a lot of work being that perfect," said Dr. Beth.

"She made it look easy," I said.

"A lot of addicts are good at making things look better than they really are," said Dr. Beth. "It's part of how they keep their secret."

I took another bite of my chocolate bar. "What if I don't forgive her? What if I'm never ready?" I asked.

Dr. Beth smiled at me. "You'll be ready when you're ready. Something tells me the forgiveness will only start to come when your mom proves to you that she is in active recovery, when she can truly show you how much regret she has. Until then, everyone else in your family needs to accept you where you are."

All I wanted was for things to go back to normal. When I wasn't worried about bringing friends home from school. When I didn't have to run around the house cooking and cleaning and doing laundry so Dad wouldn't suspect. I even learned how to order groceries online so we wouldn't run out of food. I just wanted things to be like they used to, when I only had to worry about kid stuff.

"It's not like she went to rehab because she really wanted to. After the accident, Dad said he would leave her and take full custody if she didn't go into treatment," I said. "How is she going to get better when she was forced to get help?"

"That tells me that underneath it all she wasn't totally lost because she still held on to her love for you guys. Maybe that's what is pushing her to get better," Dr. Beth said.

"What if she's not . . . better when she comes home?" I asked. "Mom probably has those rehab people fooled."

"If you see any signs, even little ones, let your father know right away," Dr. Beth said.

One thing I was learning to do was ask for help. "Can I call you if that happens? Will you help me tell him?" I asked.

Dr. Beth wrapped my hand in hers. "Of course. You have a support system now. You have me. And maybe you can open up to Bea. Wouldn't it be nice to have a friend back home who knows what's going on?"

I groaned. "I'm such a jerk. I was so mean to Bea. I said some horrible things to her."

Dr. Beth smiled at me. "You should've heard the mean things I said to Jerry when he found Burger King wrappers in my car and accused me of being a cow murderer. I really let him have it. But I was just lashing out because he had me cornered. He eventually forgave me for saying such awful things to him. He's still mad about the Whopper though."

I thought about how Bea's face was all pale and tear-streaked underneath her wild hair. "I was pretty awful to her. I said some unforgiveable stuff."

"Seems like the honeymoon period is over, kid. This is when things get real," Dr. Beth said.

"Talk about stating the obvious," I said. "How do I fix this?"

"An authentic apology is a good place to start," said Dr. Beth.

"What if that's not enough?" I asked.

Dr. Beth shrugged. "Honestly, it might not be. It all depends on what you said to her."

I let out a deep breath. "I was about as mean as humanly possible."

Dr. Beth wrinkled her nose. "An apology probably won't cut it. This might be a situation where words aren't enough. You're going to have to lay the foundation with the right words, then you're going to have to prove to her with your actions that you are truly sorry."

I grabbed a Milky Way for the road and hopped down the steps. "I have to go fix things with Bea."

I had enough with running. I walked back to the cabin while I figured out how to make Bea understand that we really were friends and were going to stay friends when we went back to Mapleton . . . no matter what.

I took my time, trying to find the right words. As soon as I saw the rocking chairs on our cabin porch, I felt like I was in my safe place. A feeling I never thought I would get at camp. I couldn't wait to say sorry to Bea. I couldn't wait for things to get back to normal.

When I opened the door, I was relieved when I saw Bea in there alone.

"Bea, thank God you're here. We need to talk," I said.

Bea shot daggers out of her eyes like it was her super power, and shouted, "Get out!"

"Please, Bea, give me a chance to explain," I begged.

"I let you talk me into your stupid plan and you almost ruined my life!" she shouted.

"I'm going to keep up my end of the pact. I'm going to fix everything when we get back to school. You're gonna be part of the M & Ms and you won't be invisible ever again," I said.

Bea's cheeks were as red as her T-shirt and the little hairs around her hairline sprang up into tiny angry curls. "Not everything's about Mapleton. You almost obliterated things with my *real* friends, my only friends. They know about the pact and I'm incredibly lucky they don't hate me! I never should've let you talk me into it."

"Bea, we can fix this," I said. "Just give me a minute to come up with a good plan."

Bea looked at me like I was a monster. "How could I have thought you changed?" she moaned.

"I have changed, I . . ." I started.

"You're the same selfish person you've been for the past year!" Bea shouted.

"I didn't mean what I said. I was just really upset about something else and I took it out on you," I said. "We are friends. Real ones."

"We are most definitely *not* friends," said Bea. "You never intended to be seen with me back in Mapleton. You are still the same weak person you've always been."

"That's not true," I said.

"Oh, really? Then what was your plan when we got back to Mapleton? Huh? How exactly were you going to make me a part of the M & Ms?" Bea challenged me with her eyes.

"I haven't figured out all the details yet. But things are in motion for when we get back home," I said. "I swear, I'm going to make it work."

Bea crossed her arms. "Just like you made everything work out here, right?"

"If you would just stop yelling for a second, you would realize things did work out this summer. We became friends again," I said.

Bea smirked at me. "You said it yourself. We're not friends. We were just using each other."

"Bea, don't say that. I didn't mean it. I was just stressed out because . . ."

"You are the most self-absorbed person I have ever met. *Every-thing* is always about you!" Bea practically spit out the words.

"I know that's how I was at the beginning of the summer, but . . ." I started.

"You know why your parents sent you here?" Bea cut in. "It wasn't because they wanted to empower you, or because they were hoping you would learn how to swim, or even because they were hoping we would become friends again. They just couldn't bear dealing with you for another day. They would've sent you *anywhere* just to get a break from you and your anxiety!"

I tried to keep my voice calm. "Things have been really bad at home. Give me a chance to explain."

"You had a chance to tell me what's going on. You had *all* summer to open up to me. You don't get to use whatever's going on at home as an excuse for your horrible behavior."

"You wouldn't be saying that if you knew . . ."

"I thought I had it hard when I was invisible, but at least I had a break from dealing with you and your nonstop drama. Just leave me alone!" Bea yelled. Then she tore out of the cabin like it was on fire.

BEA

A bit of breeze in the air tempered the hot sun blazing down on us while Hannah, Poppy, Isa, and I hung out in our kayaks. We were supposed to be doing drills around the buoys for our last practice before the tournament, but with Maisy going rogue, we finally accepted the fact that we had no shot at the Amelia Cup. I had also accepted my friendless fate that would be waiting for me back home.

"Maybe you could go to private school?" suggested Poppy.

"My mom can't afford private school. She's already stressed about paying for college," I said.

"What about a scholarship?" asked Hannah. "You are the smartest person I know."

I sighed. "I already tried applying to the private schools near me. They all gave me academic scholarships, but the tuition is so high, the aid they gave me barely made a dent. My mom said the only way to make it work was to get Dad to pitch in. He sounded like he was actually considering it, until, of course, he talked to Monica about it. The only reason he pays for camp is probably to get rid of me for the summer so he can have his perfect new family all to himself."

"Maybe you could homeschool?" suggested Poppy.

"Homeschooling won't give me a shot at the Ivy Leagues one day," I said.

I broke away from the girls and started paddling to shore. I could hear the oars breaking into the water's skim as the girls paddled behind me. I had never felt so hopeless before in my life.

Ainsley was waiting for us back at the dock. She started yelling as soon as we got close enough to hitch our boats to the dock.

"What is wrong with you guys?"

No one answered as we climbed out of our boats.

Ainsley was wearing cut-off jean shorts, a blue string bikini, and a scowl on her face. "The tournament's tomorrow and *this* is how you get ready? This was your last chance to practice the course and you spend your time floating around?"

I never know how to answer a rhetorical question, so I kept my mouth shut, and the other girls followed my lead.

"Seriously." Ainsley sounded full-on Brit as she yelled. "You guys have been checked out for days. What's going on with you?"

"We have no shot at the Cup, so why bother trying anymore?" I said.

"I thought Maisy was the dramatic one in our bunk." Ainsley rolled her eyes. "You guys have been doing great with your training all summer. Now you suddenly get cold feet?"

"Maisy doesn't care about us or the Cup. She's just counting down the days 'til she gets back to her real friends back home," I said. "There's no way she's crossing that ropes course tomorrow."

Ainsley crossed her arms over her chest. "If that's true, why has she been spending every spare second working on the ropes course with me? Why did she just practice with me for an hour this morning while you guys were all at breakfast? Why did she spend yesterday's phone block running the course with me?"

I shook my head. "That doesn't make any sense. Why would she do that?"

Ainsley looked at me as if I was the stupidest person on the planet. "Because she doesn't want to be the reason you don't win the Cup." She shook her head. "Obviously."

"But I thought . . ." I started.

Ainsley rolled her eyes. "Clearly, you were wrong about Maisy. Even smart people get it wrong sometimes."

⊱⋆ CHAPTER EIGHTEEN ⋆⊰
MAISY

THE MORNING OF THE TOURNAMENT, I SNEAKED OUT OF THE BUNK before the other girls woke up. It's not like they were talking to me anyway. After five days of the silent treatment, I was back to being invisible again at camp. I couldn't believe Bea went through that every single school day for the past year. I thought it was bad when the girls hated me the first day of camp, but it burned so much worse when they hated me after hanging out with me all summer. So it really made me think about how bad Bea must've felt when I ghosted her. Like Dr. Beth said, I was going to have to prove myself to her, and the tournament was the best way to do that.

It felt good to walk to Dr. Beth's cabin, to be headed toward someone who wanted to talk to me. Dr. Beth was waiting with a bottle of water, a banana, and some whole wheat toast. "Today's the big day! No junk food for you. We need to fuel you like an athlete for your big run."

"Thanks," I said. I started peeling the banana. "But did you really have to get yourself an Egg McMuffin? And is that a hash brown, too? You're killing me."

Dr. Beth laughed. "I'm not the one running today, so I can eat all the crap food I want."

I made a funny face at her McDonald's bag and said, "You must eat an awful lot of kale and veggie burgers at home to make up for all the garbage you eat at camp."

Dr. Beth laughed so hard that two of the rescue cats got scared and ran to the other side of the room. She told me about her latest rescue cat named Gunther, who was hiding under her porch, while I finished my banana and toast and she scarfed down an Egg McMuffin, two hash browns, and a large Diet Coke. I wasn't there to talk about cats, but Dr. Beth knows I don't like to talk about dramatic stuff while I eat. She waited until I finished before asking, "Are you sure you want to do this right before the tournament?"

I nodded. "I need to have a clear head if I have any hope of climbing to the top of that spider web."

I took a really deep breath in for three counts, then let it out for another six counts. I closed my eyes and focused on getting my heart to stop beating out of my chest. When I felt almost normal, I pulled the letter from my drawstring bag.

"We can burn it. We can rip it up. We can throw it in the lake." Dr. Beth took a long sip of herbal tea. "Or . . . we can read it."

"I already burned her other letters at the bonfire. I need to read this last one."

"I am so proud of you for taking this big step," Dr. Beth said. "It's the best way to hear your mom out with less pressure because there's no one waiting for your reaction. You can just read what she has to say and take it in at your own pace."

I picked up the envelope. It felt lighter than I expected. For some reason, I thought a letter holding so many feelings would be heavier in my hands. My heart felt like it was beating out of my chest while I ripped the envelope open and pulled the letter out. It was written on a thick piece of plain white stationary in Mom's perfect penmanship that she had learned in Catholic school.

Dear Mini,

By the time you get this letter, you will be packing up and getting ready to come home. Which means you made it a whole six weeks at adventure camp!

I am so incredibly proud of you for putting yourself out there and trying so many new things. Dad told me you've been taking swim lessons. That's amazing! Learning how to swim is a HUGE accomplishment. It means you're learning how to take control over things that scare you. That is something to be really proud of.

I heard you are the fastest runner at camp! How wonderful that you discovered you're a talented runner! Just think about all the new things you're going to learn about yourself over the next few years. I'm looking forward to being sober and present for you when that happens.

I've apologized in all the other letters about every single thing I can remember doing to hurt you. Please know I'm sorry for everything. At first, I was most sorry for the car accident, but then I realized living with me every day and keeping my secret must have been awful and overwhelming for you. I can't take back all of the terrible things I did or said, or what I put you through, but I will try my best to show you I am a different person now.

I know you have no reason to believe anything I say. But I will work really hard to earn your trust back and prove myself to you, Addy, and your father every day. I will become a mother you can be proud of.

When I checked in, it was for an eight-week stay, which meant I would've been home waiting for you when you got home from camp. I want to do that more than anything in the world. But after talking to my therapist, I decided to stay longer. I want to be the best mom possible. Which means not leaving treatment until I am as healthy as I can be. So when I do come home at some point in the near future, I will be responsible and you can go back to being a kid again. And I can go back to being your mom.

I love you more than anything,
Mom

I put the letter back in my lap and breathed out long and hard. "I still have time."

"For what?" asked Dr. Beth in her kind voice.

"To forgive her. She's staying at rehab longer," I said.

Dr. Beth reached out for my hand. "Honey, your emotional journey doesn't have any deadlines. Your mom is taking her time, getting herself healthy. You aren't bound to her timeline. You need to take your own time processing everything."

I looked up at Dr. Beth. "For now, I'm ready to go kick some Dandelion butt."

BEA

Dear Bea,

Monica and I have wonderful news that just can't wait for you to get home from camp . . . we are engaged!! Peyton and Vivi helped me propose. Monica posted the video on Instagram. You can see it as soon as you're back in the world of technology.

Monica wants all you girls to be her junior bridesmaids. The girls already picked the color of the dresses, which are going to be hot pink. You can join in on the wedding planning when you're back home.

Love,
Dad

Dear Bea,

Project Gilmore Girls marathon is under way. I have all of the supplies for our Gilmore Girls feast, burgers, fries, pizza, Mallomars, Pop Tarts, and Red Vines. I already laid out our pants with stretchy waistbands. I even bought Mr. Pebbles his favorite organic cat food for the occasion.

Get ready for our other annual end-of-summer tradition—back-to-school shopping. Can you just hurry home already???

So Gavin and I are still dating. He said he's looking forward to getting to know you outside of school. He is also more than happy to help with your math homework if you need it—which is great considering how awful I am at math.

Miss you like crazy and can't wait to see you!!! Love you so much!

Love,
Mom

Of course my own dad left me out of his engagement. Why would he include me? I am such a loser that my lifelong best friend had broken my heart not once, but twice. I'm the person who always gets left behind, for someone better, prettier, cooler. Now that Dad has two new perfect daughters to take my place, why should he worry about including me in his new life?

I didn't know which atrocity to be more worked up about. Mr. Pembrook helping me with my math homework, or the hot pink bridesmaid dress. Doesn't Mom get that the last person a kid wants to hang out with outside of school is a teacher? And hasn't anyone told Monica that just because her blonde daughters look good in any color doesn't mean that color works on everyone? How could she not know that hot pink is the enemy of redheads? In fact, she couldn't have picked a worse color to go with my curly orange hair. I really hoped Ainsley was right about Maisy pulling through for the tournament, because I needed one good thing to happen to me before I headed back to the drama waiting for me at home. But Maisy's track record didn't make me confident that she would show up for anyone other than herself.

Isa snapped a hairband at me, pulling me from my self-pity. "Think you stretched that leg enough?"

I scanned the wooded area by our cabin. "Has anyone seen Maisy this morning?"

"I don't know why we're wasting time stretching. Maisy's not showing up," Hannah said.

Isa was sitting on the ground with her legs straddled in a wide V. She leaned forward until her face reached the grass. "She has to show. We can't go down like this."

I stretched my arm across my chest and tried to sound more confident than I felt. "You heard what Ainsley said. Maisy may be a fake friend, but I don't think she's going to let us down today, if only because she wouldn't be able to bear the bus ride home with us."

Poppy bounced up and down on her toes. "If we don't line up at the start soon, we'll be DQed."

I pulled my sneaker laces extra tight and double-knotted them. "She'll be here."

I swallowed hard, hoping I wasn't wrong about Maisy once again.

As if this moment wasn't tense enough, the Dandelion Bunk girls showed up. They were all wearing bright purple shorts, tank tops, and bandanas in their hair, with matching purple Nike Flyknits. As much as I hated them, I had to give them credit for solid team spirit.

"Ready to get your butts kicked?" asked the A twins at the same exact time.

"Actually, we're ready to kick your butts like we do every summer," shot back Isa.

Tinka tapped her watch and said, "Start time's in three minutes and I don't see Ghost Girl."

"Looks like a DQ for the Sunflower Bunk," said Kaya.

Just then, Maisy broke through the birch trees. I never thought I would be so happy to see someone.

"I brought our team bracelets." Maisy opened up her hand to reveal bracelets with perfect sunflowers knotted in the middle of each one. "I spent the past few days finishing them."

My bunkmates looked to me to see how to react. I reached for a bracelet and put it on my wrist. Hannah, Isa, and Poppy all followed suit.

Isa nudged Maisy in the arm. "Way to make us sweat it out, Maisy."

Kaya pursed her puffy lips into a smirk. "Those bracelets will look good when we're running past you."

Hannah took a step forward. "None of you will get past Maisy."

"We all heard about how the least athletic girl at camp is a freakishly fast runner," said one of the A twins.

"That's so cute," sneered the other A twin.

"It'll be really cute when I pass you all at the finish line," said Maisy.

"I was medaling at the AAU Junior Olympics this spring while you were sitting home painting your nails," Tinka said. "Good luck passing me."

Maisy's tan turned the slightest shade paler, but she stood tall and puffed her chest out. "Can't wait to brag about kicking the butt of a Junior Olympics champion."

"Good luck with that," said one of the A twins. "It's not like you'll make it through the ropes course anyway."

"See you losers at the finish line!" yelled Isa over her shoulder as she took off toward the race start, with us following close behind.

All the other bunks were already lined up on the bright red line spray-painted across the field. We squeezed through the teams until we found an opening on the starting line.

Isa turned to Maisy. "Be aggressive at the start. Push your way to the front of the pack with me so we're first at the path entrance. It's a lot harder to pass girls in the woods than it is to take the lead in the open field."

Maisy nodded. "Be aggressive. Push to front. Got it."

Hannah leaned into Maisy. "Be careful in the woods. That's where everyone starts pushing and shoving."

Maisy smiled at us. "I plan to be so far ahead, no one can push me around."

I felt that excited butterfly feeling in the pit of my stomach I get when I'm about to ace a big test. We were in this together and had a chance at the Cup.

⮞·· CHAPTER NINETEEN ··⮜

MAISY

I KNOW THIS WON'T COME AS A SHOCK, BUT THE TOURNAMENT IS PRETTY much the first time I've competed in anything athletic. Seriously, the only thing that keeps me from getting picked last in PE is that I'm part of the M & Ms, and the M& Ms don't get picked last for anything. The only time I get competitive is when I'm auditioning for a show. But to prove to the girls that we were really friends, I needed to help them win the Amelia Cup. More importantly, to prove to Bea that everything about this summer was real, I needed to do this for her.

It was just my luck to be competing against a Junior Olympian in the one thing I'm actually good at. I thought about what Dr. Beth said about words not always being enough. So I took a deep breath in for three counts, then out for six. I did it one more time for extra luck. Then I put my game face on.

"How come no one warned me about Tinka being in the kiddie Olympics?" I asked.

Isa bit her bottom lip. "Because we didn't know."

Poppy put one hand on Isa's arm and one on mine. "Don't let their mind games intimidate you. She only won the Junior Olympics meet because she competed in it. Maybe you would've been the champion if you had been there."

"Poppy's right," Bea said. "If they were so convinced Tinka was going to bring them the win, they wouldn't have dropped that news on your lap right before the race."

"Exactly," Hannah cut in. "They wouldn't try to psych you out if the win was a guarantee for Tinka."

"We got this," said Isa. "Now let's get to the starting line before we get DQed."

There were thirty-some-odd girls lined up across the painted red line in the grass. Of course, the only spot we could elbow our way into was right next to the Dandelion girls. The A twins were on both sides of Tinka like two bodyguards. I had no shot of getting close to outrunning Tinka with them muscling me out of the way.

Bea looked at me, and she was cleary just as worried about the twins taking me out. "Since Poppy's sitting this event out, Hannah and I will stick close to Isa and Maisy as we cut across the field. We can't keep up with them in the woods, but we need to be their defense on the way in, so no one cuts them off at the pass," she hissed.

Hannah whispered without moving her lips. "Good plan. I'll take their left, Bea, you take the right, and we'll box out the twins."

It hit me right there on the crowded start line: we were running as a real pack. I had never felt totally part of the M & Ms. I never felt like they had my back. I couldn't think of one situation where they would look out for me like this.

"On your marks!" called Bailey.

My hands were shaking as I lined up at the starting line. I ran through a checklist in my mind—laces were tied, shorts drawstring double-knotted, hair pulled back out of my face. Everything was in the right order, now I just needed to run my heart out, and I needed to make sure Tinka didn't get ahead of me.

"Get set!" yelled Bailey.

My heart felt like it was beating out of my chest. A loud whistle sounded, and I felt the rush of the girls around me as we all pushed forward in one big clump.

I could hear Bea breathing in my ear as she made a barrier between me and the A twin who was trying to knock into me. I never realized running could be a contact sport.

"You got this," huffed Bea in my ear.

I felt claustrophobic with the bodies pushing on all sides of me, so I ran faster to get away from them. The faster I ran, the faster my bunkmates ran, even though Hannah and Bea sounded like they were hyperventilating.

I kept my eye on the opening to the woods and cut across the grass as fast as I could on a diagonal, just like Ainsley taught me. Isa was right at my heels yelling at me to not let Tinka get ahead of me in the woods.

I could see Tinka getting closer to the woods, so I ran faster, but I couldn't get around the A twins who were like a big wall between me and my competition. Meanwhile, Kaya ran in a zig-zag line in front of me so every time I got close to the A twins she would almost trip me. I watched as Tinka got into the woods on the tiny, narrow dirt trail first, with Kaya and the twins right behind her.

I pushed past all the other runners and got right behind the A twins, who had started to slow down. I couldn't see past them, but I knew Tinka was getting farther and farther ahead.

Isa was at my heels, but Bea and Hannah had dropped way behind.

This was the first time in my life when being smaller than everyone else helped, because as soon as I saw a tiny gap between a tree and the path, I squeezed past the twins.

I had to move faster if I wanted to close the gap between Tinka and me. I kept my eyes on her bright purple sneakers and pushed myself to go as fast as I could. But the faster I went, the faster she went. Her legs were so much longer than mine, that it felt like I had to take two steps for every one she took.

As the trail narrowed, I knew there was no way I could get around her until the path opened back up to the field leading to the finish line.

Tinka broke through the woods first and made her way toward the red tape.

Ainsley screamed, "You got this, Maisy!"

Bailey yelled, "She's coming up behind you, Tinka! Don't let her pass you in the chute."

I could tell Tinka was running as fast as she could because she didn't even pick up her pace when Bailey yelled. I kicked into high gear and moved within inches of her. With a final rush of adrenaline, I finally overtook her and sprinted as fast as I could toward the finish line, with Tinka now at my heels.

Ainsley jumped up and down and cheered for me at the top of her lungs.

"Go, Maisy! Go!" she yelled.

I threw myself into the plastic tape, but as usual I was too small for normal things like a dramatic finish, and my whole body bounced back. Ainsley laughed and ripped it for me so I could run through it.

Then she held up her stopwatch. "A new camp record! Maisy Winters finishes the two-mile course in 11:08!"

I jumped in the air with both my fists up to the sky.

Ainsley picked me up and swung me around. "I knew you could do it!"

She was just putting me back down on the ground when Tinka huffed and puffed into second place before doubling over like she was going to throw up.

"And Tinka takes second!" Bailey yelled.

"Isa takes third!" Ainsley shouted, seconds later.

Isa ran over and hugged me. It felt amazing. I had earned that hug.

Now it was just down to Bea and Hannah against the A twins. If Bea and Hannah caught up to them, we would be all set. We heard a rustling from the woods and we could see the brush shaking. Then Bea and Hannah shot out from the trees with dirt on their faces and bloody streaks on their knees and elbows. They shot across the field with the equally banged-up A twins at their heels.

Bea ran over to me as soon as she crossed the finish line. Her face was bright red and her sweaty curls were sticking out all over the place. "Did you do it, Maisy? Did you get first place?"

This moment was even better than crossing the finish line. "Yes!" I shouted.

"I knew you could," Bea said.

Ainsley pulled us all in a huddle. "Great job, girls! As long as Bea and Poppy come through in the swim and Isa and Hannah power through with the kayaks, we have a shot."

Ainsley put her hand in the middle of the circle. Hannah put hers on top, then came Isa's hand, then Poppy's. Bea put her hand on top of Poppy's and nodded at me. I put my hand on top of Bea's. Then we all shouted, "Sunflower Bunk!" as we threw our arms up in the air.

BEA

"You girls killed it on the swim and the kayak!" yelled Ainsley. "We're ahead of the Dandelion girls by a slim margin. Isa, this is the event that you sit out. Hannah and Poppy, you guys need to move through the ropes as fast as you can. Bea, your only job is to get Maisy through the course."

The ropes course start is staggered, so each bunk gets through it on their own and gets timed by their bunk counselor. Hannah and Poppy took Ainsley's words to heart and flew up the tree and navigated the course in record time. Which meant we had a shot at winning, as long as Maisy didn't get overcome with anxiety on the course.

As Maisy and I stood at the bottom of the tree, I said, "I've got your back."

I had never seen Maisy look so serious before. She took a deep breath and said, "Don't worry, Bea. I've got this."

Ainsley yelled, "On the count of three! Then I'm starting the stopwatch."

Maisy tugged on her helmet and double-checked that the strap was secure under her chin.

"One!" yelled Ainsley.

Maisy pulled at her harness to ensure that it was tight enough. All of her neurotic safety checks were doing nothing to assure me that she had this.

"Two!" yelled Ainsley.

Maisy rubbed her hands back and forth vigorously and took a deep breath. Then she mumbled something under her breath that sounded suspiciously like the Hail Mary. At this rate, I was going to be the one who ended up having a panic attack.

"Three!" yelled Ainsley.

Maisy stood frozen at the base of the tree. I balled my hands into tight fists and held my breath. But then Maisy put her foot in the first rung and I realized we had a shot.

Maisy had gotten much stronger after a summer of conditioning sessions and tournament practices with a bunk full of type A athletes. She climbed the tree rather quickly and I stayed right at her heels until we reached the top. I expected her to hesitate like she usually did at the precipice of the platform, but she climbed right up without pause.

As soon as I secured my place next to Maisy on the platform, I grabbed the zipline bar.

"Remember, we can't zipline at the same time. You'll have to go by yourself. Do you want to go first or second?" I asked.

Maisy blurted out, "First. So I can't chicken out."

"You can do this," I said, as I handed her the zipline bar. "I will be right behind you."

"Ready?" I asked.

Maisy nodded quickly, almost as if she was scared she would

change her mind. She stood on the platform with the bar in her hand. "Give me a push," she said.

"What? Are you sure?" I asked.

Maisy nodded rapidly. "Yes, just do it. It's the only way I'll be able to jump."

I put my hand on the small of Maisy's back. My instinct was to give her a gentle push, because she is such a delicate person. But I knew the harder the push, the faster she would propel across the zipline and get the experience over with more quickly, so I used all of my body weight and thrust her off the platform. I have to admit it felt pretty good to give Maisy a shove.

She was surprisingly quiet as she flew through the trees. But she's always been eerily quiet when she's most terrified. As soon as she got to the other side, she shot the zipline bar back to me and I grabbed it and jumped off the platform.

Maisy was waiting for me on the other platform. I could tell her nerves were kicking in because her hands were shaky, and she was Ghost Amelia pale.

"We got this," I said. "I'm not leaving your side."

"Promise?" asked Maisy.

I nodded. "Promise."

We continued to climb and zipline through the layers of ropes together, like a real team. She didn't stop and ask me a million questions about the harness or the rope. She didn't do that slow breathing thing she does when she's nervous. She just kept going.

Poppy, Hannah, and Isa screamed and cheered when Maisy and I finally reached the spider web.

I turned to Maisy. "This is it. All we have to do is get through the spider web and we're done! We got so close last time. You just need to push yourself to that last rung."

"After this, I am never climbing another rope for the rest of my life!" she said.

I neglected to point out that Project Adventure, which was essentially nothing but ropes climbing, would be part of our middle school PE curriculum.

Maisy took one deep breath, then reached for the ropes. I waited for her to get to the first layer of the web before I climbed on. I could tell she was terrified and I tried really hard to move slow and steady so I didn't shake her too much. Surprisingly, Maisy kept moving forward without stopping. She put one hand in front of the other and one foot in front of the other and moved higher up the web. Every time she climbed to the next row, I waited for her to stop, but she kept moving until she got to that last row before the top platform. I thought maybe that meant she was going to be okay, but as soon as she got to the last row, she froze.

I was inches from her feet.

"Don't look down!" yelled Kaya from below.

"We'll catch you if you fall," shrieked the A twins, holding out their arms.

"Don't listen to them," I hissed. "You can do this."

Maisy started to cry so hard, I could feel us both swaying back and forth on the rope, so that even I was getting scared of falling. "I can't do it, Bea. I can't stop shaking."

I let go of the rope with my right hand and put it over hers. Then I moved my left hand off the ropes and covered her hand with mine so that my whole body covered hers. "You can do this. I am going to stay here with you until you stop shaking and you feel like you can move. Okay?"

Her body was trembling so hard that even her teeth were chattering. "You made it up this high. How are you going to feel if you don't make it to the top?"

Finally, she took a deep breath and said, "I think I can do it. Just don't leave me."

"I'm not going anywhere," I said. "I'm just going to let go of you and move a teeny bit lower so you can move up, but I'll be right behind you."

The whole spider web shook back and forth as Maisy pulled herself to the next level of ropes and up on the platform. As soon as I got up there with her, Maisy grabbed my hand and raised it up to the sky. Then she screamed through the trees. "We did it! We did it together!"

Ainsley yelled, "Three minutes fifty seconds! You did it! We won!"

I was so shocked I just stood there frozen on the platform until Maisy shrieked, "We won! We did it, Bea!"

I didn't know if Maisy and I were still in a fight or if she really meant all those horrible things she said. But I didn't care. I gave her a victory hug just like the time we won the school talent show. All at once I could feel all of our big moments together, the time I taught Maisy how to ride a two-wheeler, when we got our second holes pierced together at the mall, that time she stayed on the phone with me all night when I slept at Dad's new place for the first time.

I don't know who started crying first, but we hugged until we both had wet cheeks and snot coming from our noses. When I pulled away, we said at the exact same time, "I'm sorry."

Bailey's voice over a microphone interrupted our moment. "The Sunflower Bunk wins the tournament, which makes them the first bunk to win the Amelia Cup in fifty years."

Ainsley yelled from below. "Get your butts down here so we can celebrate!"

Maisy and I climbed down to the ground and Hannah, Poppy, and Isa pounced on us. We fell on the ground in a huddle of hugs, tears, and screams, and suddenly, the popularity pact didn't matter.

CHAPTER TWENTY

MAISY

BEA AND I WALKED TOGETHER FROM THE SPECIAL TOURNAMENT dinner to the end-of-summer bonfire. Maybe if there were more fun celebrations instead of constant conditioning and workouts, Camp Amelia would seem less like boot camp. Anyway, the other girls gave us some space because they could tell we needed to talk.

Bea clutched her stomach as we walked. "I'm so full."

I groaned. "Ugh, me too. The chocolate fountain killed me. I think I ate my weight in chocolate-covered pound cake. Oh, and those Rice Krispies treats, and the giant marshmallows, and those double chocolate chip cookies. I never thought I would say this, but I ate way too much."

"I was all over that macaroni and cheese. I dream about the banquet mac and cheese all year," Bea said.

I stopped walking in the middle of the path. "I'm sorry. I feel so bad about the things I said to you. I am a horrible person who shouldn't be allowed around other people sometimes."

Bea shook her head. "I said some pretty crappy things, too. But I don't understand why you said all of those things first."

I looked Bea in the eyes. "I'm not just sorry about being so mean the other day. I'm sorry for dropping you. I really meant it when I told you I was sorry the first time. My apology wasn't about the pact. I feel terrible about the way I treated you."

"You broke my heart when you left me behind. It felt like when my father left, only worse because at least when he left, I still had you. When you abandoned me, I had no one," Bea whispered.

I tried to respond, but I was crying too hard.

"What did I do?" Bea's eyes welled up with tears. "What made you not want to be my friend anymore? Why wasn't I good enough for you?"

I swallowed down tears and grabbed Bea's hand and squeezed it. "You didn't do anything wrong. I swear. But, you were getting too close . . ."

Bea shook her head. "Too close to what?"

"To figuring out my secret," I said, rubbing my eyes with my sleeves.

"I'm sorry I tuned you out when you tried to tell me. I'm listening now," said Bea. "Maybe I can help."

I took a deep breath and breathed out slowly. "Even you can't help me with this one."

Bea looked me in the eyes. "You can trust me. Maybe it would help a little bit just to talk to me about it."

I clenched my hands into tight balls as I said the words out loud that I had been terrified to admit out loud to anyone. "My mom is addicted to prescription pain pills."

Bea started blinking very fast, like her brain was trying to process this unexpected news. "But your mom . . . your mom is just so . . . she's just so . . ."

"Perfect? That's what you were thinking, right?"

"And I thought your life was so perfect, too," finished Bea. Her cheeks were so red, it looked like her freckles were flashing.

"Do you remember that big fight I got in with my mom?" I asked.

Bea clapped her hand over her mouth. "That last time I was at your house, before I left for camp . . ."

"Mom wanted to drive us to the mall. But she was wasted. I couldn't let you get in the car with her like that, but there was no way I was gonna tell you what was going on."

Bea slowly nodded. "So you got in a big fight with your mom about her borrowing your shirt. Then she got so mad at you, she refused to take us to the mall."

"I didn't know what else to do," I said. "I didn't want you getting hurt."

Bea wiped her nose with the back of her hand. "You could've told me what was going on."

I looked at the ground. "I was scared. If you found out, you would've told your mom."

"I would've kept your secret," Bea said. "We always kept each other's secrets."

I sighed. "If you knew how bad it was, you would've had to tell your mom. Trust me. It was that bad."

"How did it happen? I mean . . . your mom was president of the PTA," Bea said. "She did everything. She ran half marathons, for goodness' sake. How does something like that happen to someone like your mom?"

I swatted at a mosquito that was buzzing around my hair. "Remember when my mom hurt her Achilles tendon during the Mapleton Turkey Trot?"

Bea nodded with wide eyes.

"After the surgery to repair it, the doctor prescribed her Oxycodone. At first, she made jokes about how it made her feel calm and helped her finally stop worrying about all the things she had to do. Addy and I thought it was great because Mom was finally too relaxed to micromanage us. But we had no idea what we were getting into. By the time she finished that first bottle she was addicted," I said.

"That's awful." Bea's eyes were wide and wet. "I don't even know what to say."

The funny thing was that I knew what to say. I could talk about this now. After meeting with Dr. Beth all summer, it was getting easier.

"Back when it was first happening, I was scared all the time. Scared people would find out what was going on and make fun of me. Scared that no one would ever find out and Addy and I would have to keep this secret forever. Scared that my mom . . . that my mom would die."

Bea put her hand on my back and started rubbing it in counter-clockwise circles, which used to be her way to calm me down when I was worried about something. "Oh, Maisy, I'm so sorry. I wish you had come to me."

It was finally time to get real with Bea. "I knew the second you found out, you would have no choice but to tell your mom. I couldn't risk that, so I pushed you away."

Bea's face crumpled. "For the M & Ms? To be popular?"

"It wasn't about being popular. I needed to hang out with people who don't really dig deep. Who don't notice things because they're too busy shopping and taking selfies. Girls who would never figure out my secret."

Bea's jaw dropped. "Your mom's been sick the whole time you've been friends with the M & Ms and they don't know?"

"All they care about is clothes, hair, makeup, and boys. Also, we spend most of our time at Mia's house because her brother has cute friends. I know it sounds bad, but it's what I needed. I needed to hide behind people who don't care about anything that truly matters."

Bea looked me straight in the eyes. "I care."

I smiled back at her and said, "I know."

"You have me back now. No matter what happens with your mom, I'll be there for you," Bea said.

I breathed out all of the air that had been trapped in my lungs for what felt like forever. "You have me back, too. For real this time."

BEA

The next morning, we were all on the bus heading back to our respective homes. Isa, Maisy, and I were squeezed into one seat and Poppy and Hannah were in the seat across from us. The bus smelled like Doritos, Fruit Roll-Ups, and sweaty feet, a scent I usually loved on the way to camp because it meant I had the whole summer ahead with my friends but that I hated on the way home because it meant I was leaving my friends behind. This time, however, I was ready to go back to Mapleton.

Poppy held up the shiny gold cup. "I can't wait to bring this to Nana Mary. She has her team's cup on display in her room at the nursing home. She always says earning that cup is one of her life's biggest achievements. She says it's right up there with meeting Grandfather and having children."

"No offense, girls, but I hope meeting my future husband will be more life-changing than winning this cup," said Hannah.

I nodded. "Agreed."

"My mom is already talking about putting this on my college apps. I really don't think Stanford is gonna care about some camp tournament, but whatever," said Isa.

I looked back at the normally boisterous Dandelion Bunk girls, who were unnaturally quiet, in the seats a few rows back from us. The A twins were leaning against each other, napping on and off in one seat, while Tinka and Kaya wordlessly stared out the window in the adjacent seat.

I leaned over to Poppy's seat and pushed the cup down, so it wasn't so noticeable. "Let's try to be more low-key," I said. "I kinda feel bad for the Dandelion girls. We took away their one shot at winning the tournament."

"What about next year?" asked Maisy, whose lips and tongue were bright blue from her pack of Sour Patch Blue Raspberry.

"No more tournaments for any of us. From here on out, we become senior campers, then Counselors in Training," I said.

Isa scrunched up her nose. "How can you feel bad for them? They're mean and vindictive girls who didn't deserve to win." She popped open a bag of Doritos. "Besides, we were just better than them."

I sighed. "I just wonder what they're carrying around."

Hannah laughed. "Kaya's carrying around ten pounds of makeup, hair extensions, and fake lashes; Tinka has lots of hair dye and jewelry for all her piercings; and I heard the A twins carry ten-pound medicine balls in their backpacks."

Isa gave her a high five. "Good one!"

"That's not what I meant," I started.

Maisy cut in. "What she means is that we don't know what they're going through. We don't know what kind of stuff is stressing them out. I don't even think you guys know why you hate them anymore and they probably don't know why they hate you either."

"Look at Maisy and me," I added. "We both had two different sides to the same story all this time."

The bus brakes screeched as the driver pulled into the drop-off point for all the girls living in the Five Boroughs. Isa, Poppy, and Hannah stood up and groaned.

"This is it for us," said Isa, as she grabbed her body-bag-sized duffle.

Tears streamed down Poppy's face as she stood up. "I hate saying goodbye."

"Me too," said Hannah.

"Me three," said Isa in a wry tone.

The A twins pushed past the girls and shoved them so hard that Doritos flew out of Isa's hand onto everyone within a five-foot radius.

Isa smirked. "Different sides to the same story, huh?"

We all laughed and threw ourselves into a group goodbye hug. Next thing we knew, the bus driver was yelling for the girls to hurry, and we were shouting directions to them to text in our group convo every day and to plan a fall meet-up in the city. It was always hard to say goodbye to my bunkmates at the end of the summer. But this time it was a little easier because I had Maisy. I had a piece of camp with me at school.

Maisy and I waved at the girls as the bus pulled away. Then Maisy disconnected the portable charger that was hooked into her phone and cheered. "Finally! My phone is charged."

I didn't care about my own phone. It's not like anyone had been texting me or reaching out to me on social media all summer. But Maisy's phone was our connection to the M & Ms.

Maisy groaned. "Ugh, I lost all my Snapchat streaks."

I scooted in closer to see Maisy's phone. "Go on Instagram to see what the M & Ms are up to so we can make a plan."

"I'll go on Madison's account since she posts the most," Maisy said.

"Good idea," I said. I was ready to get our plan rolling in motion. We only had a week till the first day of school so we needed to get moving.

Maisy's jaw dropped when she looked at the picture on Madison's account. It looked totally normal to me. Just a group of girls hanging out by the pool wearing the season's trendiest bathing suits and sunglasses, their skin golden from the sun, and the photo snapped before anyone got their perfect hair wet.

"What?" I asked, with a knot in my stomach. "What's wrong?"

Maisy clasped her hands on the top of her head. "No, it wasn't supposed to happen this way. This wasn't the plan. This was definitely not the plan."

"What?" I asked again, a knot forming in my stomach.

"Look at the picture." Maisy snapped a fingernail against the screen. "What do you see?"

I pulled the phone closer to my face. "Meghan and Mia floating on a unicorn float and Madeline floating on a doughnut float with Madison."

"Who else do you see?" Maisy practically shrieked.

I took a closer look. "Oh, there's Chloe Bradford-Fuller sitting on the diving board."

Maisy shook her head. "This can't be happening."

She scrolled to her DMs.

From: @madisonave
To: @maisywintersiscoming

Where have you been???? I haven't heard from you in days. I found our new girl!!

THE END

ACKNOWLEDGMENTS

WRITING IS A SOLITARY ENDEAVOR, BUT I'VE NEVER FELT ALONE on this journey. I've had help, encouragement, and guidance along the way from family, friends, and the team it takes to launch a book.

Thank you to Lauren Galit of the LKG Agency, whose keen insight always elevates my writing. Five minutes into our first conversation, I knew I had found my dream agent. Your business savvy, counsel, and friendship have been with me every step of the way. I am also grateful for all of Caitlen Rubino-Bradway's help behind the scenes.

Many thanks to Running Press Kids editor Allison Cohen. Your enthusiasm for my story, constant support, and sharp insight made me confident *The Popularity Pact* had found the perfect home. When I received the most detail-oriented email I have ever seen from Senior Project Editor Amber Morris, it only reiterated to me that my books were in good hands. A special shout-out to Christina Palaia for your top-notch copyediting skills. Thank you to the rest of the publishing team for all of your hard work—Marissa Raybuck, Valerie Howlett, Hannah Jones, Hannah Koerner, and Janelle DeLuise.

Thank you to Lisa K. Weber for your beautiful cover art and chapter illustrations that brought Maisy and Bea to life. I am immensely grateful to Kathleen Carter of Kathleen Carter

Communications for all of your hard work getting my books in the hands of more readers in such fun and creative ways.

I am profoundly grateful for my writing partner and dear friend Lea Geller for always telling me the hard stuff—whether it's about writing or life or just to grow out my bangs. Everyone needs a friend like you.

In this world of carefully curated social media feeds, it's important to have people to share in life's raw and not-so-perfect moments. A shout-out to my tribe: Elba Burrowes, Michelle Dawson, Lia Gravier, Julie Latham, Stephanie Lia, Crystal Parham, Mandy Stupart, Vicki Tatarian.

The writing community is filled with some amazing people who are generous with their time, advice, and support. Thank you to Nancee Adams, Cindy Beer-Fouhy, Pari Berk, Kathy Curto, Camille Di Maio, Veera Hiranandani, Kwana M. Jackson, Barbara Solomon Josselsohn, Susan Kleinman, Falguni Kothari, Suzanne Leopold of Suzy Approved Book Tours, Steven Lewis, Edward McCann, Cari Pattison, Melissa Roske, and Susie Orman Schnall.

The Writing Institute at Sarah Lawrence College is where I found my writing voice and later my teaching voice. Thank you to Patricia Dunn for giving me the opportunity to combine my two passions into the perfect job. Thank you again to Patricia and also to Jimin Han for starting out as my mentors and becoming friends.

I am appreciative of Marcia Bradley, Sweet Orefice, and Lucille Walker for keeping everything running smoothly at the place that has become a writing sanctuary and community for so many writers, myself included. Thank you to Annabel Monaghan and Ines Rodrigues for being wonderful colleagues and friends. I am grateful for all of my students, who inspire me with their drive and dedication. The biggest gift The Writing Institute gave me is my writing group, Ahmed Asif, Marlena Baraf, Jacqueline Goldstein, Nancy Flanagan, Rebecca Marks, Nan Mutnick, Jessica Rao, and Ines Rodrigues.

Thank you to my parents, Liz and John, who raised me to think outside the box, a necessity for a writer. Your constant love and support have carried me over many hurdles through the years. Thank you to my mother-in-law, Betsy, for always showing up for me. Many thanks to my sisters and brothers, both blood and through marriage, for all of your love and encouragement over the years. To my nieces, nephews, and godsons, thank you for inspiring me to be creative, for always asking about my books, and for reminding me what it's like to be a kid.

To Doug and Molly, thank you for always reminding me not to take things too seriously and for all the times you got me to look up from my laptop and enjoy the world around me. Thank you for walking me through some of the most challenging seasons and for cheering me on during the good ones. I know I can tackle anything life throws at me with you both by my side.

EILEEN MOSKOWITZ-PALMA

THE HARDCOVER EDITION OF *THE POPULARITY PACT: CAMP CLIQUE*
was published on April 14, 2020, during the COVID-19 pandemic.
About a month before the publication date, schools across the country closed. As a former elementary school teacher, I realized I could
help the families who were suddenly thrust into homeschooling by
offering free virtual creative writing camps and book clubs. In the
first month of the shut down, I worked with a hundred kids from all
over the country. I got to know everyone really well during the writing camps, so by the time we met for book club, the kids were really
comfortable asking me questions about *Camp Clique*. I compiled the
most frequently asked questions for this Q & A.

———.———

HOW DID YOU DECIDE TO WRITE A STORY ABOUT FRIENDS?

For many people, friendships are some of the most important
relationships in life. Having a best friend or a solid friend group
can make a person feel confident about their place in the world.
When a friendship falls apart, it can be devastating. I wanted to
capture the intensity of friendship during middle school by showing the highs and lows and the roller coaster of emotions. I hoped
to convey the message that one true friend is more valuable than
a crew of inauthentic people. I also wanted to remind readers that
friends don't always make the right choices, but, sometimes, it's
worth it to give the right friend a second chance.

WHY DID YOU CREATE TWO GIRLS WHO ARE SO DIFFERENT FROM EACH OTHER?

We all have different personalities, interests, and life experiences. I was hoping that creating two very different protagonists would help more readers feel a personal connection to the story.

WHAT INSPIRED YOU TO WRITE IN TWO DIFFERENT POVS?

Many people have experienced a friendship falling apart. Sometimes, you're the one left behind or dropped by a friend, while in other cases you're the one who left a friend behind. I wanted kids—regardless of with whom they identified—to see the other side in hopes that it might bring them closure or understanding about their own situation.

WHO WAS THE THE BAD GUY—MAISY OR BEA?

Whenever I'm asked who I think the "bad" guy is, I can't help but turn the question around on the person asking. I'm often told that, in the beginning, the reader didn't think they were going to like Maisy because of how she treated Bea; however, by the end, they couldn't help but like her. This is exactly what I wanted the reader to experience because in real life people aren't all good or all bad, and when a friendship falls apart there are usually multiple reasons why.

WHAT ABOUT DR. BETH?

I get a lot of questions about Dr. Beth. Why does she have so many stray cats? Why does she eat so much junk food? Why is she so quirky? How did you come up with Dr. Beth?

I wanted to create a quirky therapist who would be able to draw Maisy out. My mom has always been someone who lives her life the way she wants to, without worrying about what anyone else thinks of her. She is one of the easiest people to talk to, and she gives very practical advice. My relationship with my mom inspired me to make Dr. Beth the kind of character who marches to the beat of her own drum. That she was a vegan who secretly ate junk food and always had a new rescue cat in her therapy cabin just added to her out-of-the-box personality.

HOW DID YOU DECIDE THAT MAISY'S MOTHER WOULD BE ADDICTED TO DRUGS?

One of my relatives struggled with drug addiction, so I have a lot of empathy for families who grapple with this issue. My relative had debilitating anxiety and their doctor prescribed them an anti-anxiety medication, which they, unfortunately, became addicted to. At the time, there wasn't a lot of understanding about prescription drug addiction. But as the opioid crisis continues to affect families across America, I decided writing about it could provide greater understanding of this epidemic and offer comfort to any kids whose own families were affected like mine.

WHY IS MAISY SO MAD AT HER MOM?

For Maisy's entire life she had the kind of mother who was on the PTA, made the costumes for the school play, and seemed perfect in every way. Maisy's mother became a different person after she began abusing drugs and did things she never would've done sober. Maisy is angry at her mother because of the things that she did while in the throes of addiction.

IS CAMP AMELIA BASED ON THE SUMMER CAMP YOU WENT TO?

When I was growing up, my family spent summers in a lake cottage in the Berkshires, so I never went to sleepaway camp. But I based some of the Camp Amelia details on my summers in the country—lightning bugs, dirt paths, and cold lake water, always take me back to those hot summer days and cool nights. For other camp details, I talked to my daughter (who has been to camp) and my friends who have been to camp and sent their own kids. They told me about bonfires, talent nights, s'mores, and bunk rivalry. It was fun for me to create a camp world that I never had the chance to experience in my own childhood.

WHY DID YOU ADD THE CAMP PRANKS?

Even though I don't like getting pranked or playing tricks on anyone, my husband and daughter have had a pranking tradition since she was little. Every Thanksgiving weekend, they both try to pie the other person in the face. They come up with all sorts of elaborate ways to sneak up on each other and get more creative every year. While I don't like to participate, I love to watch a good prank unfold, so I wanted to give the readers a chance to experience that.

DO THE SUNFLOWER BUNK GIRLS APPEAR IN THE SECOND BOOK?

In real life, sleepaway camp and summer home friends often don't get a chance to see each other during the school year. That worked for me in terms of the *School Squad* plot because I wanted all of the Sunflower Bunk girls to stay in the Camp Amelia world, so that Maisy and Bea would get further away from who they were at summer camp as they got sucked into their life back home. The camp friend group gets replaced by the M & Ms, the school friend group. Spoiler alert: The M & Ms are *very* different from the Sunflower Bunk girls.

WILL THE SECOND BOOK PICK UP WHERE THE FIRST BOOK LEFT OFF?

Yes, *The Popularity Pact: School Squad* begins on the camp bus ride home exactly where the cliffhanger left off in *Camp Clique*.

WILL WE EVER MEET MAISY'S MOM?

Yes! Maisy spends the entire first book of the series struggling to forgive her mother. In the second book, we'll see what happens when Maisy's mom returns home from treatment.

WILL WE MEET BEA'S MOM'S BOYFRIEND AND HER DAD'S NEW FAMILY?

Yes! While Maisy is adjusting to having her mother back home from treatment, Bea is getting used to her mother having a serious boyfriend for the first time since her parents got divorced. On top of that, Bea is working just as hard at securing her place in her dad's new family as she is at fitting in with the M & Ms.

A SNEAK PEEK AT:

THE

POPULARITY PACT

SCHOOL

SQUAD

BOOK TWO

CHAPTER ONE

BEA

"I NEVER WANT TO GET OFF THIS BUS." I WATCHED THE LAST Burger King before the Mapleton exit pass by in a swirl of red and orange, the rich scent of greasy burgers and salty fries wafting through the open window.

Maisy focused her eyes on me. "It's going to be okay," she said.

I broke her gaze and looked down at my thighs. They were covered with so many freckle constellations, I almost looked tan. "Things are about as far from okay as you can get. My dad's replacing my mom and me with new and improved models. My mom's dating our old math teacher, and I'm about to start middle school with zero friends."

"That last part's not true," Maisy said, as she held out a practically empty bag of Sour Patch Kids. "You have me."

I popped a yellow candy in my mouth and felt the sour sugar crystals burn my tongue before the candy turned sweet.

"I can't expect you to give up the popular table for me," I said midchew. "So, if you want me, I'll be eating tuna sandwiches alone in the library."

"Tuna?" Maisy scrunched up her face. "No wonder no one wanted to sit with you."

"It's not funny. School starts in two days and I'm going to be just as invisible as I was last year," I moaned.

"You held up your end of the pact and made me, the least athletic and most anxious girl at adventure camp, popular. Now it's *my* turn to make *you* popular at school."

"How did I ever think we could pull this off?" I asked. "How could I ever fit in with the M & Ms?" The bus pulled off the highway onto the red maple tree–lined street that ran through the center of Mapleton. The other campers laughed and talked as if the end of the summer wasn't descending upon us like an apocalyptic plague. They may have been sad to say goodbye to the summer, but clearly they all had friends back home they were eager to see.

"We just need to come up with another plan," Maisy said. "So, put that freakishly big brain of yours to work."

I grabbed the last Sour Patch Kid. "I've got nothing."

Maisy licked her finger and ran it along the inside of the bag. "Let's list all the things we know about the situation. My dad says to do that when I'm stuck on a word problem, which is pretty much every time I do math homework."

"There's unpopular, and then there's the level below unpopular, where you're so invisible, you aren't on anyone's radar to merit the label unpopular. That's what we're working with."

Maisy rolled her eyes. "And you call me dramatic?"

"Fine, I'll play along." I cleared my throat. "Here are the known variables. Having the right friend group is the key to middle school survival. If I can get in with the M & Ms, I won't have to spend the school year hiding in the bathroom during free periods."

Maisy nodded. "We also know the M & Ms are always out for themselves."

"Exactly." I sighed. "Why would they help *me*?"

"We just need to figure out what's in it for them," said Maisy. "There must be something they could get out of being friends with you."

But I couldn't think of one thing those girls needed, especially Mia, whose popularity was matched by her Queen Bee wardrobe. I thought about Madeline with her gel manis and hair even Beyoncé would envy. Then there were Meghan and Madison, who had the kind of friendship born of having moms who were lifelong best friends. Having a person who is more family than friend is the kind of safety net that can make the difference between middle school survival and failure. Let's not forget Chloe Bradford-Fuller, who had swooped in and snatched up the spot in the group Maisy had carved out for me. These girls had everything I wanted. What could I possibly give them?

Maisy whipped her hair into a french braid at record speed. Anytime Maisy is freaking out, she plays with her hair, so this was a surefire sign she wasn't as confident about our strategizing as she was letting on.

"We need to figure out something they might want. Make them realize they want it. Then, convince them you're the only person who can give it to them," Maisy said, as she wrapped a rubber band around the bottom of her braid.

"That's genius." I stared at Maisy. "But what could I possibly give the girls who have everything?"

MAISY

As the bus thumped over the speed bumps in the parking lot, my heart pounded. I was acting calm for Bea, but the closer we got to our real life back home, the more anxious I felt.

It wasn't just about holding up my end of the pact. I needed to make up for ditching Bea last year and ruining her life. I needed to give her the one thing she wanted—a friend group at school, just like she has at camp.

"Mapleton girls!" Bob, our bus driver, called to the back. "This is your stop! Don't leave any garbage behind!"

I shoved the empty chip bags, candy wrappers, and deflated Capri Sun pouches into my bag. Bea and I stood up and brushed the Dorito crumbs and Sour Patch Kids dust off our shorts and grabbed our drawstring bags.

As I walked past the other kids, I heard another bus pull into the parking lot. I leaned out the window to get a closer look.

Bob growled, "Let's go, girls! I still got two more states to drive through today!"

I hurried down the aisle. The parking lot was filled with parents. I put my hand over my eyes to block out the sun and looked around but didn't see Dad or Bea's mom.

"We're the only two kids getting picked up from Camp Amelia," I said. "Why are all these other parents here?"

"This is where all the camps have drop-offs."

Bea sighed as our bus pulled onto the main road. "Just like that. Our summer is over."

"Not true." I dumped my duffel bag down on the hot blacktop. "We still have two days before school starts to figure out our plan."

"There won't be a plan if I can't think of something I can give the M & Ms," Bea said, just as another yellow bus rumbled across the parking lot and pulled up in front of us.

As soon as the bus door opened sweaty boy smell hit us. It was even worse than the time Addy left a pile of dirty leotards in the back of our minivan during a heat wave.

Bea wrinkled her nose. "You thought I had questionable hygiene at camp when I counted swimming in the lake as my shower? You haven't been around when the Scouts get back from their annual camping trip. We're talking about seventh-grade boys running around the woods for two weeks without running water or soap."

I shuddered. "We are so lucky we don't have brothers."

Bea squished up her whole face. "Agreed."

"That smell, though." I tried not to breathe through my nose. "It's like moldy cheese, feet . . . and . . ."

Bea gagged. "Rotten garbage."

I felt a dry heave coming on. "Ugh. That's it."

Bea grabbed my arm and pulled me a few steps back. "Let's give them a wide berth."

"Why do you always have to use big words?" I dragged my stuff back far enough so we could check out the guys without smelling them.

"It's called reading." Bea smirked. "You should try it sometime."

"You are sooo funny," I said.

Marshall Cooper was the first guy off the bus. With his thick glasses strapped around his greasy hair, his dirt-streaked Mapleton School Chess Club T-shirt over cargo shorts, and bright orange Crocs, he could've been cast in any eighties remake as head of the nerd herd.

"Things could be worse." I jerked my head toward the bus as another grubby geek walked off and said, "You could be one of those guys."

Bea shrugged. "At least they have their place in the world."

I rolled my eyes, even though she was right. "We literally just got off the bus. Give me a chance to come up with a new plan before you have a nervous breakdown."

Suddenly, a bright ray of sunshine broke through the fluffy white clouds and shone down on the bus steps. Clark Rutner stepped into the light like a superhero in a Marvel movie. He had gotten teenager tall over the summer, and his tan arms were thick with actual muscles. His red Mapleton Scouts Troop 523 T-shirt stretched across his wide chest. He had grown out his sun-streaked blond hair from a babyish crewcut into a longish surfer-boy hairstyle.

I knocked Bea's arm with my elbow and hissed, "OMG! Do you know what's happening here?"

"Ow!" Bea rubbed her arm. "What? What's happening?"

"Sometimes I wonder how someone *so* smart could be *so* dumb," I whispered. "We are getting the first look at Mapleton Middle School's Summer Glow Up."

Bea wrinkled her forehead and practically shouted, "What the heck is a Glow Up?"

"Keep your voice down," I whispered. "It's when someone goes from the awkward, ugly stage to super cute overnight."

"Oh, now I get it." Bea nodded slowly. "I'm pretty sure Hans Christian Andersen invented that."

"Who?"

Bea threw her hands up. "'The Ugly Duckling'?"

Before I could answer her, Clark turned toward us and smiled. His teeth were bright white and perfect, like a row of peppermint Orbit gum. I was just lifting my arm to wave back when he said, "Hey, Bea."

"How do *you* know the Glow Up?" I asked, trying not to move my lips.

"We were both in accelerated science and math last year," Bea said. "We're in all the honors classes together this year."

I held out my phone and pretended to be taking a selfie. Instead, I got a pic of Clark walking toward us, his blond hair flowing, his golden skin soaking up the sun.

"I think I figured out what you can give the M & Ms," I said.